W9-CHO-903

VIRTUAL MORALITY

2000

VIRTUAL
Morality
a novel

Christopher Hill

WINNER OF THE EDITORS' BOOK AWARD

PUSHCART
Wainscott
New York 11975

WHITING PUBLIC LIBRARY
WHITING, IN 46394

Winner of the 18th annual Editors' Book Award

copyright © 2000 Christopher Hill

ISBN 1-888889-18-7
LC-99 76247

All rights reserved. For information address the
publisher: Pushcart Press, P. O. Box 380, Wainscott NY 11975.

Distributed by W. W. Norton & Co.

Sponsoring Editors: Simon Michael Bessie, James Charlton, Peter Davison, Jonathan Galassi, David Godine, Daniel Halpern, James Laughlin, Seymour Lawrence, Starling Lawrence, Robie Macauley, Joyce Carol Oates, Nan A. Talese, Faith Sale, Ted Solotaroff, Pat Strachan, Thomas Wallace. Bill Henderson, Publisher.

VIRTUAL MORALITY

For my parents, of course, John and Ellen, who could teach Job a thing or two about patience.

ONE

Everett Overton Broadstreet PhD., Dean of the College of Arts and Sciences, finally resigned himself and pressed the intercom button on his telephone.

"Joyce, will you bring in Professor Stiggler's latest memo? Thank you."

Everett rested his elbows on the edge of his desk and frowned down at the blotter. The desk, which was the subject of great pride, was as large as a tabletop and he kept it as neat as the proverbial pin; pencils were carefully sorted by hardness in a lacquered sandalwood box next to his eraser, all paper clips were kept in a container with a magnetized hole in the top, and the one ornament, an antique brass compass, lay precisely seven inches in from the front of the desk and twenty-three inches in from the left hand side. Everett's mother, Mrs. Broadstreet, had been a firm believer in the dictum 'everything in its place,' and some of her mania for order had rubbed off onto her son. He didn't think much about his mother anymore, having put her in her place some years earlier by checking her into a retirement home. He spent an average of 12 minutes per month visiting his mother and an average of 78 minutes per month straightening his desk. His mother was in her place, his eraser was in its place, and Everett was in his place, behind a massively organized desk on the third floor of Old Main.

At this particular moment in his life, he was pondering his scheduled meeting with Professor Stiggler, and the more he thought about it the blacker his mood became. He had been avoiding her for several weeks as if she were a dentist with whom he had postponed an appointment for a root canal, but from the clammy feeling in his palms he knew that the moment of reckoning was fast approaching. These meetings took it out of Everett. His pulse was already starting to race and his bowels were beginning to rumble. According to the clock on the wall the meeting was less than an hour away, and as he glanced up to check the time he noticed that the clock was already in shadow, an observation that sunk him deeper into gloom.

At just that moment, as if timed to punctuate his irritation, the gargling din of a diesel engine burst into life outside, and started to rattle the huge double-hung windows behind him. He snapped around in his swivel chair and stared morosely across the quad as a cement truck chugged concrete into a mason's wheelbarrow. "Every day this week," Everett mumbled to himself. "Every single day." He wondered how the students in the nearby halls could be expected to study over the racket from this latest example of the president's obsession with building.

In the fourteen years that Everett had been at the University, he had never known a day when it had not been under construction. During his tenure no less than eight entire buildings, two parking structures, a swimming pool and a gymnasium complex had been planned, financed, and executed. The president of the school, Dr. Robert Fowler, an energetic little character known best for his pince-nez glasses and his remarkable political acumen, had at heart the instincts of a beaver. Whenever threatened with proposed cutbacks from the state legislature, which might in some way disturb the financial serenity of his domain, his first reaction was invariably to take the offensive and push the regents to approve a new building project. The strategy seemed to work; money from private contributions would keep flowing in until the budget crisis passed.

The most recent attack, launched by a Republican congressman from some insignificant town on the Western Slope, had occurred the previous year. Its immediate result was the president's new Center for Non-Traditional Studies, the tower at which Everett was staring balefully.

The structure was now eight floors high, and every morning at around eleven o'clock its shadow started to creep across the walls of Everett's office, destroying the sunshine that had made him choose the office in the first place. It was an angular building, the new tower, all cement and steel, looming like a great gray fertility totem over the grassy stretch behind Old Main. At times Everett entertained the notion that such was in fact the architect's subliminal intent; that it was designed as an enormous phallic symbol. There was even a ring of balconies around the seventh floor making the top appear somewhat bulbous. He never gave voice to this observation, of course. Gender-based elocution, or whatever it was that they called it this week, was highly frowned upon in the university community. And considering that the new structure would upon its completion house, among other things, the Women's Studies department, an openly discussed observation like Everett's would be nothing short of scandalous.

Watching the cement truck and the army of masons scurrying around, his mind flashed back to the last time a member of the faculty had been challenged on an offensive statement. So innocent it had seemed at first, so innocuous! James Biddlebody, a mathematics professor, had told a black student that there was little possibility geometry had first evolved in western Africa, and then been stolen by the Greeks. A reasonably rational conclusion, Everett had thought at the time. Everett had taken his PhD in math, and knew something about the history of his discipline. Despite the ever-increasing pressure against Euro-centrism in academia, there were simply some things which were factual, and the Hellenic origin of Euclidean geometry was one of them. Besides, Everett had thought at the time, how does one go about stealing an ability from someone else? The entire notion was absurd. But the next day four hundred students had gathered at the quad right outside his window chanting "Hey Hey, Ho Ho! Racism has got to go!" It had been an absolute debacle, press, television cameras, a nightmare of humiliating publicity. The scene was still vivid in Everett's recollection; the chanting students, President Fowler apologizing to everyone for everything, and then he himself, Dean Everett Broadstreet, swallowing another chunk of his ego and ascending the podium to join the chancellor at the microphone just like . . . just like . . .

Just like it was going to be in another forty-three minutes when Daphne Stiggler arrived with Jack Beetle, her repulsive cohort from the Political English department. Everett's stomach started to churn, and he wiped his hands absently on the thighs of his trousers.

Joyce walked in and with an instinct honed from experience carefully placed several sheets of paper on his desk. After skimming through the first page he sighed and shook his head slightly— it was the usual nonsense—but as he worked his way down to the middle of the second he froze, went back up to the top and reread it:

> *"We feel it only fair to extend to students the inalienable right to determine the acceptability or unacceptability of their peers' conduct. We therefore feel it incumbent upon us to accede to the students' demands of a student oversight committee, whose purpose will be to examine infractions of the University's Code of Speech and Conduct. The men and womyn selected for this committee will have the responsibility of hearing, judging, and ultimately penalizing offensive speech and activity among the members of the undergraduate community. Since giving token power would be construed as only token solidarity with the aims of the committee, the board should be granted full disciplinary power up to and including expulsion of offending students . . . "*

"Judas," said Everett. He had expected something mildly annoying and a little ridiculous, like most of the bat-brained ideas that Professor Stiggler bothered him with from time to time, but this, this was unbelievable. So unbelievable, in fact, that he felt sure he would be able to block it unless . . . He skipped quickly to the last page, to see how many people had signed onto the letter. His mouth went dry. At a glance it looked as if more than a hundred faculty members agreed that the administration should hand the power to expel students over to the same bunch of crazies that met regularly over at the Square. Everett cursed himself for procrastinating. How in the world was he going to fight this now? He hadn't prepared at all, and he had less than, let's see, oh God, nineteen and a half minutes. His tongue suddenly felt as if it had contracted and attached itself to the roof of his mouth.

Everett reached into his top drawer and extracted a roll of antacids, took one, put the rest back in the desk and started to work his way through the undersign'ds. Stiggler and Beetle headed the list, of course. Most of the Women's Studies department had signed on, and Everett noticed that each of the professors had spelled the department name 'Womyn's,' the way it appeared in the memo. There also appeared to be a clean sweep of faculty members both from the Center for Ethnicity and from the Political English department (of which Jack Beetle was current department chair). But there were names from other departments, too; French, Linguistics, Geology, Political Science, and even a few from his own department, Mathematics.

Everett felt frustrated and a little depressed as he put the memo back onto the blotter, although in his heart he wasn't particularly surprised. He was never sure if his fears were grounded, or if they were the normal musings of a man advancing in years, but he felt that the reasoning of the younger faculty members had become somewhat unsound lately. Daphne Stiggler, for instance, although more outspoken than most, was not terribly different from many of her contemporaries seized by the current vogue of anti-nationalism. The pendulum of rank and file public opinion may have begun to swing against "political rectitude," but the public setbacks had inspired a sort of bunker-like attitude among its adherents on campus. Throughout the 1980's they had struggled to remove any flattering portrayals of traditional western culture and society from the curriculum, and to replace them with sanitized versions of non-European cultures. In fact, largely due to their perseverance, the bulk of the old liberal arts core of the graduation requirements had been replaced by new classes that stressed understanding of the disadvantaged. It was now possible to get a degree from the College of Arts and Sciences without ever taking a course in American History; but it was impossible to get out without taking a survey Women's Studies Class. Like the one taught by Professor Stiggler. She and her associates were loath to give up either the gains that they had made or the power that came with them.

Still, Everett knew, it was pointless to dwell on these thoughts, and openly opposing the new movement could become dangerous. Faculty members on either side of the political spectrum who opposed developments like the University's new core curriculum were frozen out. They were kept off of curriculum approval committees, and out of department chairs. Although it had never happened on his own campus, Everett knew of cases where tenure and research monies had been denied to professors because they had expressed unpalatable ideas. He wondered how many of the faculty members who had signed the memo had simply gone along for fear of being ostracized.

As far as Everett was concerned, however, as an administrator, nothing was as dangerous as publicity that put the University in a bad light. Since the most vocal faculty members seemed able to produce both television cameras and crowds of chanting students at the drop of a hat, well, discretion had become the better part of valor on the third floor of Old Main.

And why not, Everett thought to himself. He was very happy with the status of his career; he had grown to crave the trappings of respect that came with the dean's office. Not the power, so much, for that was largely illusory, but he liked being a fairly large fish in a fairly small pond. Because of this, he could easily turn a blind eye to the changing season of campus activism, even if the actual process of going along gave him indigestion. Why not? The president certainly didn't mind, did he? Hadn't he commissioned the phallic symbol? That great monument to the maladjusted that had at this moment cast a shadow over Everett's entire office? Like many men in his position, Everett believed that someone would eventually stand up and put the brakes on this freight train of foolishness. But it wasn't going to be him.

Everett's telephone buzzed, and he almost jumped at the sound. His pulse shot up and a sour taste in the back of his mouth made his tongue contract. For a split second he was afraid that he would throw up all over his beautiful desk. It was like the feeling that a condemned man might have as he watches the first shaft of sunlight signal the arrival of his last day. Everett tried, unsuccessfully, to swallow, and then he touched the intercom button. "Yes Joyce?" he asked. He knew very well what she was going to say, but he also knew that Stiggler and Beetle were waiting by her desk, and he wanted to sound unconcerned.

"Doctors Stiggler and Beetle are here to see you, Dean."

"Oh, yes," said Everett with an attempt at nonchalance. "Send them in." He took a deep breath and held it, and waited for the door to open.

As usual, despite his anxiety, he couldn't help marveling at Daphne Stiggler's face as she walked in. Her hair, blond and streaked with gray, was pulled back from a countenance completely dominated by a pair of beautiful violet-colored eyes. Not that Everett was attracted to her sexually, of course. South of her neck, as the saying goes, she took on the aspect and stubborn solidity of a brick, cubic and genderless. But there was more, however, to his lack of attraction than her appearance. Aside from the fact that her politics drove him right around the bend, and that any but the most casual contact with her gave him the shakes, there was something inexplicable about her that made her seem beyond attraction, beyond lust. It seemed to Everett that she had simply turned off any sex appeal that she might have once had, with the sudden and complete finality of swatting a fly.

If Stiggler had lost any sex appeal to her years on campus, however, Beetle seemed to have gained it. Walking into the office behind her, grinning like the Cheshire cat, he was almost unrecognizable from the thin, blond man who had come to the English department in 1982. Life in the sunshine of Colorado, and the modicum of fame that he had found on the campus, had caused him to bloom. He was wearing a lime green polo shirt and a pair of trousers fashioned from Guatemalan ikat. He had gained weight without becoming paunchy. His face had an outdoorsy tan, with white circles around his eyes from wearing sunglasses. He looked, in fact, like a slightly older, better dressed version of the average student. He was quieter than most students, though, and lacked the careless enthusiasm of the undergraduate. When his face occasionally lost the smile that seemed clamped upon it most of the time, his dark eyes exuded a sort of cold, glittery menace.

Since Beetle had begun attending the meetings Everett had with Dr. Stiggler a pattern to their conversations had started to emerge. Professor Stiggler, not surprisingly, was always the more vocal of the two. Beetle would sit back in his chair and listen to the dialogue, smiling, his eyeballs as fixed as if they were trying to burn holes in Everett's forehead. It was quite unnerving. Everett would try to stay rational, but the conversation always seemed to get away from him. When he started to gibber, Beetle would step in quietly with the haymakers that put Everett onto the mat.

Stiggler walked over to the desk. Much to Everett's displeasure she pushed the antique compass from its spot and placed her cordura-cloth briefcase in its place. In mathematical terms, the vector of anger momentarily cancelled out the vector of his anxiety, and he relaxed slightly. He stood and extended his hand.

"Daphne, Jack, always good to see you two," he said. They each took his hand without saying anything, and looked as if they were embarrassed by this ritual touching exercise. "I'm sorry I've been so busy lately and

I haven't been able to get you in here, but with all the building projects and fund raising, the Regents have been taking so much of my time.

"That's quite all right, Dean," said Stiggler as she sat down. "We know how busy you are." She glanced over at Beetle who was fixing his gaze onto Everett's face. "Have you had a chance to read the memo we sent over?" she inquired.

"Yes, I have, Daphne. In fact I have it right here in front of me." He tilted his glasses to magnify the print and peered down his nose at the document. "Very intriguing. Very intriguing indeed."

"I knew that you'd feel that way, Dean, but before we went any further we wanted to get your input. Some of us thought that you might be apprehensive about it."

"Well, I don't know if I'd say 'apprehensive' exactly." Everett's pulse started to race up as he searched for a place to plunge in. "But I do have a few questions about how the, um, how the students would be chosen for this committee."

"Excellent question, Dean, and we'd appreciate any input there that you could give us," said Daphne. "When we started to draft the plans for the committee, we realized the administration might be concerned that we were putting too much power into the hands of the students. And though I know that you personally don't feel this way," she glanced at Beetle again, "we wanted to assure you that we plan to appoint the students, rather than to let the students elect each other."

"Appoint? Who would? The administration?"

"Well, no, not exactly. We thought that to get a more diverse sampling we would select the students in an open meeting of professors and associate professors.

Since the administration is still overwhelmingly mono-gendered and monochromatic, we felt that the results of unilateral administration action wouldn't reflect the multicultural flavor of the campus."

Everett had to turn this over in his mind a few times before he understood what she had said. When he did, and realized that he was one of the monogendered to whom she was referring, his monochrome flushed slightly. It was amazing how embarrassing it had become to be one of the majority, Everett thought. And then he thought, no, not the majority. He recalled a statistics problem he had often given his classes when he was still teaching. There are in fact more women than men.

"We knew you wouldn't want to totally remove the democratic process, Dean," said Professor Stiggler.

"No . . . No, of course not. But are you saying that the administration would have no say in this at all? You only mentioned professors as voting."

"That's what we had planned on, Dean."

"That doesn't seem very fair," said Everett, imme-diately wishing that he had said something that sounded less petulant.

"Well we are certainly open to discussion about this, Dean Broadstreet," said Professor Stiggler, adopting a soothing tone. "That's why we're here."

"Would you mind telling me why you had planned on leaving the administration out of this?"

"Really, Dean, there's no ulterior motive here. We just thought that since the faculty has more contact with the students they would be in a better position to make an informed choice. That's all. But as I say we are open to discussion."

In a flash Everett saw how he had been manipulated. He could not ask now, after mentioning fairness, for administration control over the decision making process; at best he could hope for one vote for each dean, a small number of votes that would be overwhelmed by the number of faculty members. Everett's stomach, which had calmed down for a few moments, growled back into life. He stroked his tie absently and tried to change the subject. "How did you plan to hold this meeting? I mean, when and how? Would you hold a special meeting of the college, or would the vote be taken during individual departmental meetings?" There. That was better. Must keep control.

"You know, we really hadn't decided on that yet, and we'd appreciate any input you could give us. Obviously, given your position in the University community you are far less organizationally-challenged than we are."

Everett stared at her for a second or two as if he couldn't believe that she was real. How did she come out with these phrases all of the time? It was as if she could speak another language, or rather that another language was being created right before his very eyes. *Organizationally-challenged.* Amazing. "Well," he said, "I suppose that holding the elections during the departmental meetings would be easiest. Each department would be responsible for discussion and then, I suppose, a secret ballot."

Beetle stirred in his chair, and for a moment he took his eyes off of Everett and glanced over at Stiggler. She headed him off with the slightest movement of her hand. "Really, Dean. I hardly think there's a need for such formality. Wouldn't a show of hands work just as well?

There would be less chance of cheating in the larger meetings. And besides, we want above all to encourage openness, don't you agree? If there are faculty members who honestly disagree with us, isn't it better that we know who they are so that we can encourage them to give their reasons? People should be proud of what they believe in, shouldn't they?" Beetle riveted his eyes back onto Everett's face.

Everett's heart thumped. He wasn't going to touch this line of reasoning with a barge pole. "Well, yes, of course . . . "

"Good. I'm so glad we agree. Some of the faculty members we've talked to were concerned that the older members of the staff wouldn't understand where we were coming from on this. I'm pleased that we can achieve an intergenerational harmony. See, Jack? And you were concerned that he'd fight us about the committee. He's already giving us good advice."

Everett coughed. "I, um, I haven't exactly said that I'm in favor, Daphne."

"You're against us then?"

"No, well . . . no. It's just that I have some reservations about this, specifically about, well, its legality. I'm sure that you are both as well aware as I am that the courts have taken a dim view of these speech and conduct codes."

Stiggler glared at him. "We mustn't be deterred by the racist rulings of a few narrow-minded judges. Nor can we allow ourselves to be frustrated because the courts refuse to recognize the real emotional damage caused by discrimination. There is a continuing crisis of hatred in this country, and if academia refuses to stand up for what is right, then who will? Or is it that you are one of the ones who fears sharing power with the less-represented peoples of our society?"

"No, of course not."

"You agree, then, that colleges have a responsibility to help sensitize young people to the plight of the institutionally-oppressed?"

"To a certain extent, yes. But . . . "

"That's certainly a relief. For a minute I thought you might be against us."

"Well, Daphne," said Everett, "I haven't exactly said that I . . . um . . . " Everett's mouth was starting to go dry again. "I have to confess to a certain degree of concern about . . . this. I'm not against what you are trying to do, but . . . These are, after all, students, and while I know about their enthusiasm, I wonder if they can be trusted to give these matters the . . . um . . . proper foresight and deliberation . . . necessary to see through the process, and . . . to the expected outcome . . . that we all have." Everett realized that he was beginning to babble, and that Beetle was beginning to stare narrowly at him, but he plunged on nonetheless. "Students, and I mean this in the most respectful of terms, students are somewhat, well, impulsive. Well, they can be, and I don't know if it's such a good idea to sit them in such absolute judgment of their peers."

"Just what are you implying, Dean Broadstreet?"

"I'm not implying anything, Daphne, I'm just . . . "

"Simply because you may personally disagree with their methods is not germane to whether those methods are right or wrong. Your way is right for you, as a middle-aged white male." Everett could again feel the sting of the label, even though it was entirely accurate. "Their way will be right for them as younger, fresher voices in society. If you are implying that these womyn and men are somehow less capable of judging fairly the misdeeds of their peers, simply on the basis of youth, I consider that to be the epitome of ageism." She and Beetle stared at him, as blank and expressionless as a wall of marble.

Everett looked from one to the other as if he were a hamster searching for the way out of a cage. His heart-rate was approaching tachycardia. How could you argue with these people? "I never said that, Daphne, and you know that I have the utmost respect for the . . . women and men who study here. But to give students the ability to dismiss other students, without any oversight from the administration is . . . well . . . it's . . . "

"It's another way to break down the wall of control that the faculty exercises over the students," interjected Beetle, suddenly jovial. "Come on. Isn't that what you really want to say, Dean Broadstreet? Isn't that your real fear?"

"No! Of course not," Everett lied. Things were getting bad. He trimmed his sails for a different tack. "But look what happened when the newspaper got ahold of the McDaniels story." Everett knew he was on dangerous ground here, but was willing to try anything to escape the corner he was beginning to feel boxed into.

"So now you want to limit the freedom of the press," Beetle said, and chuckled, his face the very picture of mirth.

"No, that's not what I mean at all, Jack, and you know it. But think about what happened." Several months earlier a young woman had accused a boy named Christian McDaniels of raping her during a fraternity party. When the campus paper released details of the allegations, including McDaniels' name, outraged protesters had mobbed and vandalized his fraternity house. A few weeks afterward the girl recanted and admitted she had made up the entire story. "That poor young man was thrown in jail with a bunch of felons, and his house was wrecked!"

"The house was insured, Dean Broadstreet," said Professor Stiggler, scowling. Then she cocked her chin upward, stared Everett in the eye, and continued in an infuriatingly rational tone, "And do you really think the incident was such a tragedy for the males involved? You know as well as I do that unreported rapes occur in fraternity houses all the time. And as far as Mr. McDaniels is concerned, I should think that this was a beneficial experience for him. Perhaps in the future he will think twice before inflicting the kind of pain that would cause a decent womyn to subject herself to that sort of humiliation. Wouldn't you agree that our function is to educate the students?"

Everett began nodding like an idiot before he could stop himself. How could you argue with reasoning like that? The time had come. "Right. Well. I'm going to pass this onto the president. He will, of course make the final decision, but I want you both to know that I'm behind this, I think it's an excellent idea, and I'll certainly recommend that we adopt it." Relief at his capitulation flooded through his body.

"Oh, we're not worried, Dean Broadstreet," Beetle said. "I spoke to President Fowler about it earlier this week at the University Club. After I explained the situation to him, he seemed grateful for the opportunity to help us."

Everett could picture that scene in his mind, Beetle cornering the president after hours, filling his head with visions of television cameras. Although, to be honest, he was never really sure how Dr. Fowler actually felt about Professor Stiggler's proposals. Or about anything else for that matter. "Well, that's fine, Jack. That's fine. I'm glad to be on board with this." Everett smiled. "Now, I hate to seem ungracious, but I have an appointment for lunch with Regent Phillips, so if you'll excuse me . . . " He stood up and started to show the two teachers to the door. "We must get together and talk like this more often. Jack. Daphne." He lifted his hand slightly, intending to rest it upon Daphne's shoulder as she passed, but almost instantly thought the better of it and let the hand drop to his side. Neither of the professors said a word. Daphne Stiggler was expressionless, and the only emotion that registered on Jack Beetle's raccoon-tanned face was a slight smirk at the corners of his mouth. His eyes were as clear and black as the night itself.

As soon as they had left, Everett hurried back over and reset the compass to its proper position on the desk. He was shaking as he pressed the intercom button. "Joyce, please hold all my calls." He felt, not for the first time, as if he had been thrown from the stern of the ship *Reason,* without a life preserver, and that the transom was disappearing into the horizon.

It took Everett several hours to fully recover from the visit, and wanting to waste no more time than necessary thinking about it, he dashed off a letter to President Fowler endorsing the project before he left for the day. As he had such mixed feelings over the whole thing, he wasn't too effuse with his praise, so the letter came out sounding quite rational and even-handed.

*   *   *

Since Professor Beetle had intimated as much at the meeting, Everett wasn't surprised when rumors started to spread that the president planned to approve the new committee.

The student newspaper, which was notorious in its support of the new academic agenda, had already written an editorial praising the president's foresight and sensitivity in choosing to endorse the "historic project." Everett had picked up a copy of the paper one morning on his way into Old Main. The article was quite in-depth, discussing plans for implementation right down to the number of students who would be involved and the room where the committee would meet. It even went so far as to suggest a list of possible student participants, the perusal of which had almost given Everett apoplexy. He had had dealings with almost all of them; several of them had tried to shout him down from the podium during the Biddlebody racism disaster.

He wondered how the editor could have known so much about the president's plans so quickly, but then he remembered that he had often seen the editor, Jerry Whiting, in the company of Jack Beetle at the University Club. For a moment he was angry, and wondered why Whiting couldn't get a job with a real paper.

The expected call came two weeks later, and Everett was summoned to President Fowler's home to discuss the tentative approval of the committee.

As he drove through the manicured grounds of the country club development where the president's mansion was located, Everett reflected upon how rarely he saw the president on the actual campus itself. Although he had an office in the new administrative building, Dr. Fowler preferred increasingly to hold appointments at his home, almost as if going to visit the school were an embarrassment to him. If such were his actual sentiments, however, he kept them otherwise well-hidden. At public functions involving officials from the state government, especially those functions covered by the press, the president was effuse with his praise of what he frequently referred to as the "growing international reputation" of the University. He took out full-page newspaper advertisements to keep the University on the minds of the voters. He had even made some television commercials extolling the University's caliber, and inviting more young people to look in-state for the needs of their higher education.

Everett had mixed feelings about the media blitz. The scholar in him found it somewhat distasteful that a prestigious institution would buy advertising time next to some school which promised the prospective student an exciting career as a medical or dental assistant. It made him feel, in a convoluted way, like the educational equivalent of an ambulance chaser. But at the same time he was aware that the revenues from undergraduate tuition were the coal that kept the University furnace stoked. Besides, he thought, with just a tinge of bitterness, somebody has to fill all of the new buildings.

Despite the endless construction and the political pandering and the sometimes maddening inability to get a commitment out of him, though, Everett found it difficult to dislike President Fowler. He seemed such a self-made man. With his little glasses and tweedy English country clothes he appeared the perfect academic, but underneath his herringboned exterior Everett could sometimes see flashes of the street-kid he had started out as. Fowler had been born in Princeton, New Jersey, but his family was from a part of Princeton so far removed from academia that it was almost conceivable he hadn't even seen the University until his teens. No doubt about it, Fowler had pulled himself up. He had earned his doctorate in architectural design in the old days, when academe still carried overtones of class-structure. He had an eye for design that was uncanny. He was even a good cook, often preparing meals for his own dinner parties. And on top of it all he had the sort of affable charm common to all born politicians; he could be so affected, so polished, that it put one at ease.

Everett parked his Volvo beneath one of the cottonwoods in the driveway and walked up to the door. His eyes were dazzled by the white concrete of the drive, reflecting a shaft of sunlight that had pierced the bank of Spring afternoon clouds. The butler (he actually had one) showed him from the slate entrance foyer, down the short flight of stairs and through to the airy comfort of Dr. Fowler's office. The Tudor facade of the mansion with its stucco and leaded windows belied the Frank Lloyd Wright feeling of the back. Fowler had commissioned the remodeling several years before and attached the spending to another on-campus building project. The president's office was at ground level, and the entire exterior wall had been made from vertical panes of glass. The ceiling had a slight vault, and taken with the gentle light pouring in through the windows the entire room gave a feeling of extraordinary relaxation to anyone with the fortune to sit in it.

Everett took a chair by the window-wall and gazed out at the immaculately trimmed lawn. He could understand why the president spent so much of his time here. The world outside was captured in the hazy green of the first warm days of Spring. Great sunbeams reached through the banks of gray clouds. Bees droned lazily over the tulips in the garden, and out beyond the trees people were wheeling their golf bags slowly down the fairway. One man stopped, took out a club and swung it in a graceful arc. A few seconds later Everett heard the quiet click of the ball.

"Ah, Everett, enjoying the view, I see," said the president as he walked into the room behind him. "Sometimes I wonder how I ever get anything done on days like this. Did you notice that I've had the tall junipers trimmed back slightly? I think it gives a better view of the mountains. Sorry to keep you waiting. Elaine had to have me approve the shopping list. We're having a few senators from the education committee up for dinner this evening and I guess I've been shanghaied into making the rack of lamb."

"How are you, Robert? I haven't seen you since, what is it, three weeks ago?"

"I believe so. That faculty meeting about the increase in fees. How did that go over, by the way?"

Everett waved his hand in a dismissive manner. "No problems at all. Everybody knew it was bound to happen, but I was certainly glad that you came over personally to help shore up support."

"Oh, it was nothing at all. Don't go making too much of it or people will start to see what an easy job I've got," Fowler said, indicating a chair. "Will you take a sherry?"

"Please." Sherry was another of President Fowler's affectations. The grounds, the light, the sherry; another relaxing meeting with President Fowler. "Here you are, Everett. And do try this cheese. It's called Stilton, and it comes from northern England. What do you think?"

The cheese was a bit salty for Everett's taste, but he felt it wise to keep his opinions to himself. "It's wonderful, Robert."

"Too salty, huh?" said Fowler, as he sat behind his desk. "Well I like it." He opened a manila folder on his desk and adjusted his little spectacles onto his nose. "Let's see," he said, "what we have here. Yes. So the students want to have an oversight board with the ability to discipline breaches of conduct. Very enterprising. Glad to see them taking this kind of responsibility. And you, as dean of the school involved, have given it your recommendation. How strong is the feeling among the faculty about this?"

"I'd have to say that it's quite strong, Robert. There were a hundred and twenty-three signatures on the initial petition."

"That's what I heard. Well, I'm not going to stand in the way of such a groundswell of support, so I'm going to go ahead and authorize it for you."

"Thank you, Robert. The professors will be pleased."

"Think nothing of it," said Fowler. "I'm pleased to do it for you. Now, Everett, let me just say that I'm holding you responsible for making sure that things don't get out of hand with this. Dan has warned me that we may be on some shaky ground here legally, since this is a state school. There might be some First Amendment problems. But I'm in no mood to jeopardize the funding for the new tower, and this recommendation that you sent over with Dr. Stiggler's memo gives me the feeling that you're fairly enthusiastic, so I'm going to let you run with it, OK?"

Everett was feeling so warm and chummy that he nodded his head in assent.

"But I wouldn't have let you do it if I didn't think you were such a stable person. I've got a lot of respect for you, Everett, and I have a lot of confidence that you'll be able to keep this thing going in the proper direction. I know that you wouldn't have gotten behind it if you didn't think you could keep it under control."

Everett shifted a little, but said nothing. Control was the one thing he was most unsure about.

"So this is what I want to have happen. We're going to give the students this oversight committee, and then nobody's ever going to hear about it again. You take my meaning? The one thing that we have to make sure of is that the students don't go off half-cocked all of a sudden and get us involved in some stupid lawsuit. God knows there are some legislators who would like nothing better than to see us on the other side of a free-speech case. I don't spend much time on campus. It's not my place. So I count on people like you to exercise their influence to shepherd these sorts of things."

President Fowler smiled suddenly, dispelling the uneasy feeling that this line of discussion was causing to grow in Everett's abdomen. "You should have heard what Jack Beetle said about you when he first came to me about this. He said something like, 'If we can get Dean Broadstreet to go along with this, then you know it's going to be a good idea.' I guess he's got a lot of respect for you."

Everett wasn't quite sure how to take this little revelation; the one feeling that he had never gotten from Jack Beetle was one of respect. But perhaps he'd been wrong. Perhaps he'd underestimated himself and his influence at the University. Perhaps he was regarded as the elder-statesman of the college. For the first time in many weeks Everett began to relax into the comfortable embrace of professional self-confidence. Yes. Of course the president can't be bothered to know the ins and outs of the campus, thought Everett. That's my job. The president was still speaking to him, and he listened attentively, readying himself to provide sage advice and counsel.

" . . . so I want you to see if you can't organize this as soon as possible."

"There are staff meetings in about sixty percent of the departments tonight, Robert," said Everett. "Campus rumor had it that you were planning to approve, so I'm sure most teachers who have a preference have given thought to the possible student participants. We could begin polling the faculty this evening."

"That's how you'd planned to do it? At the faculty meetings?"

"Yes. I thought it would be the most expedient way . . . All of the staff would be gathered anyway."

"Makes sense. I'll leave this in your hands then. I imagine you have a lot to do before this evening." President Fowler stood up, signaling the end of the audience, and Everett pulled himself out of the depths of his chair.

On the way back to campus, Everett was still gripped in the giddy rush of confidence that Dr. Fowler's accolades had given him. He picked up the cell phone that rested between the leather seats and dialed his office. "Joyce, check the schedule and see where Dr. Stiggler is right now. Jacobs 201?" Jacobs 201 was a large lecture hall in the psychology building. "Till 3:30?" He looked at his watch. "Fine. I'll catch up with her there."

TWO

Ding!

Just as soon as the door closed, Parker turned around to examine his reflection in the polished black marble of the elevator wall, and he liked what he saw. He had been wanting to steal a glance since the cute secretary got off at the eighth floor, but he'd had to wait until the other suits got off on twelve. What had she seen when she looked at him? Had she really been looking and pretending not to look, or had she actually not looked? How did he look? Powder blue pinpoint cotton shirt with a spread collar pressed just right, so that there were tiny creases along the seams? Paisley tie just slightly behind the style? Don't want to look like one of those fags in Gentlemen's Quarterly, do we! Wait. The tie's a little crooked. Hmmmmm. The knot's pointing off to one side. Was that what she had been looking at? Nah. Couldn't be. It's just a shade off the centerline. Gotta straighten it right out, though . . . There. That's better. And the medium gray chalk-stripe suit? And the socks? And the baggy white all-cotton broadcloth boxer shorts under all? Nineteen dollars a pair! Polo, Brooks, Joseph A. Banks. And the hair? Barber cut for six bucks, because the wave in it is so good that it just doesn't matter. Blow dryer? Are you kidding? Push up a couple of strands so it doesn't look too kempt. This is the nineties, for Christ's sake. Strive for that invisible mark that's just . . . shy . . . of . . . perfect.

Ding!

The door opened onto the nineteenth floor, with the flood of gray pastels and soft tube lighting that bathed the law offices of Byrd, Templeton and Diamonte, where Parker Thompson was proud to be the juniorest of junior partners. Just three years it had taken him. Three short years to leapfrog the other aspiring associates of the firm. Three years from handling cat fight and meat puppet cases for the D.A.'s office to prestige, partnership and position. In his wildest second-year law school dreams (and he'd had some wild ones) he hadn't imagined that such a meteoric rise were possible. He'd heard the horror stories of the private firms; how associates were treated like indentured servants, slaves to be cudgelled and starved into submission, partnership the only carrot on the horizon, and that to come decades in the future, if at all.

But here was Parker, five years out of school, striding confidently into the corridor, winking at the little receptionist and stealing one of her flowers for his lapel.

Parker the budding court magician of B.T. and D., as his firm was called. Parker who had apparently had the foresight to go into the D.A.'s office straight out of law school, eschewing the immediate money of private practice, and who, consequently had more in-court litigation time than anyone else in the firm. He who could quote the criminal code by chapter and verse. He who knew the language so well that he could extemporarily stretch the code when necessary, and he who had walked into B.T. and D. three years earlier with such an impressive conviction record that he could virtually dictate his own terms for employment.

Who would have thought it? Certainly not his first year Contracts teacher, who had once actually called him an irresponsible playboy in front of an entire class. Nor the fools he had done law review with, who called him an immature dope fiend, and worse. Where were they now? Chasing ambulances? Slugging it out as associates somewhere? Praying that they're on the partnership track while doing grunt work on merger and acquisition deals for eighty hours every week? Well, OK, Parker always put in sixty-five or seventy billables himself. But that's not the point! The point was that their jobs, those Harry Hairshirts who always told him that he'd never amount to anything, their jobs *sucked!* Ohhhh, *yes!* the horror stories were *true!* As the earth swung into the last decade of the second millennium, law was one of the most saturated professions in America. But the district attorney's office in almost any major city, why, they were almost always looking for a few good men (providing they had decent grades, of course.) So Parker had slid easily into the back door and had two years of the most intense legal experience possible.

Of course, he'd had to cut down on the binges somewhat. Denver was, after all, a pretty small town, and in a job where one was almost perpetually surrounded by policemen, it wouldn't do to run into someone you knew while openly blasting cocaine or chasing a little China white. But these were minor considerations. The job itself was a breeze, and reasonably fun, too. There was an esprit de corps in the D.A.'s office that he now knew didn't usually exist in the private sector, and despite the fact that he was making roughly three times as much money, there were moments when he missed the old days. You almost always knew who the good guys were in criminal law; if the D.A. were taking the time and expense to prosecute a case, there was very little doubt that the defendant was as guilty as sin. So the hot conviction record had been pretty easy to amass, and where the average young lawyer might not see the inside of a courtroom three times in a year, Parker had spent three or four hours every working day arguing before the bar. In his short career with the city, he had tried more than two hundred cases, acquired the ability to recite the procedural rules as easily as his address, and had discovered the benefits of a certain creative attitude toward the interpretation of case law. For this was Parker's most important lesson: that most judges didn't know the cases any better than he did, and that, within reason, they were almost all open to the power of suggestion.

And if that elastic interpretation had put a few people away who might otherwise be walking the streets, so what? It wasn't as if any of them were actually innocent. And law was hardly concerned with any esoteric idea of truth, anyway; that reality was drummed with the subtlety of a freight train into the head of every first year law student in the country. No, every case is winnable and every case is loseable, and the only thing separating one from the other are the brains and the resourcefulness of the attorney. Parker Thompson had plenty of both.

It is perhaps then understandable that humility was not one of his weaknesses. On spring mornings like this, after nights like last night, Lordy, it felt so good to just be alive and young and almost immortal.

And what a glorious morning it had turned out to be, all peach-colored sky and damp, sage-smelling air. He had dropped the girls off at some condo complex around an hour after sunrise, and had killed the two hours before work just driving like the wind over the plains south of Denver, flying out to Franktown and Castle Rock, winding the engine out to a scream thinned by the rush of the wind, the air whipping around his face until his cheeks were numb from the cold and sore from squinting his eyes. And the drive back up I-25, through the Castle Pines at ninety, the Porsche feeling like it was a bullet built around him and all his senses plugged into the dash waiting for the radar detector to go off, and why the hell not? What more could there possibly be but this feeling where you are one hundred percent pulsing life, milking the sensation until you are a part of some cosmic extreme, beyond thought or worship, dancing on the edge of pure physical ecstasy, just you and a car and a road and speed.

And a job, of course, which you have to get to by ten o'clock. So Parker stopped back at his house to shower and shave and put on the starched blue cotton shirt and the rest, and then drove a lot more sedately to the firm downtown. Gotta pay those bills. Porsches and houses and drugs and women do not come cheap. And unless one exercises great care, they do not come at all. And they are always much easier to lose than they are to gain. Parker had learned that lesson in spades as a summer intern in L.A. a long time ago. Now, six years older, and perhaps just a little wiser, he never screwed around with his career. If being a lawyer meant that for sixty hours a week he had to toe the line and wear the suit and walk the walk, well then by God he toed the line and he wore the suit and he walked the walk. And that was that. Life was good.

Parker walked the walk down the glassed hall toward his office with his morning-after euphoria intact. He didn't have the corner office yet, the one that belonged to another, slightly older comer in the firm, but it was his own office, the first he had ever had to himself, and outside the glass door was his own secretary, also a first. A pang of anxiety shot through him when he saw her, but he squared his shoulders and walked up to her desk.

"Morning, Linda," he said, a little more brusquely than he should have, and hoped that he was controlling his face enough that it wouldn't betray his uncertainty. It was hell being the consummate young legal shark, and also being afraid of one's own secretary, especially when she was petite, attractive, and only twenty-three years old.

"Good morning, Parker," she said with a tinge of arctic frostiness. "You look like you didn't get too much sleep last night. Anyone you knew?"

Good God! The woman had x-ray vision! How did she know? Still, it was no good trying to hide it. "No . . . They . . . She was . . . no. Just someone I met."

"Oh it was a 'they,' huh? You may have outdone yourself this time." She fixed Parker with her level gaze, and assembled her mouth into the tightest of smiles, keeping all of her dangerous jagged edges submerged beneath the surface like an iceberg.

Of course he had only himself to blame. He had made the single executive's universal mistake of sleeping with her about three months earlier, after the office Christmas Party. Even at the time he had known it was a mistake. She was just so pretty though, that thick honey blond hair, so lovely, the lipstick and the perfume, and she had always seemed so inviting . . . He had finally broken down and done it. The event had been actually kind of weird to him, like it had all been ordained. He knew, for instance, the minute he got to the bar that night, that he was going to sleep with her and she had seemed to know too. She would touch his arm with just the slightest bit more pressure than necessary when she wanted his attention, looking into his eyes, brushing by him when she got up. Nothing overt, but little things, another language that they both temporarily understood.

And then later that night, while they were making love in the darkness of his room, she had whispered to him, "Oh yes, I've wanted you for so long. Oh God. Oh yes, Parker. Oh yes." And then she had started to laugh when they had finished, laughing like it was from some total relief after stress. She seemed so utterly happy. And her reaction had made Parker feel extremely uncomfortable. Each time they made love that night she had been reduced to this intense laughter afterwards, and then a dreamy, happy peace. Strange.

He had spent a lot of time that weekend thinking about it. He liked her, and he liked making love to her, and he wanted the option of making love to her whenever he felt like it. But the more he thought about it, the more he realized that there were complications. She worked for him, for one thing. He had never really had this sort of "I say—you do" relationship before, not even with the pool secretaries in the D.A.'s office. He didn't want to abuse it. And he also never wanted to worry whether she was with him because she wanted to be, or because she felt as if she were obligated. No. That wouldn't do. And then he began wondering if she had slept with him because she hoped for some kind of advancement. It seemed a strange idea at first; what could he do for her? But then again . . . You never know. Girls do strange things. And that thing she had said to him while they were in bed, about wanting him for so long. It had seemed almost too sincere, like she'd planned to say it. In Parker's experience the only name commonly spoken during the throes of passion belonged to the lord on high. Who could remember someone's name at a time like that? What if she were faking? Who could tell what girls were faking and when? What if she were just trying to use him somehow? How could he know? And what if she had really meant it? Could he manage to hold her off, and still have her whenever he wanted? And, horror of horrors, what if she really fell for him? He liked her well enough, he supposed, but he didn't think she was what he was looking for, if indeed he was looking for anything. He foresaw the inevitable break-up. She worked in his office. She would know things about him, things she could lob around the office like hand grenades. Like his occasional taste for heroin. Christ, if that ever got out . . . Good-bye Colorado Bar Association. His life would become a minefield. And then the dread phrase started to creep into the legal departments of his brain. "Sexual Harassment Suit." No way! Get me out!

So he had come to work the next Monday, lamely equipped with a bunch of daisies hidden in his briefcase, in the foolish hope that things could work out nicely, and had called Linda into his office. She had come in with such a beautiful, trusting smile on her face that he had instantly had second thoughts. But no, he thought. I just can't take the chance. He watched the look on her face fall away as he told her that he didn't want a relationship. The look told him that she had been on the level, that she really had liked him. She told him that she had been thinking about him all weekend. And that was all she had said. "I'm sorry," he had said. "I don't want you to feel sorry for me, Parker," she had told him as she walked out of the office.

He never did give her the flowers.

Like a lot of young men in his position, he soon learned that in the act of disrobing with her he had both laid bare his chest and handed her a dagger. Not that it was her fault, of course. It would have taken a more than human effort on her part to resist turning the knife a little when she felt like it.

"Have you got any coffee for me?" he asked with studied nonchalance.

"Sure," she answered, displaying about a thousand teeth. "It's in that urn right over there."

How embarrassing. As he walked over to the coffee pot, he saw one of the senior partners of the firm, Jim Diamonte, walking toward him with an armful of file folders. As Diamonte looked at him, and then over toward Linda, Parker could tell what was running through his mind. Diamonte never got his own coffee. He fixed Parker with a quizzical expression, glanced back again at Linda, and then nodded in the direction of

Parker's office. Parker charged his cup with sugar and followed him in.

"Now, Parker," said Diamonte distractedly as he looked through the files in his arms. "How are you coming with Mr. Batelin's case?"

Parker shrugged. "I've got a pre-trial with the other guy's attorney this afternoon and I'm sure he's going to settle. I'm going to crucify him if this thing goes to court and he knows it."

"Well that's good, Parker, because you're going to have to drop it."

"I'm what?"

"Hold on for a second. I have to get rid of these files." He walked down the hall to his office. When he came back a minute later he didn't have the files in his arms anymore. "Now," he said, "Where were we?"

"I was just picking myself up off the floor, because you just ordered me to drop a case I've been working on for a month and a half."

Diamonte grinned. "Sorry. You know I can't order you to, but I'd appreciate it if you would. I've got a case I want you to take, and I want you to have a clear plate for it. It's for an old friend of mine's son. It seems the boy has gotten himself kicked out of college, and they want to sue for readmittance."

"Sue? On what grounds? I mean, if he's out he's out. Unless there's some discrimination angle. Is he black or something?"

"No," said Diamonte. "That's one thing he isn't. I went to law school with his father and he's the original Wasp. Do they still say 'Wasp'? Anyway, it's not about grades. His father tells me he got into an argument with one of his professors during a class and wound up making an allusion to her sexuality, if you get my drift."

"And they kicked him out for it?" The legal departments of Parker's brain started to click through the possibilities. "Did the administration claim harassment?"

"No, not exactly, and that's one of the things that's interesting about this. The administration wasn't even directly responsible for his expulsion. Evidently, the school created some sort of student review board and gave it the power to expel students for making offensive statements."

"Oh really?" said Parker. "One of these politically correct things? Yeah, that does sound interesting. I've read about some of this stuff. Was there a specific list of words or something they weren't supposed to say?"

"I'm not sure, but I don't think so. As I understand it, the students have been given the latitude to simply expel people who make offensive statements," Diamonte said.

"Offensive as determined by whom?"

"Why the other students, of course," Diamonte said with a touch of sarcasm in his voice. He raised his hand to forestall the expression of disbelief growing on Parker's face. "No kidding. I know it sounds absurd, but there it is. The school has some sort of speech code, and they've handed the right to interpret it over to the students. David, that's the boy's name, was kicked out a few days ago. As I understand it, this review board was just created within the last few weeks, and David is the first person to be disciplined. I would imagine that the students on the review board wanted to flex their muscles a little bit and set an example." Diamonte looked speculatively out of the window for a moment. "I don't think they could have realized just how badly they blew it when they decided on him as the best candidate to dismiss. His father's a hell of a lawyer."

"But this doesn't make any sense," said Parker. "It's a state school. They get funding directly from the government, don't they? They had to know there would be a First Amendment conflict. There was that, um . . . That University of Michigan case a couple of years ago. Even a one-L in their cockamamie law school up there could have told them there was going to be a problem."

"I'm at a loss to explain it myself, Parker. But don't be too quick to assume that this is a cut and dried issue. I remember reading something a few years back where the law school faculty someplace in New York tried to set up a similar speech code. As I recall, they came right out and said that the students shouldn't expect First Amendment protection. Something about the intellectual community having a higher standard of values than any naive commitment to unrestrained debate." Diamonte chuckled ironically and raised his bushy eyebrows. "How about *that* for convenience? And this was at a law school, for heaven's sake. Here were these supposed jurists, supposed American jurists, who decided that their private sense of values should supersede the United States Constitution. But I don't need to be telling you this. You were still doing law review five years ago. You know as well as I do what kind of lunatics there are in this profession."

Parker smiled. He was very fond of Diamonte. "Still though, Jim, if they were discussing, I mean this kid David and his professor, if they were discussing anything of an even remotely political nature, this has to be a big S speech case."

"The boy even remembers his Con Law lingo," Diamonte teased. "Yes, I'm inclined to agree with you about the higher standard. But as I say, you never know."

Parker stared blankly out of the window digesting the information. Like Diamonte, he had heard of some unusual things going on at college campuses, but didn't think too much about them unless they made the news. He seemed to remember there being some sort of tussle at the University a few months before about racism or something. The whole thing had looked monumentally stupid to him at the time and he had changed the channel. He had handled a few discrimination cases before, and had come to the conclusion that colleges were among the least likely of places to be guilty of it, and the most likely of places to agonize over it. As far as the other barbs that came under the blanket heading of "political correctness," these speech codes and the like, there were ample protections in the Constitution. So for the case he was being offered, it seemed too simple, too obvious. There had to be something else that he wasn't being told. "What's the kid like?" he asked.

"I know what you're thinking, and no, he's not some sort of troll. In fact he's a reasonably level-headed young man as I recall. Fraternity boy. He's fairly cocky, and he probably drinks too much, but so did you when you were that age. And so did I," he added with a grin. "I went to Columbia with his father. As I say, he's what we used to call white bread when I was your age. Extremely bright man, but one of those lawyers who went in for money more than for the esoteric aspects of our trade. He's with Beauchamp Tyler. I imagine you've heard of them before."

"Who hasn't? Wall Street firm," said Parker. "But I always thought it was pronounced 'Bow-champ' or 'Bow-shamp.'"

"No, it's 'Beechum.' Believe me, I know. I'll tell you a story. When I was just out of Columbia, old Horace Beauchamp was still alive. Terrifying man. Huge head. Meaner than you can imagine. I heard him give a speech one time at a bar association dinner, and the kid who introduced him pronounced his name wrong. I'll never forget it. Beauchamp corrected him, and then, with the microphone on, asked him if he'd been in New York long. The young lawyer, and remember, he was only a little younger than I was, told him he'd just graduated from Yale the year before. Beauchamp looked him in the eye and said 'It's a pity your visit will be so truncated.' Then he just turned away as if the kid had vanished. Which, as far as his career was concerned, was just about what happened."

"You mean he ruined the kid? Got him blacklisted or something?"

Diamonte spread his palms upward and shrugged. "What I mean, is that the word is pronounced 'Beechum.' Anyway, Art Shore had the temperament to succeed in that sort of environment. He's a partner now. We keep in touch. And David, his son, is coming in today at one. You can form your own impressions then. Assuming you want the case, of course."

Parker was a little bit nervous, since the case involved a personal friend of his boss's, but he was excited, too. First Amendment cases didn't come along every day, and if there were any complications to them they could very easily go before the state supreme court, or even higher. It was actually quite an honor for a person in his position to be offered such a plum. "What, are you kidding? You bet I'll take it. Who can you give me for staff?"

"Take Rick and Aimee."

"Both of them?"

"Yeah. I'll get them off of whatever they're working on. And if it's all right with you, I'll put Stevens on the Batelin case. Call the opposing counsel and reschedule the pre-trial. You can brief Stevens on the particulars later. If Batelin gives you any static, have him come talk to me. And Parker, this one's important. I've always been impressed by the work you do here, but I also know that you have a pretty active social life. I want you in early on this, OK? And I want you to give me progress reports personally. Shore's father's going to be here on Friday, and I don't want him to think I've handed his son's future over to a bum. I want you looking a little more bright-eyed than you do right now."

Parker bristled at the implication. "I'm all right."

"I know you're all right. I wouldn't be offering you this if I didn't think you were all right. But I want Shore to know you're all right, too. Clear?"

"Clear."

"Good. Then I'll leave it to you." Diamonte rose and started to leave.

"Hey, Jim?" asked Parker.

"Yes, Parker."

"Why me? Why not one of the full partners?"

"Oh, a couple of reasons. If this thing actually goes before a judge, it would look better to have a younger attorney representing him. That way it won't look so much like the old establishment coming down on the free-thinking younger generation. Besides, I thought it would be good for you to take a case like this. You're a good lawyer, Parker. You've got the potential to be a really good lawyer. I thought it was about time that you had a case that dealt with the fundamentals. Let you start to see the overview of what the law is and what it can do. Good luck with it." Diamonte turned and walked out of the door. Parker could hear him calling out, "Mrs. Pringle! Where are those files I just had?"

Parker got up and walked over to the bookcase on the wall opposite his desk. The shelves contained the sum total of his legal experience; thick volumes on Colorado and federal statutes, procedural rules and jury instruction, and on the bottom shelf, rarely used, were the books he had accumulated while still in school. He knelt down and scanned the titles, and then extracted a copy of *Emanuel's Constitutional Law Outline*. The faded green cover was a mass of scribbles, notes from research done long ago and now forgotten: "cite F Supp 823—estblshmnt?" "US 186 SC 23—29-35." *Emanuel* had been one of his saviors in law school, a constant companion, and looking at the book brought a flood of memories of when he had still believed that the law had anything to do with right and wrong. The one book he most wanted, however, was Lawrence Tribe's *American Constitutional Law,* and Parker couldn't find it anywhere. He couldn't even remember the last time he had seen it. He took the copy of *Emanuel* back to his desk and began to read.

About an hour later, the two associates assigned to the case, Rick Friedman and Aimee Clarke, arrived in his office. In any law firm there is a pecking order as rigid and inviolable as the Vatican's, and B.T. and D. was no exception. In fact, if anyone in the firm cared to see where in the hierarchy they stood, they could simply look at a piece of office stationery. Along the left-hand margin the names of the partners were printed, starting, of course, with the named ones like Jim Diamonte. He, John Byrd, and Robert Templeton held the greatest amount of stock in the firm, and answered to no one. Below their names in descending order of seniority and shareholding were listed the other partners. Parker's name was now listed on the left-hand side, too, albeit at the bottom, but in that simple shift was reflected a great deal of office prestige and power. Just six months earlier he had been listed on the right-hand side of the page, meaning that he was simply a lowly associate, and had theoretically to do the bidding of any of the people listed on the left-hand side of the page. In practice it worked somewhat differently, because certain associates were understood to be in the sphere of certain partners. Parker had been one of Diamonte's crowd, and had worked almost exclusively for him since he had come to the firm. But even among the associates there was hierarchy, and since the last printing of office stationery, when Parker had made his triumphant jump to the left, the top two names listed belonged to Rick Friedman and Aimee Clarke. That Diamonte had chosen both of them for this case said quite a bit about the importance he placed on it, a significance which was not lost on either of them, or on Parker.

"Where's the fire?" asked Rick, as he and Aimee took the chairs in front of Parker's desk. It was an awkward moment, because they had both been listed above him when he was an associate, and Parker knew that they now had some animosity toward him. For this reason he had avoided them as much as possible. Now, however, the moment had arrived.

"I was on my way over to District with Johansing when Diamonte told me to stop whatever I was doing and come see you," Rick continued. "What's the story?"

"The story," said Parker, "is that the son of one of Diamond Jim's law school buddies has gotten himself thrown out of college, and it has fallen upon us to have him reinstated."

"What'd he do?" asked Aimee. She crossed her legs seductively, causing Parker to glance at them. There had been a time when Parker had considering making a play for her, because she was the only sort of woman whom he could see himself with in any sort of lasting relationship. She wore black-framed glasses and red lipstick, exuding a business-like sexuality. She was also brilliant. And unfortunately she was fairly friendly with Linda. He got the uncomfortable feeling that she knew everything, *everything* that had gone on between him and his secretary. Part of his mind actually feared the sorts of things that women whom he had slept with might say about him; not so much that he honestly felt himself to be a poor lover, but because it is the one area of a man's life where he cannot be absolutely certain of his ability. In Parker's case, this was especially troubling, since a great part of his ego was based on the belief in his own infallibility.

"Evidently, he used some sexual allusion while he was talking to one of his professors. I don't know all the particulars. The professor's a woman, and the boy was tossed by some sort of student review board. Some politically correct nonsense. I don't know. I won't have all the facts until I talk to the kid this afternoon."

"Harassment statutes?" asked Aimee.

"Maybe. I know most of them in this state anyway. But I have a feeling that this is going to be more First Amendment stuff. I've been reading through *Emanuel,* and there're a couple of things I want you to check. I haven't been able to find it yet, but it seems to me that there was a case in about 1989 somewhere in Michigan where one of these speech codes was thrown out."

"Wisconsin," said Rick. "And it was a US Supreme Court case. I had to look it up a couple of months ago."

Parker was annoyed at the correction, but he decided to let it pass. "OK. I'm going to want to see it. See if you can dig up anything relevant on strict scrutiny speech cases. I'm hoping there's going to be some political angle I can use to demonstrate chilling effect. I'd also appreciate it if one of you could dig me up a copy of Tribe. Mine seems to have disappeared. And one other thing . . . I know this is a little unusual, but could one of you prepare a little background information on these speech codes in universities? I want to know how many of them there are, ballpark figures. And I'm also going to want to know how they've been attacked in the past, successful strategies, you know?"

"I've got a friend over in the morgue at the *Dispatch* who can probably give us the numbers," Aimee said with a smile. "He owes me a favor or two. It'll at least give me a place to start looking."

"Great. I'll have a talk with the kid this afternoon. Then I want to reread the First Amendment entries from Tribe before we do the brief, and if it's at all possible I want to file it by lunchtime tomorrow. So what do you say, tomorrow morning?"

Rick and Aimee looked at each other and nodded. "Yeah," Rick said. "Eight o'clock?"

"Fine." Parker looked at his watch. "I gotta go. Lunch date. See you kids later."

*   *   *

Parker found his best friend and sometime crime partner, Clayton "Pidge" Segal, seated on the sunlit terrace of Welton Place, the fern bar across the street from their shared athletic club. Welton made a convenient rendezvous for the two of them, especially after heavy evenings, since if one or the other was too hung over, they could finesse the weekly squash game and pass an hour comparing headaches. Parker took one look at Pidge and knew that the game for today was definitely off. His friend had taken a table in the corner of the patio, under a Cinzano umbrella, and was staring morosely through his aviator sunglasses into the depths of a Bloody Mary.

"Did your boss change the dress code, or what?" asked Parker as he sat down. Instead of displaying the woolen plumage of the young stockbroker, which Pidge was, he was casually upholstered in Levis and a sweatshirt.

"I've got to stop going out Monday nights," said Pidge, and shivered. "Or maybe I have to stop going out with you."

"Question number eight:" Parker intoned gravely, "Have you ever missed work because of drinking?"

"Not funny. This is the first time, and I intend it to be the last. We didn't have any issues this morning, and I couldn't hack sitting around the office. Maybe I should just quit drinking."

"Question number four: Do you ever swear to quit drinking?"

"Oh, fuck off. What's your story, anyway?" Pidge shivered again, and massaged his temples. "I seem to recall you disappeared pretty early. Oh, wait a minute. Didn't I introduce you to Mary last night? I can't imagine you were able to score with her so quickly."

"I can't imagine anyone scoring with her," said Parker. "No offense, Pidge, but stop trying to set me up with your friends."

"She's new in town. She doesn't know anybody. She's pretty, and she'd be good for you."

"Pidge, she asked if I was a Catholic."

"Well you are, aren't you?"

"More or less," said Parker. "Less. Look, I'm not anti-religion or anything, but it's just not the sort of thing you talk about at a bar. Or anywhere else, for that matter."

"Why not?" asked Pidge.

"What's the matter with you? Come on, man, snap out of it. You look like hell."

"I feel like my eyes are about to pop clean out of my head. So what happened to you last night?"

One of the fern-bar waiters drifted up. His face was beautiful and evenly tanned. He put his hand on the back of Parker's chair and looked into his eyes. "May I get you anything?"

Pidge groaned. "I think I'm going to barf."

Parker smiled at the waiter. "Give us a minute, would you?"

Pidge turned his eyes to the waiter and said, "You know, if you tip your barber next time, that won't happen to you."

"I'll come back in a few minutes," said the waiter.

Pidge watched the waiter depart. "I can't stand them."

"It's not his fault," said Parker.

"I don't care. I just can't stand them. I feel too crappy to be tolerant. What happened to you last night?"

"Well, I talked to your friend for about twenty minutes before I realized she was a vestal virgin. Then I went off and had a religious experience of my own."

"Did you fix?"

It amused Parker to hear his friend use drug slang, since drugs were so much not a part of his life. The first time Parker had ever used opium, in Thailand, Pidge had been with him, and had even taken a few drags on the pipe, but true to form that had been the only foray into narcotics he had ever made. Pidge drank, occasionally to excess, and would sometimes do cocaine, but never touched the hard stuff. "No. A little blow. Nothing major."

"So?"

"Soooo," said Parker. "Then I went home with these two girls. It was a pretty early evening. I think I was in bed by ten."

"You what!"

"I went home with these two girls. We didn't talk much about religion."

"You *what!* You mean you took two girls home, to their home, or you took two girls . . . home?"

"Man, I took 'em *home.*"

Pidge was smiling now, despite his hangover. "You disgusting, miserable dog. Why does that always happen to you? I've never known anyone else in my life who was able to pull that off, and you . . . How many times have you done this now?"

"I don't know. I think I should start writing an advice column. Come on. Let's go play some squash. You need the exercise. Besides, if you stay here, the waiter will put something gross in your drink."

"Let him try. Nah, I feel too cruddy. You go on. See if you can pick up a game. I think if I hit a ball right now my whole body would shatter." Pidge laughed again. "You disgusting pig."

THREE

When Parker got back to the office it was already after one. He had found someone milling about the courts, and the two of them had played until the twosome in the next time slot came and kicked them out. After taking a shower he was running late, his hair still wet, dripping into his perfectly ironed collar, and when he got back to the firm he hustled down the corridor. Through the windows to his office he could see a young man with longish blond hair sitting in his desk chair. A baseball cap perched atop his head, and his wiry frame was cowled in an extraordinarily wrinkled yellow shirt with a frayed button-down collar. A pair of mirrored sunglasses hung down against his chest from a neon pink cord looped around the back of his neck. He appeared completely engrossed in the magazine which he had propped up on edge on the top of Parker's desk. The cover was titled "*Rock and Ice*," and pictured another wiry young man splayed out like a spider on the overhanging face of a cliff.

Parker stepped into the doorway, a little breathless, and ahemmed good-naturedly, with a look that was supposed to say 'OK, kid, out of my chair.' The young man, however, did not smile. He looked up as if Parker had disturbed an important train of thought. He stared for a long half-second and then asked, "Yeah?" in the tone normally reserved for bothersome waitresses who hover around in coffee shops when you are trying to read the paper. Even in the short syllable uttered, Parker could hear the boy's accent, which was of the sort that some dedicated New York City dwellers, even educated ones, seem to raise as a shield in an effort to seem world-weary and invulnerable.

"Yea-a-ah," said Parker. "My name is Parker Thompson, your name is David Shore, and you're sitting in my chair."

"Oh. Sorry," said the young man as unapologetically as possible. He stood up, marking the place in his magazine. "I figured you were just some loser who wanted to see if I wanted anything. Yeah. My name's David. I guess you're my lawyer."

"I guess I am." They shook hands, and Parker noticed that his new client needed a shave.

"Did you oversleep or something?" asked the boy.

"Pardon?"

"Your hair's all wet. Did you just wake up or something?"

"Oh. No, I was at the gym. We ran a little overtime on the court."

"Really." It was a short word, but Shore was able to pack a lot of New York boredom into it.

"I'm glad to see you've been making yourself at home."

Shore shrugged. "You were late."

"Uh . . . right," said Parker, beginning to feel irritated at the boy's arrogant demeanor. "Right," he said again. "Well why don't you sit in that one over there for awhile and we'll have us a little talk. OK, Sport?" 'Sport' was a derisive term that Parker and his friends had used in college.

Shore's eyes flashed up sharply, and then, with apparent effort he pushed something between a smile and a grimace onto his face. "I'll make you a deal . . . Parker, is it? Parker. You don't call me 'Sport' and I won't call you 'Tiger.'" He said it coolly, but his voice quivered just a bit, like a person nervously trying to sound clever in front of someone he wants to impress. Parker concluded that at least some of the snobbishness was probably bravado.

"I think we can get along with that. You call me Parker and I'll call you David. And by the way, David? I'm not your waiter, I'm your attorney."

At that the young man smiled naturally. "Where are your people from?" he asked as he sprawled into one of the chairs across from Parker's desk.

"Chicago. Look, I'm not trying to rush your fraternity, OK? And I'm not going to tell you how much money my father makes. I understand you have a problem so why don't we start off talking about that, all right?"

"Fine."

"Great. What's the latest you've heard from school?"

David pursed his lips and blew his cheeks out thoughtfully. "Nothing. This speech board or whatever told me I was out last Friday, and that's about it. I called my father about it and I guess he talked to the dean, but the dean wouldn't budge. Dad just about hit the ceiling because my family makes endowments to the school."

"What do you mean, 'endowments?'"

"You know . . . like contributions and stuff," said David. "Give's 'em money when they ask."

"Did he know the dean personally?" asked Parker.

"Yeah, I guess they've met. But they weren't friends or anything."

Parker nodded his head. "How about you? Did you know the dean?"

"No. I mean, I've seen him before. In fact he was in the classroom the afternoon when all this started," said David.

"How did all this start? Why don't you just start at the beginning and tell me what happened." Parker took a new legal pad from a drawer in his credenza and began writing on it.

"Sure." David took a deep breath and blew it out slowly, inflating his cheeks again. "About a week and a half ago I was in my Women's Studies class. Well maybe I better start before that. God this is so complicated." He stopped for a moment and a frustrated look chased over his face as he tried to collect his thoughts. Then he started again, slowly. "OK. I'll try to explain this to you. To graduate we all have to take this one class in women's studies. It fulfills one of our core graduation requirements. The class is called The Women's Experience in America. Now, I can't stand this class, none of us can. I mean, you know, like the guys in my fraternity. Basically if you've got anything on the ball, and you're a guy, this class is going to make you feel like crap. And it's all bullshit anyway. You know, the typical feminazi junk. But we all have to take it in order to graduate, right? Most people take it in the first or second year, but I kind of put things off sometimes. Especially if I know I'm not going to like them. So I'd heard from all the guys about how much of a drag this class is supposed to be so I waited and waited until now, last semester of my senior year. Are you with me so far?"

"Yeah," said Parker. "Go on."

"OK. About a week and a half ago . . . that would be the Friday before last . . . I was in my Women's Studies class. It's a big class, you know, lecture hall. There must be two hundred students in it. And I always sit off to one side with my friends and some of the sorority girls who are in the class with us. Most of them hate it, too, 'cause the teacher works out on them if they're pretty and have money. It's all such a bunch of crap. So there I am in this class. The professor, her name's Stiggler, by the way, is giving a lecture on how all, well, male-female sex is uh . . . is really rape. No shit. She was saying how some women don't realize it because they're in love, but that any time a woman has sex with a man it's really an act of rape."

"I hadn't heard that one before," said Parker.

"No, I'm serious. You wouldn't believe some of the stuff they tell us. It was in our textbook and everything. Here's this fat old broad, probably never been laid in her whole entire life lecturing us on how we're all a bunch of rapists. You have to understand, we've heard this junk so many times . . . So this friend of mine who was sitting with us, this guy Rock, he's in my fraternity, he's a real joker, he goes 'Well Polly Quinn wanted me to rape her before we even left the bar last night.' You'd have to know Polly. She's this . . . She's got kind of a reputation. Anyway, it was really funny, and we all started laughing, even the girls. Well Ms. Stiggler," he drew out the 'Ms.' so it buzzed like an egg timer, "Mizzzzz Stiggler just loses it. I mean she freaked. I don't think she heard what Rocky said, but she knew that somebody said something 'cause we were all trying so hard not to laugh. I guess she gets it in her head that I was the one who started it, so she's like looking at me and saying all this stuff and we, I mean we all shut up."

"What sort of stuff? What did she say?" asked Parker.

"Just all this stuff about me. Like uh . . . 'Pay careful attention, women. This is what you want to avoid.' I mean what a lame thing to say. And I was trying to just look off into space and ignore her but she just wouldn't let it go. She looks up at me all serious and says 'Be honest. How many women have you raped?' I knew I shouldn't have done it, but I'm like, 'I never raped anyone in my life.' And she goes 'You people disgust me. I'll bet your father never worked for anything in his life, did he? And now he's sitting on top of the same male-dominated power structure.' And that just did it. I mean, my father works so hard I hardly ever see him. Not that I'm crying about it or whatever. He's got a big job. But he's a great guy. So before I could even think about it I said something like 'And fat old dykes wind up in power in boho universities like this one.' I was, man I was pissed. I just got up and walked out. That's when I saw the dean sitting there in the back of the room. He looked like he'd swallowed his dentures."

"Do you have any idea what he was doing there?" asked Parker. "Does he often come and audit classes?"

"No, not that I know of. I'd never seen him in a class before."

"Did he say anything to you at the time?" asked Parker.

"No. He hardly even looked at me. But I suppose I probably looked pretty mad."

"But he heard all this, right?"

David knitted his brows and nodded. "Oh yeah. He heard it all right."

"What happened after you left the room?"

"Well, nothing. At least not right away. My friends told me later that night that she was pretty pissed after I left. At first I was worried that I'd blown my grade in the class, but I went climbing over the weekend and pretty much forgot about it. I mean, I didn't care. What the hell? Dad's got connections everywhere to get me into law school and my LSAT's are good. I figured what's the worst that can happen? So I guessed I'd just lay low in the class and mark time until the end of the term. But then that Monday . . . last Monday . . . a funny thing happened. This squid showed up at our house and told me I had to show up at the speech code board, and I'm thinking, you know, whatever the hell that is."

"Did you know him? The guy who delivered the summons?"

"No, it was just some hairy little loser with dreadlocks wearing a tie-dye and Birkenstocks. You know. Typical granola."

"Did he tell you what it was about?" asked Parker.

"Yeah, I believe he said that it was about how I had grossly offended my fellow classmates, or something to that effect. And he told me it was about Stiggler's class, so I knew what he was talking about."

"Did he mention if you should bring counsel with you?"

"What, the little crunchy guy? No way. He was trying to act all important, using all these big words and stuff, but I don't think he knows what the word 'counsel' means the way you're saying it. But the letter he gave me told me specifically that I was not to bring anyone with me."

"No one at all? Parents? Anyone?"

"Nobody."

"OK," said Parker. "Go on."

"So last Wednesday night I go to this room in the University Center, that's the main student center on campus, and Stiggler's there, and the dean, and some other people who I guess were professors, and behind this long table were seven students who I later found out were the speech code board."

"Did you know any of them? I mean had you any dealings with any of them before?" asked Parker.

"You might say so," said David. "One of the girls, this girl named Gretchen. I did her after a party last year."

"Did her? You mean . . . " said Parker.

"Yeah. She's one of these granola girls who comes from a rich family but wants to do the sixties rebel thing. You know. She used to come to our parties sometimes. I think she probably got tired of those wimpy guys who she hangs around with. So I did her after this party."

"I don't mean to pry," said Parker, "But did you ever call her afterwards?"

David shifted a little in the chair and looked down at his feet with an embarrassed smile. "No, I didn't. And, yeah, she was probably pissed off about it."

"OK. Did you know any of the others?"

"The granola who delivered the letter was there. And that one guy, Georg, I knew him." David pronounced the name the German way, with two hard 'g' sounds, and he elongated the first syllable so that it sounded like Gay-Org.

"Who's he?"

"Oh he's this German fruitcake who's always getting involved in campus politics. You know, gay and lesbian concerns and all that. I mean, I didn't know him personally or anything, but he's always in the school paper."

"And you didn't know any of the other people?" asked Parker.

"No."

"Well what happened then?"

"It's kind of hard to explain," said David. "They told me that I had been summoned because several students in my class, and the professor, had been, I think they said, 'deeply offended' by my conduct in a certain class, and what did I have to say about it. And at that time I started thinking about what Stiggler had said about me and about my dad, so I said 'What about my being offended by what she said?' And Georg, the homo, said that they hadn't received any complaints about Professor Stiggler, and that if they were to receive any at this point they probably wouldn't take them seriously because it would look like I was just trying to get even. And then he asked me if I denied using, I can't remember how he put it, a 'trans-genderal epithet' or something like that. And I said, 'cause I thought the whole thing was pretty ridiculous, I said, 'you mean, did I say "dyke?"' And that really pissed them off. But all the time I was thinking what's the worst they can do to me? I guess I found out."

"Did any witnesses come to describe what had happened in class?"

"That girl, Gretchen, she's in the class, and she talked about what I had said, and about how I had used the word 'dyke.' When I tried to ask her about what Stiggler had said to me, to get me angry, one of the professors said that it was irrelevant."

"How did the meeting end?" asked Parker.

"After about an hour or so they told me to leave, and said for me to come back the next day and that they would inform me of any disciplinary action. So the next day, Thursday night, I went back and they told me I was out. I couldn't believe it. I guess I was kind of in shock. I mean this is my last semester and I've put four years of my life into that school." David looked up at Parker with something like appeal in his eyes. "Can they do this to me?"

"No," said Parker. "At least I don't think so. You're probably studying political science, right?"

"Yeah."

"Did you ever happen to take a Constitutional Law class?"

"I took the survey class when I was a sophomore," said David.

"Well this should be a pretty straightforward First Amendment case. I was talking about this with Jim Diamonte this morning, and we both agree that this is probably what we call a 'big S' speech case."

"What does that mean?"

"Well, you know about the First Amendment, right?"

"A little, yeah."

"I'll see if I can explain this easily. The prevailing view of the courts is that the First Amendment was designed primarily to protect political speech. But that being said, there has been a great deal of debate over protection of other kinds of speech. The classic example is yelling 'fire' in a crowded theater. Obviously, the founding fathers did not intend such speech to be protected. Another example is speech designed to incite people. Fighting words, as they're known. Can you stand outside of a bar and call someone's mother a whore, with the intention of starting a brawl? Probably not. So the courts have evolved this dual nature of free-speech cases. OK?"

"OK."

"Now, because of this dual nature, there are two potential tests that a restriction of speech might have to pass, depending on the nature of the infringement. If the statute's infringement is incidental and unintended, and infringes on all points of view equally, then whoever created the infringement must only prove that there was what we call a 'rational basis' for it. Do you understand?"

"Sure," said David, though it was obvious that he didn't.

"I'm not doing this very well. How about this. Suppose some government agency tries to stop people from placing handbills on cars in its parking lot, in the interest of cutting down on litter. This restriction might stop people from expressing a political statement. And somebody like the ACLU might actually try a test case in a situation like this just to see what the courts would say about it. This is the sort of case where the courts would probably use the rational basis test, and they would balance

67

the potential infringement against the potential benefit of such a policy, in this case a cleaner environment."

David nodded his head.

"OK," Parker continued, "Now what if that same government agency made a rule that prevented people from placing anti-abortion literature on people's windshields?"

"That would be unfair," said David.

"That's right. It would be. Here, in legal terms, the agency would be attempting to stifle the free exchange of ideas. There would be what the courts call a 'chilling effect.' To deal with this sort of infringement, the courts have developed a more vigorous test than rational basis. The government would have to prove a 'compelling interest' in having such a policy. Not just a legitimate reason, but a compelling one. The courts would apply 'strict scrutiny,' to such a rule. And in the history of this country, I can only think of a few First Amendment cases where the government has been able to meet the compelling interest standard. That's not to say that there aren't more, but for the government to demonstrate compelling interest is extraordinarily rare."

The young man looked out of Parker's window, and for a moment Parker was afraid he'd lost him, but then David said, "But it's not a law that was passed in either case. Just a rule. How can the courts get involved?"

"You catch on quick. Excellent question." Parker gave a wry smile. "In reality, the courts can get involved anywhere they want to. In this case, they have interpreted the First Amendment to apply to any organization acting as an arm of the state. Your school gets direct government funding."

"Yeah, I guess it does, doesn't it?"

"Yup. So we have that going for us," said Parker. "As far as your particular case is concerned, there is at least one case that I know of that applies specifically. I'm going to have to look it up to get all the particulars, but there was a case in Michigan or Wisconsin where one of the universities created one of these speech codes, and if I'm not mistaken, the U.S. Supreme Court threw it out on appeal. After all, the very nature of such codes is to prevent debate in certain areas that may very well be political. I've got some people looking it up right now. I think there may be some latitude on the part of private universities, but with state schools, which get funding directly from the government, I don't think there's any question. In fact, I can't understand why your school did this. It's almost laughable."

"I know I'm not laughing," said David. "And I hope you aren't either."

"No, no. Not at all. I'm just telling you this because in the end I don't think there's any way we can lose. And if they somehow managed to evade the First Amendment question, there are other ways we can fight them: due process, for one. As a government agency, they can't just kick someone out with no established policy. You weren't allowed counsel. You weren't aware of the board's existence, and were never advised of the change in policy. If I understand correctly, the students on the board have no written code to go by. This is vague to the point of absurdity. There's . . . there's a lot."

"So what happens now?"

"Well, the most important thing is that we want to win decisively as soon as possible, so you won't miss too much school. We'll file tomorrow in District Court. With a little luck, we should get a hearing within a month or two."

"A month!" said David. "Those fuckers! I can't just miss a month of classes. I won't be able to graduate!"

"I know, it stinks. We may be able to get an injunction that would force the school to let you back in while the case is pending."

"When would that happen?" David asked.

"Maybe as early as Monday. There's an obvious time constraint here, and the courts are usually sympathetic. The hearing would only take about twenty minutes or so. And if the court doesn't enjoin, we can always threaten the University with a suit for damages."

"Really?"

"I don't know if we'll get anything, but it's worth a shot," said Parker. "At the least it'll shake them up a little. It all depends on the strength of their case. The fact that you slept with that girl on the board will go against her credibility. And I'm going to want to talk to that dean who was there. Get a formal statement from him. If he says the same thing that you do, and it becomes apparent that you were goaded into your actions, that should take most of the wind out of their sails. They may want to drop the case right then."

"And how long will all this take?" asked David.

"Maybe a couple of weeks, if all goes really well. It depends on what the dean says. David, I know this isn't easy for you, but you may not be able to graduate until this summer."

"Great."

"But cheer up. You have an outstanding lawyer. Me. *And* you have a laughably easy case. We just have to convince the University of these facts, and I don't think that's going to be too difficult. If things turn really ugly for them, they may be receptive to the idea of modifying your graduation requirements somewhat."

"So I might be able to get out in May after all?"

"Stranger things have happened. I want you to write out exactly what happened to you, the same way that you told it to me, so that we have a record. Try and be as accurate as possible. You can bring it with you on Friday. I also want you to leave me a phone number where I can get in touch with you if I need to. What are you going to be doing for the next couple of days?"

"Climbing, most likely," David answered, picking up his magazine. "And of course I'll be down here with my father on Friday. Right now I have to go get a present for my girlfriend. It's her birthday tomorrow."

"What are you going to get her?"

"A .357 with a laser sight."

Parker started to laugh, but the smile left his face when it occurred to him that the kid wasn't joking.

FOUR

"WHAT THE HELL IS THIS!"

Everett could have heard the thunder in President Fowler's voice even if he had laid the telephone down and stood across the room. That same gentle voice that one month earlier had graciously offered sherry and Stilton was now a roar competing with the endless construction noise in Everett's office. The New Jersey back-alley instincts were dominating any pretense of gentility as Fowler bawled into the phone. "I just got a call from Dan, and he tells me that the Shore kid's lawyer filed a suit against us in Denver this morning. What the hell is this!"

"Oh dear Lord," said Everett. Well, there it was. Since the student hearing the week before where young

Mr. Shore had been given the boot, Everett had lived in terror that something like this would happen. That whole evening had been a disaster, with Stiggler working herself into a righteous rage, practically ordering the students to expel while Everett sat by, utterly impotent to stem the tide. The account given there of the classroom confrontation didn't exactly square with Everett's own recollections, but fortunately, he was not called upon to speak. In the end, not a single member of the board had dissented in the vote. Shore's father, a contributor to the athletic program, had called two days later demanding his son's reinstatement, and Everett had had the unenviable task of explaining to him that it was impossible. "What do you mean impossible?" Shore senior had stormed. "You're the dean of the fucking school! Do you have any idea how much money I've given you!" And so on. The yelling was bad enough, but the vulgarity was even worse. Like a dwindling number of older academics, those who still believed that they formed a special branch of the upper class, Everett found such language distasteful. Shore had eventually hung up on Everett, leaving him feeling somewhat emasculated, his nerves steadily being beaten to a frazzle by the now perpetual din of construction noise in his office.

"'Oh dear Lord' is right," Fowler hissed, his voice quieter now, spitting the syllables out. Everett had to put a finger in his other ear to hear what Fowler was saying. "I don't know what the hell's going on over there, but you had damned well better find a way to put an end to it. This is unbelievable. When I heard that they'd expelled somebody, I was a little concerned, but I figured you knew what you were doing. This . . . Jesus! Everett? Are you there?"

Everett was rubbing his hand over the crown of his skull, trying desperately to think. "Yes, Robert. I'm here."

"Well? What are you going to do?"

"I don't know what we can do. We gave the students the power and they used it. You yourself approved."

"Don't you try to put this off on me! You're the dean of the college. You said you could keep a lid on this thing. Why'd they expel him anyway?"

"The boy called Professor Stiggler a . . . a dyke."

There was a pause at the other end of the line. "Well," said Fowler, "He might not have been far wrong."

"Pardon?" said Everett.

"Nothing. Wait a second, I've got another call. Let me put you on hold." A moment later the line clicked back. "Everett? Are you there?"

"Yes, I'm still here, Robert."

"I've got Dan on the other line. I'm going to see if I can put him through onto our line. Let me see. How do you . . . " The phone went dead for a second, and then came back. "Dan?" Fowler was saying.

Dan Patterson's courtroom baritone answered, "Yes Bob, I'm here."

"Okay," said Fowler. "Everett says that the boy called his professor a dyke, and that's why they tossed him. What do you think?"

"Hmmmmm. There were witnesses?"

"I was there myself," Everett replied. "It was in a classroom full of people."

"The young man might not have a case, then."

"You really think so?" asked Fowler.

"It depends on the circumstances, of course," said Patterson. "But it is reasonable to assume that a university might have a code of conduct, and that a reasonable person might accept that calling one's professor such a name might violate that code. There's also the potential for a harassment angle. Yes. I'd say that the University could be shown to have acted responsibly."

"Whew," said Fowler. "Thank God. Everett, I'm sorry. I thought that the board might have acted capriciously. I see now that you're on top of it."

"It's quite all right, Robert. I understand your concern." Everett was also relieved, and he grasped at this bit of good news like a drowning man.

"What do you recommend we do now, Dan?" asked Fowler.

"For the moment, nothing," came the lawyer's reply. "Have you been subpoenaed yet, Everett?"

"Subpoenaed?"

"I can see that the answer is no," said Patterson. "You're going to be. Thompson, the attorney for the student, wants to get a deposition from you. I didn't understand why when I first read the complaint, but it's evident that he knows you were present when the incident occurred."

"What do you know about him?" asked Fowler. "The boy's lawyer, I mean."

"I don't know him personally, but I've heard of him. He's with a pretty well established Denver firm called Byrd, Templeton and Diamonte. He's quite young. Used to work for the District Attorney's office."

"Is he good?" asked Fowler.

"So they say."

"You mean I have to go to court?" asked Everett. His brain had virtually ceased functioning upon mention of the word 'subpoena.'

"Oh, no. Nothing like that," said Dan. "It'll probably be in Thompson's office. The student may or may not be there. There will be a court reporter. I'll be there with you. They just want you to tell what happened. I'd also recommend that you refrain from discussing this matter with anyone. In fact, it might be better if you could pass the word to the entire faculty not to talk about it with anyone outside of the University. Just tell them to say that it's under adjudication, and refer any inquiries to me."

"You mean there may be . . . there might be . . . press?" asked Fowler, hesitating over the pronouncement of the dreaded word.

"At this point I can't see why anyone would be interested, but it's best to be sure."

Everett hung up the phone a few minutes later, without hearing much of the rest of the conversation. He wasn't thinking clearly. 'Subpoena.' 'Testify.' 'Testify.' For some reason he recalled that he knew the derivation of the word, which came from the Latin, when, during Roman times, a man would take his private parts into his hand while giving information before a court. The ultimate oath, as it were. A picture of Everett assuming this posture before a packed, walnut-panelled courtroom bubbled up into his brain. He shook his head in horror and tried to concentrate on other things. 'Pass the word.' Yes. Tell the faculty not to talk to anyone. Arrange a meeting of department heads this afternoon. He put his finger on the intercom.

"Joyce? Could you come in here please?"

There was a muffled commotion outside, and the door opened onto a faintly comic scene. His forty-year-old secretary, who stood about five feet two, was trying to push an enormous man in a business suit out of the doorway.

"Dean Broadstreet?" asked the man, over Joyce's head.

"I'm sorry, Dean," said Joyce. "I tried to tell him that he couldn't see you without an appointment, but he refused to leave."

"Dean Everett Broadstreet?" asked the man again.

"Yes?" said Everett.

"Shall I call security?" asked Joyce, determinedly holding the large man by the lapels.

"Let's see what this is about, first."

Joyce released the man and stood back, glaring up at him. The man shrugged his shoulders to put the line back into his suit and carefully straightened his lapels. One of the workmen outside gunned a diesel engine, producing a particularly pregnant burp that shook the windows of Everett's office. "You've got a lot of noise in here," the man in the suit called out.

"I am uncomfortably aware of that. What is it that you . . ."

"I have a brother that does sound insulation. You might want to talk to him. He could probably help you out."

"I'm calling the police," Joyce declared.

"By the way, Dean, this is for you." The man extracted an envelope from his jacket pocket and handed it to Everett. "It's a summons to appear at the Denver law firm of Byrd, Templeton and Diamonte next Thursday, the twenty-second of March at two PM. Should you fail to appear, a warrant may be issued for your arrest." The large man gave a sunny smile. "Have a nice day," he said as he walked out of the office. "You too," he said to Joyce.

Everett stood beside his enormous desk, holding the envelope as if it had been painted with Drano.

"Dean . . . ?" asked Joyce.

"It's uh, it's nothing. I'll explain later." Everett put the envelope down and stared at it thoughtfully.

"Dean . . . ?"

"I said it's nothing!"

"I'm sorry, Dean. What was it that you wanted to see me about?"

"Oh, yes. Forgive me. Could you please arrange a meeting of the department heads for this afternoon? Tell them it's about the expulsion of David Shore. I know it's short notice, but do the best you can. And make sure it's somewhere far away from Old Main. This noise is going to be the death of me."

"Yes sir." She hesitated for a moment, giving Everett a curious look that made his skin crawl. Then she too turned and walked out of the office, leaving Everett alone with his thoughts in a sea of sound.

* *

To the uninitiated, the words 'department head' have an honorific ring to them, as if the title is bestowed upon the leading scholar in the group, the professor most likely to win this year's Nobel or whatever. This is usually a fairly accurate appraisal, but for academics in a few large universities, like Everett's for instance, being named department head is as calamitous an event as a major airline disaster. To the person so-named falls the unfortunate duty of presiding over the squabbles in the department, riding herd over often-jealous professors who run the personality gamut from quiet and uncommunicative to overbearing and pompous. The head also has the final word on scheduling conflicts, allotment of facilities, and often, allocation of funds. The hours are long, the headaches great, and the appreciation usually nonexistent. In short, it is a lousy job, and the person who winds up with it each year is generally the poor unfortunate in the department who could think of no plausible excuse for turning it down.

There are exceptions, of course. In academe, as in any endeavor, there are always those who, with the best of intentions, make their own the business of others. If a professor has an interest in influencing the general direction of work in a department, the power wielded by the chair can be attractive enough to offset the hassles that go with the job. Jack Beetle, for example, headed the Political English department almost every other year; enough English professors agreed with his vision to allow him a virtual dynasty. But such unanimity of opinion is rare. Most professors are canny enough to realize that the same urge that makes people want the job can quickly turn them dictatorial or even vindictive. In most departments, therefore, the person who most wants the job is usually the last one to get it, and, therefore, most professors saddled with the responsibility grudgingly accept the 'honor' and do as little with it as possible.

It is perhaps understandable, then, that when unscheduled meetings pop up it is easy for the average department head to find a reason for not attending. As Everett walked into Room 214 of the Teller Bioscience Building, the cavernous hall where Joyce had arranged the impromptu meeting for him, he was not surprised to see that, at best, half the actual department heads had shown up. There were about thirty people clumped together in groups of friends at the long tables. Everett could probably have joined almost any one of them, but in official settings like this one he liked to hold a certain degree of reserve between himself and the faculty. He took a seat near the front of the room.

Surveying the crowd that had gathered, his eyes were drawn to a girl who looked to be in her late teens, sitting with Beetle and his entourage at a table on the other side of the room. He recognized her as Gretchen Van Doorn, one of the members of the speech code board. She had coincidentally been present in the classroom where David Shore had uttered his now-infamous remarks regarding Professor Stiggler and her allegedly aberrant sexuality. Van Doorn's kinky hair framed eyes that wandered from face to face, following the conversation around her. By accident or design she was seated next to Daphne Stiggler, (not a department head, but present anyway), who seemed to be doing her best to coax her into the discussion, lost to Everett in the general blur of voices in the room. The girl remained stubbornly aloof, however, answering usually with simple nods of her head. To Everett it appeared obvious that she was shy, slightly overwhelmed by being in a new environment and completely surrounded by faculty.

At length she happened to glance over and see Everett watching her. When their eyes met, Everett panicked slightly, with the sudden realization that he had been staring, and quickly smiled to dispel any notions she might have had about lecherous intent on his part. The girl's face froze, an icy curtain falling over her features. Her expression told him, "Not on your life. Ever. And especially not with you." And though Everett had few immodest misconceptions about his attractiveness to the opposite sex, in this case he got the strange feeling that it had less to do with his age or appearance, and more with the fact that he possessed a Y chromosome. The girl turned and said something to Stiggler, who looked over expressionlessly at Everett. She shook her head sadly, and patted the girl on the hand. Everett could feel his face burning with embarrassment. He turned away quickly and faced the blackboards with an attempt at nonchalance, feeling as though he had been caught trying to catch an unauthorized glimpse of a woman's breasts through the top of her blouse.

A hand suddenly slapped him on the back, startling him, and a voice boomed behind him: "Everett, you old slug. How are you holding up?" Everett turned sharply and saw with a mixture of relief and surprise that the hand and the voice belonged to Dr. Sigemund Stein, his oldest and closest friend on campus, who was standing behind him in his characteristic tweeds. They had known each other since graduate school at Northwestern, where Everett had been struggling with his thesis on statistics, and Stein working on his dissertation in Medieval History. They had been friends even then, a study in contrasts; Everett formal and serious, Stein colorful and brilliant. It was strange that after so many years apart, each following the branching stream of his life, that they should have arrived on the same campus late in their careers.

"What are you doing here, Stein?" Everett had known him long enough to know that everyone, including his wife, called him by his last name. Somewhere during his formative years he had put his foot down and re-fused to go through life as a 'Siggy.'

"Oh, you know," Stein replied. "Usual story. Patty had plans for the afternoon and asked if I couldn't cover for her. I wanted to see what was going on with all this nonsense, anyway. Is it true? Is that kid suing us?"

Everett lowered his voice. "Yes, I'm afraid he is."

"Great. That's just great," said Stein. "I knew something like this would happen. I bet Fowler's going out of his mind."

"I had a talk with him this morning. I would say that your assessment is correct."

"Well, he can't be too upset with you. This stupid review board wasn't your idea. If he's looking for some-one to get angry at, he ought to be talking to those dimwits over there." Stein jerked his forehead toward Beetle's table.

"Shhhh," said Everett, although it took effort to keep from smiling.

"What's that kid doing here, anyway?" said Stein, ignoring him.

"I don't know. I assume she came with them."

"This is a faculty meeting, for Christ's sake. Who is she? She looks familiar."

"Her name's Van Doorn," said Everett. He didn't want to look back over at the table again. "She's on the speech code board. Listen, Stein, just let it go for now."

"So what'd Mr. Let-me-just-say have to say?"

"I don't know. Not a lot. To tell you the truth I found it hard to concentrate. I was subpoenaed this morning."

Stein's eyes widened. "Really? How come? Ohhh, that's right. You were there, weren't you. You know, you never told me what happened that day."

"And I'm not really at liberty to talk about it now, if you know what I mean. In fact," said Everett, checking his watch, "I think I should get this started."

He considered going up to the podium, but since Stein was there he decided against it. Stein had been telling him forever to guard against taking himself too seriously. Instead, he picked up his chair and moved it to the other side of the table so that he was facing the room and said, "If I could have your attention . . . Thank you all for coming on such short notice. I'm sure you all had better things to do this afternoon than to come here, but a situation has arisen that requires the attention of everyone in the college. You've probably heard the rumors so I'll go ahead and confirm them. David Shore, the student who was expelled last week, is suing the University for readmittance." Everett watched the murmurs and 'I told you so' nods ripple about the room.

"Do you know the grounds of the suit?" asked Dr. Rasnikov, in his slightly accented English. He was representing the Political Science department, was famously conservative, and had been one of the few outspoken critics of the student review process.

"I don't know all of the particulars," answered Everett, "but I believe his attorney is challenging the constitutionality of our new Code of Speech and Conduct."

"Such a surprise," Rasnikov muttered, turning to stare pointedly at Beetle. "I seem to recall hearing something about such an eventuality."

Beetle ignored the challenge. As an English teacher who taught from an openly Marxist perspective, it was clear that he considered Rasnikov, who had fled the Soviet Union in the fifties, to be beneath contempt; at best Rasnikov was annoying, at worst he was a traitor.

Everett stepped in to head off the conflict. "Now isn't the time to go into that," he said. "What we have to concentrate on now is that the University may be put into an unpleasant spotlight. As I'm sure you can imagine, President Fowler is less than pleased. I had a talk with him and Dan Patterson, the University's attorney, this morning. We were all in agreement that those in the University community have nothing to gain by speaking to anyone regarding this matter."

"Surely you can't mean that we will be unable to defend ourselves from verbal assaults waged by those persons who disagreed with our decision," said Stiggler, with a glance at Rasnikov.

"Which decision was that, Professor?" asked Rasnikov. He ran his hand over his slicked, inky-black hair. "The one where you repealed the First Amendment, or the one where you tried to destroy a young man's future?"

"I must say that I find it insulting to be addressed in so judgmental a fashion, considering that it was I who had to endure Mr. Shore's verbal equivalent of rape."

"Rape?" asked Rasnikov. "I had no idea your classes were so . . . what iss word . . . steemulating."

"I don't find that in any way amusing," Stiggler hissed.

"You peeple duhn't find anything amusing," Rasnikov replied.

"Dean Broadstreet," said Stiggler. "Will you please ask Professor Rasnikov to keep his blatantly offensive remarks to himself?"

"Yes, Dean. Better to silence dissension. Is current trademark of acadeemia."

"I have no desire to silence you, Boris," said Everett. "However I wish we could stick to the subject at hand, which is . . ."

"But leesten to her, Dean Broadstreet," said Rasnikov. "This sort of nonsense treevializes the suffering of women who have actually endured such horror."

"I think I am in a better position than a fascist male like you to discuss the horrors of rape, in whatever form," said Stiggler.

"Oh really?" said Rasnikov, staring down at his table, his voice becoming flat and bitter. "When I was a leetle boy, I saw some Russian soldiers in Ukraine rip a woman into pieces. They used daggers to cut openings in her body because she didn't have enough orifices to accommodate them all. I was five years old and I hid because I was afraid. You duhn't think that a child understands these things, but I saw them and I knew what they were doing. And they were also backed by a regime that silenced dissension." He looked up at Stiggler. "So don't you tell me that you have any exclusive right to sensiteevity, you pathetic, spoiled leetle fool!"

Good God! thought Everett. What an appalling image! He stared at Rasnikov with the sort of horrified respect he had once felt when he had seen a woman of about his own age with a number tattooed onto her forearm. He had never considered what Rasnikov had been through as a young man. The old Ukrainian rarely spoke in specifics about his life.

Stiggler, however, was furious at having been so upbraided, especially since it had taken place before one of her star pupils. "Who the hell do you think you are, talking to me that way? You call me pathetic? Pathetic is running away from a country where such things take place, instead of staying and trying to change them. Pathetic is deserting one's homeland in cowardice."

"Cowardice?" asked Rasnikov, flushing with anger. "Cowardice! Don't talk of cowardice until you know something of fear. My entire veellage was starved half to death and then murdered by those . . . those *animals* in the Kremlin!"

Everett had to step in before this escalated any further. "I think we're getting off the subject," he said, his voice rising a note or two.

Beetle however had lost none of his composure. "We certainly are, Dean," he said with an indulgent smile. "But I do wish you'd clarify what you meant. Do you mean that we are not to discuss Mr. Shore's expulsion within the University community?"

"No, Mr. Patterson was referring primarily to the press, should there be any interest in the case. But I must say that I wish we could limit discussion of it, even amongst ourselves, as much as possible."

"I see your point, Dean, of course," said Beetle, "but I can't say that I'm sure I agree with it."

"What do you mean?" asked Everett. He braced himself for impact.

"I mean that Daphne may be right. We have to look at this incident in a larger context. I think we're all in agreement that the speech code was an attempt to foster understanding and sympathy for the disadvantaged, and that its creation was not an isolated thing. The faculty has been steadily moving in this direction for as long as I've been at the University. The majority of the faculty felt strongly about the creation of the review board. They may not like being prevented from speaking about something that they firmly believe in. Such a gag order will make them feel that they have done something wrong, and they haven't. And it will open the doors to the perpetual onslaught against them from the right." Beetle turned and smiled at Rasnikov, as if to say that he meant it sarcastically, and that there weren't any hard feelings. The Russian looked back at him as though he would gladly have separated Beetle's head from his shoulders.

Stiggler chimed in, "That's exactly right, Dean. And we feel that it's critical that the faculty not be dissuaded or in any way chastised for their actions. We want people to understand exactly what happened in my classroom that day, and why what we did was right. To that end we have invited Ms. Van Doorn here to explain to the department heads what went on that afternoon, since she was present and observed the entire proceeding, and is also a member of the student review board."

"Pardon my confusion, Dean," Rasnikov said. "But I was under the impression that this was a faculty meeting to discuss a serious problem facing the University. Do we also have to leesten to this child rationalize the actions that created the problem in the first place?"

"I'm hardly a child, Dr. Rasnikov," said Gretchen. She looked surprised that she had spoken. "And I'd appreciate it if you wouldn't call me one." Stiggler patted her hand.

"Please, Dr. Rasnikov," said Stiggler. "It has taken a good deal of courage for this young womyn to come forward into what is clearly a hostile environment for her so she could explain what happened. I think the least that we can do is to exercise a little tolerance and understanding."

"Oh put a sock in it, Daphne," said Stein. He had been watching the debate silently and now came in on Rasnikov's side. "If you had an ounce of tolerance or understanding in your body, and if she had any courage, the University wouldn't be in the mess that it's in."

"Just how serious is the situation?" asked Donna Milton, a thirtyish professor representing the Philosophy department.

"It's difficult to say," said Everett, grateful for the opportunity to steer the conversation away from the shallow and controversial waters it was drifting into. "Mr. Patterson feels that we may well win the case. But I can't stress enough that it's the publicity which has the greatest potential for damage to the University. And that's why we're asking that you tell your departments to keep discussion of it to a minimum. At least with respect to people outside of the school," he added, in deference to Beetle.

There was a general nodding of heads, and Everett took this as an opportunity to close the meeting. "That's really all I had, so if there's nothing else . . ."

"There is indeed something else," said Stiggler. "There is Ms. Van Doorn, who has given up her afternoon to come here. I think we owe her the opportunity to defend herself."

"From what?" asked Stein.

"From the groundless, ageist accusations that will undoubtedly arise among the faculty when they speculate on what happened at the student review board meeting," Stiggler answered. "As you all know, the proceedings were closed in order to give the students the freedom to discuss the matter without fear of recriminations from the faculty and administration power-base.

But with the crisis of suspicion endemic within the University community, what was given to the students with the best of intentions will now obviously work against them. We must give the members of the review board every opportunity to tell what actually happened."

"I'm sorry," said Rasnikov. "Sometimes I find it deefficult to follow this woman's English. Do I understand that these students were given the freedom to discuss the fate of other students, completely without rule of procedure, with no impartial bystanders, and now you will give them the opportunity to say whatever they want with no way of telling if what they are saying iss fabrication?"

"Here is precisely my point," said Stiggler, looking appealingly around the room. "Dr. Rasnikov, and others like him, have already made up their minds that the students are lying. If he is free to spread such venomous accusations about the campus, without giving the students the ability to openly rebut, why, I can think of nothing more damaging to the students' perception of the American system. The students on the review board were chosen because they were leaders in the undergraduate community. What message are we to send them?"

"Oh, bullsheet," muttered Rasnikov.

"That may be the message you want to send, Doctor," said Stiggler, "and I understand that that is basically what you teach in your classes. But I hope for something more from the rest of the faculty. Dean? Shall we do the right thing and give Ms. Van Doorn the opportunity to speak?"

All eyes turned to Everett. While he hadn't the ideological fervor of Rasnikov, he had little doubt that Van Doorn's presence was a propaganda ploy on the part of

Stiggler, and, probably, Beetle. He had no interest in hearing a recounting of the events that had led to Shore's expulsion. In fact, he figured the less said about the entire incident, the better. Every fiber in his being clung to the possibility, however remote, that the entire affair, the lawsuit, the faculty arguments, everything, might still somehow magically disappear. But on the other hand, the faces of the other professors assembled told him that they were eager for the details. Look at them, he thought. Buzzards! Fruit flies! Their faces glowed with the anticipation of schoolyard boys watching an argument that might escalate into a fistfight. C'mon! We wanna see!

Well. Everett, always mindful of appearances, didn't want to seem obstructionist. In the final analysis, he reasoned, having the girl tell her story probably couldn't do any harm, and he was never in the mood to openly cross the two professors who had brought her. "Never let it be said that I stood in the way of fairness," he said, in a tone that was supposed to convey self-deprecating jocularity, and didn't. The faculty members looked at him blankly. "But we'd all appreciate it if she could keep her remarks brief, all right?"

Stiggler whispered something into Van Doorn's ear, and the young woman nodded silently. She looked about the room at the professors and then began to speak in a voice now thin and reedy, slow and cautious. "I'd like to thank Professor Stiggler for giving me the opportunity to address this meeting, and I'd like to also thank all of the professors who voted to give the students a voice in what happens on the campus. Right now I want to tell everyone that we had grounds for doing what we did, I mean for dismissing David Shore. What he said to Ms. Stiggler was completely inexcusable."

"What exactly did the young man do?" asked Milton, the philosophy professor. She said it in a kindly voice, with a deep, soulful expression on her face, but Everett thought he could detect a hint of hunger; she wanted to hear the dirt as much as anyone else.

Gretchen turned in appeal to Stiggler, who nodded firmly. "Well, while we were in class, discussing Dr. Wickham's theory of rape and sexuality, a group of . . . um . . . Mr. Shore's fraternity brothers began laughing loudly. Daphne tried to bring some order back into the room, but that group of boys wouldn't keep quiet. They were just really rude. Then, when she asked David to leave, because he was the instigator of the trouble, he stood up and said, 'I don't have to take this from . . .'" She looked appealingly again at Stiggler, Do I *have* to say it?, but her mentor stared serenely at the front of the room. "He said: 'I don't have to take this from a fat old dyke like you.' And then he stood up and walked out. You see, we really didn't have much choice but to do something about it. I mean, I'm on the review board, and I heard it, and of course Daphne heard it, the entire class heard it. And I knew David from a long time ago . . . This really is the sort of thing that he'd do. He can be really . . . uncaring."

At this, Stiggler came back to life again, to the apparent relief of Ms. Van Doorn, who fell quiet immediately. "I'd also like to stress," she said, "that the review board would probably have been lenient with Mr. Shore, had he exhibited even a hint of contrition. He did not. His speech at the meeting was gender-specific and gender-hostile. He used the same trans-genderal epithet during the meeting that he had used in my classroom. It was truly a disgraceful performance."

"But you have no minutes from the meeting," said Rasnikov.

"We already explained that we do not and why," said Stiggler, with the voice of one wearily pointing out the obvious and irrelevant for the fifteenth time. "But if you have any doubts, I'm sure that Dean Broadstreet will verify what we've said."

Several pairs of eyes now turned their beams onto Everett, who had been listening to the account with the same morbid fascination that he had when he had heard Gretchen tell the story to the review board. He coughed. "Well," he said, "I'm afraid that that really isn't possible right now, since I was subpoenaed this morning. And I'd appreciate it if you all would keep that information to yourselves," he added, although he knew instantly that none of them, with the possible exception of Stein, would.

FIVE

It was fitting, Parker thought, that Arthur Shore had arrived with the storm clouds. Friday had started off clear enough, but the warm weather of the previous two weeks was giving way to rows of gray clouds streaking the sky like autumn smoke, harbingers of a coming snowfall. And Shore, to whom Parker had only been introduced a few hours earlier, was doing his best to match the mood of the participants in the conference room with the changing weather. He was howling like a blizzard blown in from the northeast, dumping a foot and a half of criticism on anyone within reach.

There were six people present, seated around the beveled glass top of the conference table. Shore the elder had taken, characteristically, Parker imagined, the seat at the head. Diamonte, to his right, was staring blankly out

WHITING PUBLIC LIBRARY
WHITING, IN 46394

the window at the clouds, as if to let Shore bluster until his energy was spent. David Shore was seated across from Parker, watching the proceedings with serenity, and if he didn't seem embarrassed by his father's explosive temper, to Parker's relief, neither was he looking at all critically at his attorney. His father's anger was either so strange that his senses refused to register it, or was so commonplace that he found it unworthy of consideration. He occasionally focused his eyes on Parker, but the gaze was impassive, almost as if he were a medical student observing a routine procedure he had seen many times before.

The only people in the room who seemed to be enjoying the performance, with the exception of Arthur Shore, who was, after all, the leading man, were Rick Friedman and Aimee Clark. They were rooted in the two chairs beside Parker's, had been there for the last two hours, and were hanging with appreciative fascination on every word issued by this newcomer as he systematically tore Parker into pieces. This was a big day for the two associates. Through some divine providence, some perfect alignment of the planets, they had been placed at this particular spot at this particular time to watch this particular attorney get his comeuppance. And what a heavenly show it was. It was one of those rare occasions where irony makes something sweet seem sweeter. Neither of them could have realized, indeed Parker hadn't realized, just what sort of scene this was going to be. But then, how could they have? It was beyond their professional experience. They had expected a rather dull pretrial conference with an older attorney, probably someone like Diamond Jim, who would listen patiently to Parker explain his strategy for the handling of his son's case, and then politely accede to Parker's brilliance. Boring to the point of distraction. But instead, wow! Here comes the tiger! This great white shark of a Wall Street lawyer, sinking his jaws into Parker's flesh, tearing off chunks, swallowing, wallowing viciously in the blood, and going in to tear off some more. What a great afternoon!

Parker glanced over at them from time to time and could see all of this on their faces; their teeth set, lips parted, eyes aglow with ill-concealed pleasure. As for Parker himself, he was becoming jaded to the attack, staring bleakly out the window at the gathering clouds, the same way Diamonte was. Now and then Parker would cast his eyes around at the others, doing his best to seem unaffected by the astonishing barrage of vulgarity being leveled at him by this silver-haired, blue-suited fury of litigious anger.

"I can't *fuck*ing believe this!" Shore exploded. "I came out here expecting this thing to be settled! To be finished! And now I find that my son's future is in the hands of some cerebral jackass who thinks he's Clarence god-damned Darrow talking some high-flung garbage about the fucking First Amendment! Jesus!"

And so on. At their introduction earlier in the afternoon, Parker had tried to project the image of the confident but professionally aloof attorney. It seemed the proper way to handle the situation. After reading the relevant case law and drafting the brief the previous morning, he had no doubts at all about his ability to win the case. Furthermore, he had gotten a hearing on a temporary restraining order scheduled for Monday morning, at the conclusion of which he was certain David would be reinstated at the University, which meant that the first major hurdle, and much of the urgency that went with it, would be removed. The last thing Parker wanted now was for the boy's father to stick his nose into it, and start telling his son's attorney what to do on his own turf.

Shore, however, wasn't having any of it. Instead of meekly assenting, he had run his eyes over Parker as if the younger man were a stubborn mildew stain, and, to Parker's short-lived amusement, had begun shaking his head. Seating himself at the head of the table he had worked himself into a rage over what he perceived to be the mishandling of his son's case.

"What choice do you think I had?" asked Parker, who, working to control his anger both at Shore's dismissal of his strategy and at his seeming determination to publicly humiliate him, adopted an insolently bored tone. He took his eyes from the window and rested them on the older lawyer. "Given these circumstances, how would you have proceeded?"

"What I would have done is immaterial. But I'll tell you one thing. I never would have filed, like you did, you fucking moron!" Shore howled, his face pale and mottled with blotches. It was bizarre to see a person Shore's age come so completely uncorked. He looked as if he were about to spontaneously combust. "Like any person with half a brain I would have been down at the fucking opposing counsel's office that fucking morning threatening them with eighteen different countersuits for damages. I would have scared the living shit out of them and gotten the settlement immediately! On the spot!"

"As I have explained three times now, we have a contingency for a countersuit if we fail at the T.R.O. and the injunction," said Parker.

"But by then it will be too god-damned late!"

"For what? The University will be more likely to settle with the tangible certainty of the T.R.O. and the injunction. We need the restraining order so your son can get back into school as soon as possible. How could it have possibly been better if we'd waited to file?"

"It would have been better, you moron, because now we have to go through with it!"

"So what!" said Parker sharply. He was getting tired of being called a moron. "Excuse me, sir, but with all due respect, I think I can guarantee that I am not going to lose this case."

Shore enunciated his syllables individually. "That is not im por tant. Of course you can't lose. That's not a fucking issue here. We all know, hell, even the *school* probably knows it can't win. That's not the question. The question is my son's future, which you seem bent on destroying."

"We get the restraining order and your son goes back to school next week. He graduates in May. The court case works itself out, the school probably settles anyway, and that's it. Where's the problem?"

"You know, I really ought to thank Diamonte here for giving me the opportunity to meet you. I haven't met anyone as stupid as you in years. I'll see if I can go through this really simply for you, OK?"

Diamonte did not stir at the mention of his name, and Parker stared at Shore.

"OK," Shore continued slowly, as if he were speaking with a four-year old, "You know what court is, don't you? Well? Come on, Counselor. You can do it."

Parker sighed. "I know what court is."

"Great! Now we're getting someplace. Did you know that what happens in a courtroom is made public?

It's true! Anybody can go and watch court. Isn't that amazing? You know, you could even go watch court sometime. You might learn something."

"Can we get on with this, please?" asked Parker

"OK, you little shit. The public goes. That means the press can go, too. And they get to write about it in their newspapers."

"Oh, that's what you're worried about. Well, I hardly think there's going to be any interest in this," said Parker.

"If this were about you, I'd say that, too. Partly because you're a nobody, and partly because I'm beginning to hate your fucking guts, and if you were my client I wouldn't mind taking the chance and running the risk of destroying you. But this is about my son, and I care about him. And he's not a nobody. He's the son of a partner in one of the most prestigious corporate law firms in the country. I think the papers might be very interested."

Parker thought that this was absurd, but tried to mollify the man by agreeing with him. "I suppose I see your point," he said. "But I still don't think it's that big of a deal."

"Oh, that puts my mind at ease," said Shore sarcastically. "You don't think it's that big of a deal."

"No, I don't."

"Having your name dragged through the mud isn't that big of a deal."

"For God's sake, Mr. Shore, this isn't Victorian England. He's going to look like the victim in all of this."

Shore ran his hand through his hair in exasperation, and the blotches on his face flushed a darker tone. "Look at my son. Does he look much like a victim to you? He sure as hell doesn't look like one to me. He looks to me like what he is: a rich kid who called his teacher a dyke during what was basically a sensitivity training session!"

Parker pointed out the window at the city. "If you think that the people out here are sympathetic to this politically correct bullshit, I think you have seriously misread the public mood. At least you have for out here. And assuming that he's going to do corporate work, like his father, I'd think this would be a badge of honor. I hadn't noticed that sensitivity was much of an admired trait on Wall Street."

"What the fuck do you know about Wall Street? You don't know shit. If you knew anything you'd realize that there isn't a company between William Street and Nassau that would have anything to do with a kid whose name was in the papers for any reason outside of getting married. At least not any company that I want him to work for. But even if this stayed quiet, we'd still have another problem, thanks to your astounding lack of foresight. Where is he planning to go this fall? Assuming, of course, that by some miracle you don't screw up and he is able to graduate."

"He's going to law school, isn't he? So what? What earthly difference does it make?"

"Aaaahhhggg, where the fuck did you go to school, anyway? Fucking Wyoming? I want my son to go to an Ivy League law school. It was enough that I let him come to this frontier outpost for his undergraduate degree. You better believe that he's going to a real school to get his J.D.. Back in the real world, on the other side of the Hudson River, that sort of thing still matters if you want to get a job with a good firm. Do you have any idea what's going on in the Ivy League these days? Or maybe I should put it this way - do you know what kind of people staff their admission programs?"

"Oh." Parker's blood ran a little cold as he realized what Shore was driving at.

"That's right! I think we're beginning to see some daylight here. The Ivy schools are filled with people just like that broad who my son had his little altercation with. And I'll tell you something. They're not going to look too kindly on a rich young white male who got famous by calling his fucking Women's Studies teacher a fucking dyke!" Shore slammed his hand down onto the conference table. "Have you finally begun to understand? Christ, Jim," he said to Diamonte, switching off his anger, "You deserve a medal for dealing with this fool on a daily basis."

"You're overstating the case, Art, and you know it," Diamonte said quietly. "David's got the L-Sat's and he's got the grades. And he's got you for a father. He's not going to have any problems getting in anywhere he wants to go."

"I just don't know anymore, Jim. I just don't know. It's not like the old days. All these damned racial quotas and everything. I can remember a time when I could have made a call and gotten him in anywhere, just like that." He snapped his fingers. He paused for a moment, as if reliving an experience, and a look of disgust creased his features. "You know, I went up to Columbia last fall for the alumni dinner. I hadn't been up there in years and it was a real eye-opener. Before they hit us with the money talk, some woman gave a talk on the 'Womenist' direction in legal interpretation. It scared the living shit out of me. And what really got me was that this is what they're feeding the alums, for Christ's sake. God only knows what they're doing in the classrooms. You bet I'm concerned.

"And let's see if we can't take this a little bit further," he continued, glaring again at Parker. "Suppose, somehow, that he gets into school and graduates, and suppose, somehow, that this little scheme of yours works. We go to trial, and you win. What happens if they appeal and the case is reviewed? What if you win, and admittedly this is an unbelievable stretch, considering your intelligence quotient, what if you win and it sets precedent? *Shore v. Western University*. A new standard guiding free expression in publicly-funded institutions of higher learning. You were hoping for that, weren't you, Thompson?"

Parker tried to avoid his gaze, because this was, in fact, something he had dreamed of.

"C'mon, Thompson. Don't be shy. We're all attorneys here. We know it's what you want. Gives you a fucking hard on. Parker Thompson, First Amendment lawyer. You win a big case, everybody slaps you on the back and tells you what a great young litigator you are. Well the other half of that story is that my son walks around for the rest of his life with this big sign over his head. He starts going to interviews to find a good internship: 'Uhhhhh, let's see, son, your name is Shore, is it? You wouldn't by chance be the Shore of the Western University case would you? Oh. I see. Well, we'll let you know.' Who the hell would hire him? Have their potential clients say, 'Oh yes, I remember him. Reactionary. Impulsive type. Understand he hates woman and minorities. Can't keep his mouth shut. Don't think he's quite what we had in mind for our thirty million dollar account. Don't think we want any firm that would hire him, either.' 'Thanks very much for coming in, David. And don't let the door-knob hit you in the ass on the way out.' "

There was silence around the table for a moment. Parker, angry at himself for not considering these possible eventualities, could almost hear his heart beating. He was too nervous to say anything. Finally, Diamonte said, "So how do you want to play it, Art?"

Shore looked at his watch. "Hell, it's after six now. The T.R.O. hearing's Monday morning. I don't think there's any way we can get in touch with opposing counsel before then, is there?"

Diamonte shook his head.

Shore hesitated a moment, and then blew his breath out slowly. "Well then, it looks as though Mr. Darrow here's going to have his day in court. But I'll tell you this, you little twirp. If you fuck this up, I swear to God I'll ruin you."

Parker ignored him.

"Did you hear me, you little worm?"

"I heard you."

"Then I think I've said all I needed to," said Shore. "Why don't we call it a day?" He pushed his chair back from the table. "Oh, by the way, Jim, I'd like to speak with Thompson alone if you don't mind."

"Sure," said Diamonte, with an uncertain glance at Parker. "David and I'll wait for you downstairs, Art." He filed out with Shore's son and the two associates, leaving Parker alone at the conference table with the old lawyer, who regarded him without comment for a moment or so.

"So what do you think of your new client, counselor?" Shore finally asked.

"Are you referring to yourself or your son?"

"Me."

"I think you're a jerk."

Shore laughed. "At least you're a good judge of character."

"I mean, I don't know you too well."

"No," said Shore, still smiling. "I think you've sized me up perfectly. I'm glad to see Jim hasn't lost his touch at finding astute people to work for him. He says you're very good by the way."

"Oh, yeah?"

"Yeah. And he wouldn't lie to me either. I understand that he was the one who put you up for partnership. Jumped you over those two associates who were just in here. I'd keep an eye on them if I were you, because I get the feeling they don't like you too much. Anyway, let me tell you something, Thompson. Right now I'm a jerk with a problem. And that problem is you. Because I don't know you, and I don't know what you're going to do. And I can't stay here and keep tabs on you. I have to trust you. And boy do I hate trusting people. Now, if this were my own firm, and you were one of my minions, I could simply guarantee that if you fucked up, your desk would be cleared out before you got back from court. But in this case I don't have that sort of power, seeing how this is another law firm and you're a partner. So last week, when Jim informed me that you would be handling my son's case, I said to myself, 'what am I going to do?' "

"Look, let's cut the patronizing shit," said Parker, his annoyance getting the better of him. "I've been taking your crap for two hours now, and I've put up with it because you're a friend of Diamonte's. But you're right. I don't work for you. And I'm not going to put up with it for much more. I'll admit, maybe I should have gone after the settlement more aggressively, but I can still take care of your kid's problem, providing you get the hell off my back. If you don't want me to represent him, just say so. Believe me, this is one case that I wouldn't mind giving away."

"God, you really are young," said Shore half under his breath. Then he continued, "No, it's too late for that now. And anyway, I'd have the same problem with anybody else out here. Besides, I've already checked you out." He let the phrase hang in the room for a moment until Parker got the full gist of what he was saying.

"What do you mean, 'checked me out?'"

"I mean that I found it a little unusual that this supposedly shit-hot attorney didn't go to work for the firm where he did his 2L internship. So I called up my old buddy Jack Porter over at Talbot and Reeves in LA and asked him why you hadn't, and he told me . . ."

"You fucking bastard," said Parker, as he felt a hand closing around his heart.

" . . . that you were arrested for possession of heroin while you were interning for them. Heroin, no less! He said that they had been able to take care of it, but under the circumstances, it wouldn't have looked too good if they had offered you a position. Now, in New York, getting arrested like that might not even be that big of a deal, as you say, but out here . . . Podunk town, who knows what kind of Victorian values they might have? The people in the bar association might be very interested, huh? Not that they could dump you just for getting arrested. You were never convicted, so I'm sure you're innocent. But you lied on your Bar application. Didn't you."

Parker digested this bit of news, seething. Shore stared at him with a grin of pure malignancy. After a moment, Parker said, "Well, I have to assume that you have no desire to use that information, or else you would have done so already."

"Very astute. And by the way, I really don't care about your private life. You don't much strike me as the junkie type, so I'm assuming that you're, at most, a casual user. All I care about is that you dispose of this case as rapidly and as effectively as possible."

"Then why tell me?"

"Just to let you know, you little turd, that I don't boast idly, and that when I said that if you fuck this case up I'd ruin you," his voice dropped to a whisper, "I meant it." He picked up his coat from the back of one of the chairs and walked out of the room.

A minute or so later, Parker made his way through the darkened hallways to his office, steaming. The fear passed quickly, because his faith in his own ability was so deeply ingrained, but this feeling . . . He hadn't been treated in such a manner since law school, and back then it had been assumed that certain professors would work on you, to toughen you. It was all part of the program; once you understood the drill, no problem. But that was then, and even fresh out of school, when he went to work for the D.A., no one had ever made such a stinging and pointed attempt at humiliating him. And now, a practicing attorney for five years, in walks this bastard from out of nowhere who cleans his clock thoroughly for a couple of hours, and then finishes up by putting a gun to his head. Parker wasn't really concerned about the possibility that he might actually lose, but this feeling of . . . what was it? anger? frustration? of knowing that someone else *had* something on him that was horrible. It felt exactly like it had when he had been tossed in the clink in LA and the iron door had closed behind him. Was this what those poor guys in the big money firms had to put up with? Mortgaging their manhood all for a chance to someday be the one in the big chair, working out on whoever whenever they felt like it? Parker suddenly realized how lucky he was, how that even with the setbacks he had had, his disastrous internship, the resulting job with the city, how everything had worked out for the best. Did I ever really want to work in Los Angeles? he asked himself. For what? Slave away for twenty years for some bastard like Shore? Swallow all your anger and resentment until you're fifty years old, blood pressure about to blow your eardrums out, measuring the passage of the hours by dosages of Prozac and Tagament? And then to still have that bastard sitting over you with the whip, still worrying you about your fucking billable hours?

He stormed into his office, tore off his coat, wadded it into a ball and threw it, with all his might, into his chair. He pounded his fist onto the top of his desk. "Jesus Fucking Christ!"

There was a voice behind him, soft and feminine: "Excuse me, Parker?"

"Get the fuck outta here, Linda," he said, without turning around. "I'm not in the mood right now."

"Sorry, I'm . . ."

"I said get the fuck out of here!" he shouted, and then, whirling around, he caught himself.

There in the doorway, standing as if there were a light around her, was the woman Pidge had introduced him to on Monday night, before the last debauch. She was wearing a sundress and sandals, and looked earthy and casual and utterly out of place in the hard chrome and glass of his office. She made the room feel as if it had been sterile before her arrival, and was suddenly struggling to spring into life. Parker was so surprised by her presence that he almost forgot he was angry.

"I'm sure glad I'm not Linda," she said.

Parker smiled slightly. "Sorry about that, I uh . . . sorry. It's Mary O'Neill, isn't it?"

"Uh-huh."

"What are, I mean, what are you doing here?"

"Clay told me to meet him here. He said we were going out."

"He did?"

"Yes. I take it he didn't tell you?"

"I'm sure it just slipped my mind." He smiled again. "Did the Pigeon also tell me what time he was coming by?"

"Yes he did. About a half an hour ago."

"That's right. Hmmm. Do I still think he's coming?"

"No. You think that he's probably gone on ahead to someplace where we are supposed to meet him later. You also have the feeling that we are being set up. Again. I have that feeling, too."

"Maybe it's not such a bad thing." Parker noticed that her dark hair curled a little where it fell to her shoulder, and that her dress gently followed the curve of her breast. He wondered why he hadn't noticed when they had first been introduced. Her clear, blue eyes grasped his with fearless candor, and she answered slowly:

"No, maybe not."

They looked at each other for a moment. Parker was not exactly sure of what he should say, and for the first time in recent memory, he was honestly concerned that if he opened his mouth the wrong words might come out of it. She smiled. "What do we do now?" she asked.

"Um. I have to change my clothes. Did you drive?"

"No, I walked over from my office."

"You better come with me then. We can meet up with Pidge later."

"Don't forget your jacket."

He picked the coat up from his chair and put it on. As they walked down the corridor, she slipped her arm into his, and he felt himself becoming aroused by the gentle pressure. It was a very clean, very simple sensation.

"Bad day?" she asked.

"Baaad day."

They took the elevator to the parking garage under the building, and he steered her toward his car.

"That's yours, isn't it?" she asked as she saw the Porsche.

"That it is," he replied, a bit of swagger creeping into his voice. He would never have admitted to such a thing, at least not while sober, but he loved the effect his car had on women. Women were so easy to impress.

"I might have known," she murmured.

"Known what?"

"What is it, a seventy-five? Seventy-six?"

"It's a seventy-five," said Parker, surprised. "You know about these things?"

"Let's see . . . I know that that would make it the 2.7 liter, right? The year after they changed it. The newer emissions package required that year by the DOT resulted in a loss of power that they compensated for with an increase in displacement. I can't be sure without looking inside of it, but I'd bet that this is an 'S' series, the hot package with the Webers. And . . . I think seventy-five was the first year that Stuttgart offered factory air."

Parker stared at her in amazement. "Stuttgart offered factory air on the American version back in 1970," he said.

She hit her head with the heel of her palm, in mock dismay. "I hope you don't think less of me."

"No, don't worry. I'm . . . I'm impressed all right. Would you mind telling me how you know all that stuff?"

She giggled. "Osmosis, I guess. I've got two brothers who think that Ferry Porsche was the second coming and we all missed it. One of them got a junked speedster when he was in high school, and restored the whole thing. He still has it."

"He got a Porsche in high school? You guys have money?" Parker asked.

"No, you don't understand. When he got it it was wrecked. Totaled. He and my other brother did all the work themselves. Scrounged for the parts. I mean, they love that car. They didn't just get it to look cool or anything."

"Which is cool itself," said Parker. "Half the guys in the Porsche club in town are such losers. They buy all the latest garbage, and it's all insanely overpriced. New chain oilers or better dry sumps or whatever, and they never do their own work. If I had the time, I'd do like your brothers did. I do my own work on this one, but it's not such a big deal. Parts are a little bit easier to come by."

She walked around the car looking at it from all sides. "It's a beauty. How much have you gotten into it?" she asked.

"To tell you the truth, I redid the rings over the winter. The compression's a lot better now. It goes like a bat."

"Now I'm impressed. Did you drop them down through the pan or did you pull the whole engine?"

"Boy, you know all the right questions and everything," he said, grinning. "I don't know what it's like on the 356, but on this one you have to remove the whole power train, including the transmission. There's just no room to fool around in."

"Big job. How long did it take you?"

"About a month of evenings and weekends. That's what I mean about having time. If I had to do any major body work as well I'd never get it done. Don't ever go into law. It's a thankless job and the hours are miserable."

"Then why did you?"

"I don't know. I guess because I'm good at it," said Parker.

She stopped her examination and looked up at him. Her eyes had that fearless look about them again, and Parker had the uncomfortable feeling that she was looking at his insides.

"OK," he said. "So I just didn't know what else to do. Come on. We can get the top out of the trunk."

"No, let's leave it off. So we can feel the air blowing on us."

"It's pretty chilly out. You haven't been living here very long. Even when it's sunny in the daytime it still gets cold at night. And I think it's going to start snowing."

"Trust me, it won't snow. I don't want it to. And don't you love the way it feels with the top down?"

"I like it very much. But you're not exactly dressed for it."

"Oh, that doesn't matter. I'm pretty tough."

Parker took off his jacket and handed it to her. "Put this around you then."

"O-Kayyy." An enormous effort. "Clay didn't tell me you were such a gentleman."

"I'm not. You have to open your own door."

"Can I drive?"

He actually considered for a moment. "No. I don't think I know you that well."

"Chauvinist."

Mary had been right about the weather; as they drove from the parking garage, the long, wave-shaped clouds had blown over the city, leaving a stretch of iridescent blue between themselves and the mountains. The bright twilight of the cold, setting sun cast the world in a surreal radiance, brightening the colors of the buildings and the cars on the road. The wind whipped about Parker and Mary, chill and fresh and full of promise. Twenty minutes later, as the light began to fade from the sky, they drove down the alley behind Parker's house, and turned into his garage, where his other car, a dilapidated jeep, occupied the other space.

Mary climbed out of the Porsche, and ran her finger over the fender of the jeep. "Where'd all the sawdust come from?" she asked.

"That," said Parker, pointing to a table saw pushed up against the wall of the garage.

"You do carpentry, too?" asked Mary.

"Wait'll you see the inside of my house." He led her through the mud room, which he was currently using for storage. Pieces of furniture were stacked to the ceiling on one side of the room, covered with a plastic drop cloth which ballooned out into the passageway. On the other side were cans of paint and a few power tools. The floor was rough plywood and the walls were unfinished. "Sorry about the mess, but I've got so many projects going on I never seem to get around to cleaning up. Come on. We have to look at something." He walked through the kitchen and through a smallish family room, each of which were furnished, and into the front living room, which was currently empty. The air smelled strongly of paint, and their footsteps sounded sharp in the darkness. He flicked on the light and knelt down. "Hah! It's perfect," he said.

"What is?" she asked, looking around her at the empty room.

"This!" he said excitedly. "Look! It's perfect!"

"It's a floor."

"Of course it's a floor. But this morning, at five o'clock, when I got up, it was an unfinished floor. I laid the urethane on it before I went to work."

"What's urethane?"

"I swear. Women never know about the important things in life. Urethane is an environmentally safe wood finish."

"And you put it on by yourself?"

He nodded proudly, like a first-grader who had been given a gold star. "And it came out just right." He ran his fingers over the silky finish for a moment. "I guess I should explain. I bought this house a year and a half ago, and I've been working on it ever since. It's finally getting close to being done."

"You mean you've done all the work yourself?"

"Yeah, and you should have seen it when I started. It was dark, the rooms were too small, the floors had linoleum on them. It was a pit. I've removed walls, and put in a bathroom, and redid the kitchen and . . . Oh Christ, the cat." He walked over to the door to the basement and opened it. His tabby emerged from the darkness, ignored Parker, and hustled around the corner toward the kitchen. "I had to put him down there so he wouldn't walk on the floor while it was drying."

"Can I ask you something?"

"Sure."

"What don't you do?"

Parker thought for a minute. "Plumbing and drywall."

"What's that?"

"I said plumbing and drywall. They both defeated me."

She rolled her eyes. "Noooo. What's drywall?"

"It's the boards they use to finish walls. I can set them in place, but I can't mud them."

"Meaning . . ."

"Well, when you finish putting the boards up, you have to cover the seams with mortar, and I've tried it but I just can't get the knack. I think you have to be some kind of an artist. I remember watching a couple of kids mudding a room on one of those construction shows on PBS. They couldn't have been more than eighteen or so, you know, wearing old T-shirts and with these cigarettes hanging out of their mouths, but they mudded a whole room in half an hour. I'll tell you, it was like watching somebody write poetry." He started to chuckle. "I'm sorry, you must think that's about as boring as can be."

She smiled at him and said, "No, I like listening to you. You're a good talker. Anything else you can't do?"

"I can't sew."

She laughed.

"I'd really like to learn how, though. Seriously. I'd really like to learn how. I don't suppose you . . ."

"Not at all."

"We can't have everything." He led her through the family room and into the kitchen, where his cat was sitting on the tiled counter. "Hello, cat," he said, and gave him a stroke. "He's angry at me for locking him up. You want some wine?" he asked, opening the refrigerator door.

"Please," said Mary. "Nice cat."

"He pulls his weight," said Parker. "He goes out and kills things and brings them back. He's a charmer." He poured some chardonnay into two glasses and handed one to her. "Make yourself at home. I'm going to change."

"Oh, here," she said, and slipped his jacket from her shoulders.

"Thanks." He took the coat upstairs to his room and closed the door. He took off his shirt and trousers, and changed into a pair of wrinkled khakis and a polo shirt. He washed his face, and ran his wet hands through his hair. He looked at himself in the mirror, at the crows feet just beginning to grow in the corners of his eyes. There was a seal of cocaine on the vanity. He picked it up and put it in the medicine cabinet, next to his razor. When he came back down, Mary had put on his *Exile on Main Street* CD, and was sitting on the sofa, talking to the cat. She had chosen one of his favorite songs, a fake-country tune called "Sweet Virginia," and the plaintive, bitter voice of Mick Jagger wailed softly over the speakers. "Drop yo reds, drop yo greeeeens an' blues."

"So how come you do all of this stuff?" she asked, as he took a swallow from his glass and sat down on the other end of the sofa, and gently tugged the cat's tail.

"I don't know. I guess it's a holdover from the days when I didn't have any money."

"Which was when?"

"After I graduated from college. I finished in three years, and then spent the next two bumming around trying to decide what to do. And I was broke like you read about. That's when I decided to go to law school."

"I can't figure you out," said Mary.

"How so?" he asked.

"I don't know," she said. "Just you. You're not really what Clay described."

"What did he tell you about me?"

"Quite a bit. He said you were a really good lawyer, and that you partied pretty hard. I guess I figured you'd be kind of cold or, I don't know, fake. But you do things. It's strange. Like, you made these tables, didn't you?"

"You can tell, huh?"

"No, not really. They're beautiful. I could just tell. I don't know. There's just this other part of you that doesn't fit with the image I had of you." She ran her finger along the inlay of the coffee table. "You took a lot of time to make these. I can't explain it. Don't take this the wrong way, but it seems like everything I was told about you seems so superficial, but now I get to know you, you're not very superficial at all."

"Don't kid yourself. I'm very superficial. And I think I'm going to have to have a word with Pidge about the press he's giving me."

"He was pretty honest. He also told me that there was more to you than a lot of people know, and that I'd like you when I got to know you. What did he tell you about me?"

"Terrible vision. Poor posture."

She giggled. "No, really."

"He said that you were a very nice girl, and that you'd be good for me. See, Pidge wants to straighten me up. He thinks I'm too wild."

"Are you?"

Parker considered for a moment. "I don't think so. I just want to experience everything, you know? And be able to do everything. I've always had this . . ." he stopped, weighing whether to continue.

"What?" she asked. "What is it?"

"I don't know. It's hard to explain. I've just seen so many fifty year-old men who look back and regret, you know, not doing something when they had the chance. I never want to be in that position. And I really hate talking about myself. Could we talk about something else?"

"How about dinner?" she asked.

"That's a good thing to talk about. I like talking about dinner. We could go out if you like, but to tell you the truth, I had a pretty lousy day, and I'd just as soon stay home."

"OK," said Mary. "But I can't cook at all."

"Can't sew, can't cook."

"I'm more of a watcher than a doer."

"I can cook."

"Why doesn't that surprise me?"

"Are you a vegetarian or anything?"

"No," she said with a little surprise. "What gave you that idea?"

"No reason." He walked into the kitchen and opened the refrigerator. "I've got a couple of steaks," he called. "Would that meet with your approval?"

"Sounds wonderful," she said, coming through the doorway. She sat herself up on the counter and crossed her ankles, dangling one of her sandals from her toe. She watched as he took down the pans from the rack over the butcher block. After a moment she said, "Are you going to tell me what happened to you today?"

Parker lit the stove and set the pan down on the burner. "Oh, just this case I'm working on. This kid got himself kicked out of college, and I'm trying to get him readmitted."

"Is it really hard or something?"

"No, it's not that," said Parker. "But the kid's got connections to my firm, and I was asked personally to handle it for my boss. It's just a pain, that's all."

"Do you think you're going to lose?"

"I never lose," he said, a bit too sharply. He looked up quickly at her, to make sure that none of the warmth had gone from her eyes. It hadn't, but she looked at him with an expression of concern. "Sorry," he said. "I'm not usually so much of a jerk, but this one's really got me worked up." Parker washed a head of broccoli and put it on the stove to boil. "The kid's father is an old friend of one of our senior partners, and he flew in this afternoon to discuss his son's disposition. He's a lawyer, too. He spent about two hours trying to tear me a . . . trying to make me feel as stupid as possible. And then, right before he left, he laid kind of a bombshell on me."

"What was it?" she asked.

"I'd rather not talk about it. Let's just say that he dredged up something unpleasant from my past. As if it's going to make me work harder for him or something," he added bitterly.

She slid down from the counter and walked over to him. "Don't worry," she said. "I'm not going to ask what it was." She slid her arms around his neck and pulled him to her. He could smell her perfume. Her lips felt wonderfully soft and warm, her tongue small and gentle. He felt himself getting hard again.

"Hm. That was really nice," he said. "We could just skip dinner . . ."

"Are you kidding? You haven't even taken me out yet."

"I'm making you dinner," he said hopefully.

"That doesn't count. You have to actually take me out."

Parker disentangled one of his arms and checked his watch. "I think there's a movie starting in twenty minutes. We could be back here in . . ."

"Shut up and kiss me some more."

Two hours later, dinner long finished and by an unspoken understanding neither interested in going out, they were again sitting in the family room, though by now, Parker was holding her hand on the back of the couch. He found that talking to her was pleasant in a way that he had forgotten that talking could be. Not cute or contrived, but natural, as if they were picking up a conversation that had been interrupted during their childhood. As time went by, he found his lawyer's instinct for snappy repartee dissolving out of him and being replaced by this natural simplicity. It was very relaxing. Eventually the conversation washed back over the meeting he had had with Shore that afternoon. He never brought up the specific card the old lawyer was holding on him, it didn't seem appropriate to, and she never asked, but as he talked the situation out with her, his remaining frustration gradually melted away, and the discussion fell into a comfortable silence.

Not wanting to take the chance of ruining the moment by pushing too hard, he asked if she wanted to go home. She squeezed his hand and told him she thought she had better. He got her his heavy fisherman's sweater, and she pulled it on over her head. It made her look small and vulnerable and appealing. They drove to her house in the icy breeze, and he kissed her goodnight on the front step, just like he would have if he'd been in high school, but somehow it didn't feel parochial. And as he made his way home through the dark streets, he sometimes thought he could still smell her perfume hanging in the air like a very pleasant memory.

SIX

The grandfather clock standing in the foyer of Everett's home beat the seconds by with agonizing lassitude, as its owner sat in his living room feeling completely and utterly tangibly alone. This feeling of overwhelming solitude had begun upon receipt of his subpoena, and in the subsequent days deepened into a degree of mordant dread that he had never imagined possible. What made the feeling so acute was that there was no one with whom he could discuss it, not even Stein, because any open mention of his dilemma would have paradoxically made it more real than Everett wanted to believe that it was, as if the very action of putting it into words would have somehow confirmed that it existed. Still, as much as he tried to deny it, his entire being was consumed with worry over the coming week and the unpleasant reality of his pending testimony. For the more he thought about it, the more he realized that *reality* was what it was. A very unyielding reality that had always been far removed from the cloistered environment of the University. In Reality there were people who plodded along through their day-to-day existence, who never came into contact with the world in which he made his home. These other people might never even consider his world at all, and the sudden, sharp realization of this, given undeniable credence by the subpoena sitting on the coffee table in front of him, made Everett feel terribly small.

More immediately troubling, in this new reality there were courts, and there were people who worked in the courts, and there were people whose fates were determined by courts. And most troubling of all, actions in this new world resulted in tangible consequences, a very alien idea to a person who had spent his adult life in the dreamy world of the theoretical. To Everett, who had never had so much as a traffic ticket, the sudden cognition of the outside world was a serious blow. It tore away the layers of insulation in which the years had steadily cloaked him, and forced him to remember a time when he had been closer to that other world, and more aware of it. The memories that he had from that time, which might have been cheery under other circumstances, memories of a young man's perceptions long buried in his subconscious, flooded back to him. Courtrooms, for instance, to the best of his knowledge, were greasy, poorly painted places filled with dirty little squealers, fat, fraudulent businessmen and scheming lawyers. As far as Everett saw it, courtrooms were the lint-traps in the great laundry dryer of society.

Of course, there were also the great moments of law in history, which took place in enormous paneled rooms where important men took important decisions (as opposed to making them); a picture in which Everett could place his dignified self, if he chose to give his imagination a stretch. But in the other court, little court, which to Everett meant anything below the black-robed justices in Washington DC, there was simply no place for a person such as himself.

Seated on his couch and listening to the clock tick, head in his hands, the God angle began to creep into his thoughts as well, and this also caused him a deal of concern. To testify, after all, in the strictest sense, meant to make an oath before God. Not that that should have bothered him, of course. In the day to day workings of the twentieth-century university, the very idea of God had been relegated to at best a sort of popular superstition, and at worst to a dangerous concept which had caused untold suffering in human history. Well, that wasn't exactly true, Everett knew. In one of the patronizing ironies of academe, organized religion was accepted, and even encouraged, among black people and among other groups which intellectuals regarded as 'disenfranchised' or 'indigenous.' But that was the extent to which the academic mainstream allowed itself to bend. Everett's friend Stein was a conservative Jew, but he was highly unusual in this regard. Most academics considered themselves above the base belief in such foolishness, and for much of his life, Everett had fit comfortably into this category. But now, in later middle age, Everett was facing the yawning expanse of eternity, and doubt had crept into his mind. It might have been considered cowardice by the strict atheists, and it probably was, but it was nonetheless true that Everett had begun to wonder whether the old stories were based on some reality. What if they were true? What if there were a force in the universe, a binding force that determined truth? He could not quite bring himself to believe in a hell filled with fire and torment, but he could both understand and fear an eternal loneliness.

And besides, though Everett had never been religious, at least not in a way that anyone would recognize, he had always liked the *idea* of God, in an abstract way. It fit in well with his structured view of the world. Whether he believed or didn't believe, to make such an oath was a solemn thing to do, and all the more disturbing when one was not exactly sure of what one was going to swear to.

For Everett was not at all certain of what he was going to say in his deposition. He had been present in the classroom. He had had the misfortune of seeing what actually happened, and he knew that the accounts given by Stiggler and Van Doorn were not exactly correct. Somehow, though, the incident and the subsequent student meeting had been unreal to him; worrisome, to be sure, but on the whole tolerable since somewhere deep down Everett did indeed separate the doings of the University from the world of consequences. Now, however, he and his recollections were being thrust into that world, with no safety net between his precarious position and the jaws of disaster.

Everett was rushing to the point where he could see clearly the nature of the cage in which he was confined. If he chose to blindly back up Stiggler's account, everything he wanted desperately to believe in, the moral underpinnings of his dreamily structured universe, would be destroyed. Furthermore, he would no longer have the comforting egotistical faith that he was a better man than most. He would become one of the dirty little squealers of his tortured imagination, and his internal dignity would be destroyed.

But if he didn't, what then? Looking back on the meeting in Teller, he suddenly realized that the doe-eyed student's statement must have been for his benefit. There was no question of the little excrescence explaining her agony for the faculty. No. It had nothing to do with that. It had been a command performance directed by Beetle solely for the purpose of laying out what he himself was supposed to say. They had practically written his script. They must have heard somehow about the subpoena. Of course . . . Joyce! Joyce must have told someone about the incident in his office. Beetle had already known, and had taken the opportunity to give Everett his lines. And if Everett chose not to read his lines . . . He could see the whole showdown. Fowler would have to be called in to state the University's position. If there were even a glimmer of possibility that he could do so, he would come down on the side that brought in the most money, without question. And Everett had himself provided that doubt by failing to take steps to block the expulsion of the student during the conduct board meeting. As far as the bringing in of money was concerned, unfortunately, in the arena of linguistic hermeneutics, Beetle was famous. He published constantly. It was due in large part to his renown that several respected English scholars had joined the faculty, and indirectly that the new tower had been funded. Fowler would never back a . . . a balding, middle-aged, dime-a-dozen white male (ugh!) against a man responsible for raising an obscene quantity of dollars. Everett's only hope lay in the possibility that the opponents' reform might come forward to save him, but the more he thought about it, the more remote this eventuality seemed. The Rasnikovs of the University rushing in to his aid? Forget it. Everett had never once used the power of his office to slow the path of academic reform even though he privately disagreed with it. There would be no groundswell of support for him; indeed, they might be glad of the opportunity to take their chances with a new dean. If the crunch came, Everett's career would sink like a stone in oil, without leaving a ripple.

His options were terrible. He struggled through the week trying to determine what the least damaging course would be. The deciding factor came on Wednesday, when he picked up the campus paper and learned, care of the front page, that David Shore had been reinstated. The story had all the hallmarks of a Whiting special; the tone seemed to indicate that the school had wanted this all along, and that the University had practically begged the court to rule in the student's favor. Fowler was even quoted: "Let me just say that we welcome the opportunity to demonstrate the impartiality of the student governing board." Everett, however, knew otherwise. Fowler was more than likely standing in his backyard at this very moment, screaming like a maniac at his geraniums. Reading between the lines of the story, Everett could see that the court had found sufficient grounds to question the nature of expulsion, which probably meant the constitutional challenge that Fowler had feared from the beginning. Fortunately for Everett, Fowler's anger was most likely being directed at Patterson, since Everett didn't hear from the president all day. He did, however, receive a hand-written note from Beetle. It said simply:

Regarding the recent development in the Shore case, we look forward to reading the notes from your deposition.

Regards,
J. Beetle

And there it was, the discreet message, the veiled threat, the loaded gun. Everett had reached the end, and his esteem, his dignity, his very soul plummeted when he realized that he was the same as any other man. In the final analysis, it was better to be an employed squealer than an unemployed anything.

But if this realization brought resignation, the resignation brought no peace. The day still dragged forward into evening, and evening into Thursday. He could almost feel the time passing as if a weight were anchored somewhere in his skull, dragging downward and inward as the moments crept by. By the time Everett got out of bed on the morning of his deposition, his shoulders and neck were aching from the prolonged tension and lack of sleep. He took a hot shower and tried to get down a cup of coffee, but it was black and sour. It upset his stomach and made him shaky. He drove the two hours to Denver in a jittery silence. In the expanse between stations, he didn't even have the radio to keep him company.

Everett always felt a little lost in big cities, even minorly big cities like Denver, and it took him a half an hour of swimming through the one-way streets to find Patterson's office, and then another ten minutes to park. He stepped from the quiet interior of his car into the sounds of traffic and construction, of the day-to-day existence of the real world where he was now a hopeless prisoner. The sunlight was blocked by the high-rise buildings, and as he walked along the sidewalk, surrounded by other humans unconcerned with his internal struggle, the chill, March winds blew down the street and into his clothing. He shivered.

Patterson's bulky frame filled the doorway to his office seconds after his secretary alerted him to Everett's arrival. The lawyer ushered him into a seat in his office, next to a stuffed pheasant. The office was quite large, with an enormous half-moon shaped desk, a pair of leather wingchairs, a library table, and a spectacular view of the mountains. The walls of the room were papered in a delicate floral pattern, and hung with antlers and tasteful pictures of game animals and fish. Everett hadn't realized that Patterson was such a sportsman. In fact, he realized that he didn't know Patterson at all, having only been introduced to him once, several years earlier. He seemed larger now, or perhaps Everett felt somewhat deflated by his predicament. The dead pheasant stared at him.

"Now don't worry, Dean. I can see that this might be a little unnerving for you, but you have nothing to be concerned about." Everett was startled, because in his feverish state he thought that the bird had spoken to him. "Dean? Dean Broadstreet?"

"Yes. Of course," said Everett.

"Are you all right?"

Everett pulled himself together and tried to smile. "Yes, counselor. I'm fine. This is all very . . . different for me."

"I'm sure it is," said Patterson, his round face radiating concern. "A lot of people feel nervous when they have anything to do with the law, but believe me, there's really nothing to worry about. We're not even going to court. Just think of it as going to someone's office to tell about something that happened to you. Because that's really all it is."

"How far away is . . . What's the other lawyer's name?"

"Thompson."

"Yes, of course. How far away is Mr. Thompson's office?"

"About two blocks," answered Patterson. "It's over on Tremont Street."

"I see," said Everett, because he didn't know what else to say.

Patterson looked at him. "Yes, very close to here. Listen, Dean, there's nothing to be nervous about. Everything will be just fine. I've known so many people to be nervous about giving depositions, but there's really nothing to it. You know what happened. Just tell the truth the same way you told me over the phone."

"Yes," said Everett. He could feel himself getting shakier.

Patterson looked at him again, a little narrowly this time. "It *was* the truth, wasn't it?"

The institution of direct assault brought Everett back to attention. "Of course it was," he snapped, trying to project indignation.

Patterson smiled his soothing smile again. "Then there's nothing to worry about, is there? It's just a case of nerves. I've seen it before. As soon as you start talking the anxiety will pass. You'll be fine." He glanced at his watch. "It's almost one," he said. "Why don't we see about getting some lunch. There's a place right around the corner."

Some fragment of Everett's remaining ego found it hard to believe that others were so unaffected by his torment that they could eat at a moment like this, but he accompanied the lawyer to the restaurant and picked a salad while Patterson wolfed down a steak. The conversation dragged, and Everett felt certain that the gulf of silence at their table was his fault. He searched his brain for some avenue of discussion to break into. At length, he asked Patterson about the fact that Shore had been reinstated.

Patterson paused with a forkful of roasted flesh halfway to his mouth. "We may have lost the battle," he said, "but we haven't by any means lost the war. To tell you the truth, I had almost expected to lose at the T.R.O.."

Everett wondered what a T.R.O. was, but let it pass.

"You see," Patterson continued, "Judges are usually pretty receptive to stopping any action that would change the status quo. Since Shore had been removed from school, the probability of indirect damage to him, should he win the case, would have been quite high. So even if the court finds the possibility of his winning the case remote, they err on the side of caution. That's what happened here. Thompson's a good lawyer. I'm sure he understood this when he filed the motion." Patterson attacked the steak again, and took a few bites from his potato.

"How did President Fowler take the news?" asked Everett.

Patterson shook his head. "Bob?" he said, pausing a moment to clear his mouth of foreign matter. "Oh, Bob came unglued. But what do you expect? He called me up yesterday in a panic, but I explained everything to him."

"So you think we'll win?"

The lawyer laid his fork down and grinned. "You betcha. I've been putting out some feelers, and from what I understand, this kid Shore's kind of repulsive. Rich, prep school, fraternity, always gotten everything he wanted. Now, if he were up for some sort of violent felony, that sort of background would work in his favor, because he's not the kind of person who's going to knock over a Seven-Eleven. He'd stand before the bar in his khaki pants and his blue blazer and his rep tie and the judge would probably dismiss on sight. But what we're talking about here is a form of defamation, and that's exactly the sort of thing he would do. We have a professor, who teaches a class on tolerance, for Christ's sake, who says he did it. We also have at least one student who says he did it. And the lynchpin is you. Even if Thompson were able to demonstrate that Stiggler was predisposed against him, and I'm not ruling that out, and even if he were able to in some way discredit Van Doorn, we still have you. I can't for the life of me think of a reason you'd perjure yourself."

The word 'perjure' caused Everett's blood to chill. Was that what he was about to do?

"Which reminds me," said Patterson. "There's something I wanted to talk to you about. Is it true that you know Shore's father?"

"We have met, yes."

"And do I understand rightly that he's a pretty heavy hitter with your athletic department?"

"Yes, he's given us quite a bit of money," said Everett.

"Wonderful. Now this is important. Did he ever contact you and ask that you get his son reinstated?"

"As a matter of fact he called the next day."

"But did he put the screws to you? I mean, did he in any way indicate that he might withdraw funding if his son's expulsion were permanent?"

"You might say so, yes," Everett answered. "He was quite belligerent."

"Yes!" Patterson exclaimed, a grin spreading across his face. "I *knew* it! Oh, this is outstanding. This is really outstanding. If anything, you have reason to corroborate Shore's story in the interest of securing University funding. Oh yeah. I think we're going to win. And I think I'm going to have some dessert."

Fifteen minutes later, after the lawyer demolished a substantial chunk of tiramisu, and then graciously paid the check, the two of them walked over to Tremont Street. As the doors of the crowded elevator closed on them, Everett felt as if he were being buried alive. His face must have registered the emotion, because Patterson smiled at him and shrugged, as if to say 'Relax! This is nothing!' The dean closed his eyes. He didn't open them again until the bell tolled at the nineteenth floor.

* * *

Parker Thompson, on the other hand, was twice as elated as Everett was miserable. The successful injunction hearing wasn't exactly a legal coup, but it was something, and it showed at least a preliminary inclination on the part of Judge Brewer, who was handling the case, to be open to the First Amendment argument. The jurisprudence looked good as well. The case Parker had asked Friedman to dig up, which turned out to be called Doe v. Michigan (not Wisconsin, Parker noted with satisfaction), seemed to fit fairly well with the circumstances of Shore's dismissal. In the University of Michigan case, the administration had outlined an entire

140

code of unacceptable speech and conduct, with items ranging from certain sexual advances, to speech which created a "hostile" environment. Compared with the situation on David Shore's campus, where they didn't even bother writing a code, the Michigan case seemed to represent cautious certainty. Yet the presiding Judge in the case had flatly ruled that Michigan's experiment in censorship was excessively vague, excessively broad, and clearly unconstitutional.

As Parker read the twenty-page record of the case in the *Federal Supplement*, he became more and more fascinated by what the administration had tried to do. Since the person who had filed the suit, an anonymous psychology student, had done so on the basis of potential infringement, and not on a specific damage to himself, his attorneys had to show a "genuine and credible threat of enforcement," which meant that they needed to demonstrate the intent behind the University's policy. To do this, they subpoenaed notes from administration meetings, letters and inter-office memos, anything they could find to show what had been on the minds of the framers of the policy. The picture that emerged was stunning. It reflected an almost straight-jacketed political viewpoint among the top administration officials, and an attempt to make the concept of victimization both definable solely by the victim and punishable by the full weight of authority. There was one particular memo cited where an attorney for the University, who had assisted in researching and drafting the policy, had actually recommended that the University ignore traditional First Amendment interpretation. How in the world could a decent lawyer say such a thing? Parker wondered if similar discussion had taken place at Shore's college. In any event, the presiding judge at the district court, while declaring himself sympathetic to the University's desire for equal opportunity of education, declared that such desire could not be furthered at the expense of free speech. The University lost the case, and the US Supreme Court let the decision of the District Court stand without comment.

In an interesting footnote to the case, Parker also learned that the University still refused to be completely undeterred, and had later attempted to set up another code dealing with faculty and staff. He was unable to find out what had been the final disposition of the new code, but it was at any rate unimportant to the case at hand. As far as the court was concerned, blanket censorship in the name of civilizing boors was still too racy a concept for the legal system to tolerate.

It did not, however, seem too racy for many universities. Aimee Clarke's contact at the newspaper had come through for her and found articles estimating several hundred such speech codes scattered among the American institutes of higher education. The number of these collegiate Star Chambers, moreover, was quietly growing. The decision in Michigan seemed to have had little or no dampening effect on the fervent righteousness of the campus censors. It was somewhat puzzling. As he leafed through the articles, Parker found several instances of constitutionally questionable practices which were simply allowed to stand. They didn't only deal with speech codes, either. He read stories about freshmen being subjected to 'orientation' sessions which sounded more like indoctrination camps from the Eastern Block. Some students had been forced to room with homosexuals. Entire social codes had been designed at some universities, with the clear intention of exacerbating race relations, and obviously counter to the spirit of civil rights rulings of the 1960's. It was insane. He had to conclude that college students were either more disposed than the average person to suffer while evils were sufferable, or that they simply took for granted the truth in what they were told by officialdom. If so, the more cases challenged publicly, the better informed the students and their parents would become. It was an interesting feeling for Parker, this measure of moral certitude. He had to admit that he felt a rush of professional excitement at the thought that he might be holding onto a case that could set precedent in the constitutional arena. Diamonte had been right. He had needed to handle a case like this, and despite the pressure Shore's father had tried to exert over him, he looked forward to coming to work each morning. So much so that he had curtailed his normally late nights.

But he had another reason for staying home as well, in the form of Mary O'Neill, with whom he had spent every evening since Friday. This, too, was an unusual situation for Parker. It had been a very, very long time since he had entered into a relationship with so few reservations. He had grown too old to feel the helpless immersion that younger men wrongly label as love, where one is so overwhelmed by the desire for physical union that caution is abandoned, but Mary had awakened in him a tenderness, almost a paternalism, that was new to him. It was as if she made him remember something about his childhood, something that had been burned out of him over the years. He was not naive enough to believe that the feeling would last forever, but when he held her in his arms and made love to her, something he had waited several days for, it truly felt different to him. After the first time, he realized with a sort of shock that she had been the only thing on his mind.

Patterson arrived promptly at two, and Parker had the receptionist show him and the Dean to the conference room. When he came in with Friedman a few minutes later, the court reporter was already present, setting up her tape recorder and steno machine. Parker grinned at Patterson. "How are you doing, Dan?"

"Can't complain, Parker. You ready to drop this nonsense yet?"

"Funny, I was going to ask you the same thing."

"Oh, I don't think so. Let me introduce you to Dean Broadstreet."

"It's a pleasure, Dean." He took the hand extended to him, and was surprised by how cold and clammy it felt. Balding and in tweeds, the older man looked like every picture of an academic that Parker had ever seen. He looked somewhat ratty, though, and as thoroughly out of place in the gleaming conference room as an insect in a laboratory.

"How do you do, Mr. Thompson," said Everett. Parker noticed that his high voice quivered slightly, like that of a man accustomed to being in authority, and unsure of what he should do when he wasn't. Parker wanted to relax him, but didn't know exactly how. Despite the rumpled demeanor, Parker got the feeling that calling him by his first name would have jarred the room like an explosion.

"I do very well, Dean," Parker answered with a reserved smile, trying to offer the man as much dignity as he could. "This is my associate, Rick Friedman. He'll be sitting in with us today. And I'd like to thank you so much for taking time to come and talk with us." It was a ridiculous statement, considering that he was under subpoena, but Parker wanted to offer the man an illusion of power.

Everett took the bait. "Yes," he said, his chin lifting. "I'm certainly glad to offer any assistance I can."

"Hopefully this won't take too long," said Parker. "If you would be so kind as to take a seat there, there are just a few questions I'd like to ask you." He nodded to the court reporter, who poised her hands above her stenograph machine. Parker began, "For the record, it is the twenty-second of March, Nineteen Ninety-Four, at two-o-five PM. This deposition is being taken at the offices of Byrd, Templeton and Diamonte on Tremont Street in Denver, Colorado. Present are Parker Thompson, representing plaintiff, appearing for Byrd, Templeton and Diamonte. Also present are . . ." Parker looked at Friedman.

"Rick Friedman, also of Byrd, Templeton and Diamonte," said Friedman.

Parker then nodded at Patterson, who said, "Daniel Patterson, of Gamble, Patterson and Pierce, Stout Street, Denver, representing Western University."

Parker then looked at the dean expectantly, who said, "Everett Overton Broadstreet, Dean of the College of Arts and Sciences, Western University."

Parker grinned at the dean and flashed him the OK sign while he continued in his sing-song, official voice. "This deposition is being taken in evidence for the case of David Shore, plaintiff, versus Western University, defendant." Parker looked again at Patterson. "Has the witness been advised that he is under oath?"

Patterson looked at Everett. "He has."

Parker opened the folder in front of him, which contained David Shore's written account of the incident. "Very well. I ask the witness, Dean Broadstreet, where were you on Friday the twenty-seventh of February at three o'clock PM?"

Everett swallowed. "I was in Room 201 of Jacobs Hall."

Parker smiled and held up his hand. "I would note for the record that Jacobs Hall is a building on the campus of Dean Broadstreet's university. Could you please tell us what was happening there?"

"There was a class in session."

"Who was teaching the class?"

"That would be Dr. Daphne Stiggler, of the Women's Studies department."

"How many people were present?" asked Parker.

"It would be difficult to say, but approximately one hundred and fifty."

"Do you often make it a habit to audit classes?"

"No," said Everett. "But I had to speak to Professor Stiggler, and I had been informed that I would find her there."

Parker was pleased to note that the dean seemed to be relaxing, so he asked him directly, "Did you happen to notice an altercation in the classroom, and if so, could you please tell us about it."

"Well," the dean stammered. "You have to understand that I was right in the back of the classroom, and I, well, I didn't hear exactly what happened."

This answer annoyed Parker, and he had to suppress his courtroom instinct to rip into him about the acoustics of the room. Formality and clarity in response was one thing, but hedging under oath was something else. Parker pushed the warm smile back onto his face and said, "Just tell us what you did see and did hear."

Everett swallowed again. "Well, as Professor Stiggler was lecturing, it seemed that some boy, some young man, I should say, made some sort of comment that several of the students around him found amusing. They began to laugh in an, in a most disruptive manner." He fell silent.

"Please go on, Dean," said Parker. So far, so good, he thought. The dean was beginning to describe the confrontation, and he was doing so without any bluster. He seemed nervous, but rational and honest. These depositions were usually very interesting, because they gave people an opportunity to describe single events from their own perspectives. After sifting through the different angles, the lawyers were usually left with a core of truth, the limits of which they could fight out between themselves.

The dean hesitated a moment before continuing, and then looked out the window. "You have to understand, this sort of thing happens fairly frequently. There are always these self-styled comedians in any classroom."

A faint warning bell started to go off in Parker's head, and he glanced at Friedman. "What happened then, Dean?"

The dean closed his eyes, which Parker took to mean that he was visualizing the scene. "For the moment, nothing at all. I thought that Dr. Stiggler showed admirable restraint."

Parker suddenly felt that he'd been kicked in the stomach. Friedman looked over at him in alarm; whatever his personal feelings toward Parker, this was a case he was also working on, and he had no more wish to lose it than Parker had. Parker cut him off with a look that said both 'Oh Lord,' and 'Keep your cool.' "Did the professor make any mention of the people who were laughing?" he asked. "Did she say anything to them?"

"Eventually, she had to," said Broadstreet. "I believe, and remember, I was in the back of the room, I believe she said, 'if you cannot sit here like an adult, I must ask you to leave.' "

Parker was thinking furiously. "And that was all? No preamble? Nothing? She just asked him to leave?"

"Yes."

Parker perched on the edge of his seat, waiting for Broadstreet to continue. "Yes?" he finally said. "And then what happened?"

Everett sat in his seat, rooted.

"What happened then?" asked Parker, trying to keep his voice under control. He had no idea whether the man was lying to him or if he were telling the truth. He couldn't think of a reason why the dean would lie to him, but, God, if this were true his entire case would go out the window, and Shore might well destroy his career. "What happened then?"

The dean looked straight at Parker and said, "Then the young man stood up and said 'I don't have to take this from a fat old dyke like you.' He stormed out of the room."

Parker was rocked, but he had to continue. "Did you recognize the student?"

"Yes, it was David Shore."

Friedman, unable to contain himself any longer, said, "Let me remind you that you are under oath. Are you saying that there was no provocation at all? That the student just blew up and walked out?"

Patterson broke in. "This is a deposition, Mr. Friedman, not a cross examination. My client is fully aware of his responsibilities in this matter. He has been asked the question and he has answered it. If you badger him, I promise you that statements made afterward will be inadmissible."

"Pardon my colleague's enthusiasm, counselor," said Parker, "but this is a very delicate point. Dean Broadstreet, you are completely certain of this, under penalty of perjury, that there was no further provocation?" Parker rifled through the notes in the file. "The professor made no comments regarding the student's background? His father? Nothing at all?"

Everett took a deep breath and stared down at the table. "No."

Friedman, evidently, still believed the student's account. "Do you expect us to belie . . ."

Parker grabbed his arm to shut him up. He hissed in Friedman's ear, "Would you calm down? We're in a deposition right now, and this is my ballgame. Don't screw it up."

Friedman glared at him, and whispered back, "He's full of shit! It doesn't make any sense that the kid would act so rashly. Press him!"

Patterson cleared his throat. "Is there some problem, gentlemen?"

Parker nodded at Friedman. "No, counselor. None at all. But I would like to ask Dean Broadstreet if he found the student's behavior unreasonable."

The dean raised his head. "In what way?"

"Doesn't it seem strange to you that this student would become so agitated so quickly?" Parker asked.

"I'm going to have to object," interjected Patterson. "Relevancy, and it calls for speculation."

"Objection noted for the record, but I can and will argue that this man has extensive teaching experience and is therefore an expert in the field of classroom interaction. I am bound to ask again. Did it seem unusual to you?"

"No, not particularly," said Everett.

"That a student would make such a violent outburst in class didn't strike you as odd?"

"Asked and answered," said Patterson.

"Fine," said Parker. There was no point in pursuing it. If this were the dean's statement, and he were planning to stick with it, there was nothing he could do about it at this time. "Let's move on to . . ."

Friedman drew in his breath with a sharp hiss.

Parker said to Patterson, "Do you mind if we take a short break?"

"I have no objection."

Parker nodded to the stenographer, who lifted her hands from the machine and stopped the tape recorder. He led Friedman out of the conference room and down to his office. He closed the door. "What the hell is the matter with you?"

"That guy is lying. I mean, I know that guy is lying," said Friedman. "It's all over his face. He's scared to death."

"You're basing a conclusion that a man is committing perjury on his demeanor and facial expressions? I can't wait to get into court with that."

"I know what I know. And you know it, too."

Parker settled into his chair. The full weight of the dean's testimony was beginning to sink into him. "Look, I'd like to believe more than anything that you're right.

But there's not a fucking thing we can do about it right now. Come on, Rick. Sit down for a minute. If you have any brilliant ideas, I'd love to hear them."

Friedman rubbed his chin for a moment, and then said, "You've met Shore, and you've met Broadstreet. Of the two of them, whose account are you more inclined to believe?"

"Personally," said Parker, "I'd have to say Shore. But I'm not exactly unbiased."

"Seriously," said Friedman. "Shore's account is more detailed. It holds together better. Hell, it just makes more sense. Why would this kid, who's been sitting in this class which he hates for a whole semester up and explode over being asked to leave?"

"Maybe for just that reason. Maybe because he was tired of swallowing this nonsense for so long."

"You don't believe that," said Friedman.

Parker chuckled. "What I believe or don't believe is immaterial. It's what Judge Brewer believes that's important. And I'll tell you, the kid has a lot more reason to lie at this point than Broadstreet does."

Aimee Clark entered the room. "Hello boys. What's going on? I went into the conference room and nothing's happening. Did you finish already?"

"We hit a bit of a snag," said Parker. "Broadstreet's statement doesn't corroborate Shore's at all."

"Yeah," said Friedman. "And the fat old bastard's lying through his teeth."

"Or at least that's the considered opinion of Rick Friedman, the human polygraph," said Parker.

Aimee took the other chair. "Do you believe him?" she asked Parker.

"Who, Rick or Broadstreet?"

"Either one."

Parker drummed his fingers on the desk for a few seconds. "To tell you the truth, I have to go along with Rick. I think the fat old bastard *is* lying. But why? If we're going to discredit him, we're going to have to find some motive for why he would deliberately mislead."

"How about subornation? If somebody's forcing him to concoct this story, it would explain his nervousness," said Rick.

"I've considered it, but from whom?" asked Parker.

"How about the woman? This Stiggler character."

"Is she the professor?" asked Aimee.

"Yeah," said Friedman.

"But he's her boss, for Christ's sake," said Parker. "What could she possibly have on him?"

All three of them thought of the same thing at the same time. Aimee arched her brows and looked at Parker. "It has been known to happen," she said pointedly, running her hand through her hair and glancing out the glass wall at Parker's secretary, who was at her desk typing something. Friedman looked down at his toes, obviously trying not to laugh.

"O-kay, O-kay," said Parker, grinning. "So we all know about Parker's private life. But that was different." The two associates laughed. "She was beautiful. She still is. I would remind you that the only point on which these two statements agree is on the specific phrase 'fat old dyke.' "

"Stranger things have happened," said Aimee, still smiling. "When I saw him, he didn't look like much of a player, but . . ."

Parker held up his hands. "OK. Patterson's gonna scream about relevancy, but I'll go into it. But if it doesn't pan out, I'm going to get the hell away from it as fast as possible, and I don't want to hear any static from you," he said to Rick. "And, Jesus, if it's not that, we are way up a creek. We better get back in there. You want to come?" he asked Aimee.

"You're going to ask that old guy if he's been having an affair with an alleged lesbian? I wouldn't miss this for the world."

*　*　*

A strange sort of calm had descended upon Everett the moment he began to tell his story. For the first time he could remember, he was living completely in the moment, and it was . . . *easy*! He had entered the other world, the darker world of his fevered dreams the night before, and he found it was simple, gentle . . . *easy*. He had walked through the doorway, and lightning hadn't struck, his tongue hadn't snapped. He was at peace.

Everett knew that the other attorneys suspected him of lying, especially the one who had been introduced as Friedman, but what of it? He was on the winning team, now. As long as he stuck to his story there was nothing they could do about it. After they left the room, Patterson looked over at him and told him he was doing very well, but Everett almost ignored him. He was beyond the need of Patterson's help.

Thompson and Friedman returned about fifteen minutes later, with a young woman in tow. They did not introduce her, and she did not smile at Everett. The three of them sat down at the table, and Thompson asked the stenographer to begin. He started speaking again in his fast, official voice: "This deposition is commencing again at two-fifty PM. In addition to the people previously mentioned also present is . . ."

At which the young woman said, "Aimee Clark, of Byrd, Templeton and Diamonte, appearing for the plaintiff." How formal this new world is, thought Everett.

Thompson then began, "Dean Broadstreet, you earlier stated that you were present in the classroom by chance. Is that correct?"

Everett wondered what this was about. "Yes, that is correct," he said.

"And that you had to speak with Professor Stiggler. You never told us why, and I would appreciate it if you would."

Patterson looked sharply at Thompson, as if he were about to say something, but then appeared to change his mind. He remained silent. Everett immediately felt that this was some attempt to trip him up somehow, and he thought for a moment before answering. "I had to speak with her," he finally said, "about the establishment of the student review board."

"And that was all?" asked Thompson.

Everett shrugged his shoulders. "Yes."

"Wouldn't it have been just as easy for you to leave a message for her in her department mailbox?"

Everett considered this, and answered, "Possibly, but I wanted to speak with her face to face."

"Why?" asked Thompson.

"It just seemed easier."

"I see," said Thompson. "Dean Broadstreet, what is the nature of your relationship with Professor Stiggler?"

"Objection," said Patterson. "Relevancy."

"It may be highly relevant," said Thompson. "And in any case we'll let a judge decide. I ask the question again. Dean Broadstreet, what is the nature of your relationship with Professor Stiggler?"

This was a troubling question for Everett. Patterson had said that he could think of no reason why Everett would lie, but suppose this Thompson person had figured it out? Could he know? A parcel of doubt crept into Everett's peace, and he hesitated. "I don't think I understand your meaning. She works for the University, and is a respected member of the community."

Thompson looked at his associates and smiled slightly, which unnerved Everett a little more. "I didn't ask you about Professor Stiggler's relationship to the University," the attorney said sharply. "I asked you, and I'm asking you again, what is the nature of your personal relationship to her?"

Everett tried to control his voice, but stammered. "I . . . I don't think I take your meaning."

"Then let me spell it out for you. Do you or do you not have a romantic relationship with Professor Daphne Stiggler?"

"Objection!" cried Patterson, as relief suddenly coursed through Everett's body. "Objection, objection, objection! Are you kidding? This man is not on trial, and his personal relationships are absolutely no concern of the court. I will not allow my client to answer the question."

Thompson was at him in an instant, almost shouting, with the rapidity of machine gun fire. "It has every relevancy! You will direct your client to . . ."

"Dan!" said Everett, so overjoyed that he slipped into a first name-basis and didn't even realize it. "I don't mind answering. Believe me." He threw back his head and laughed, to the obvious alarm of Thompson. "No. I do not have a romantic relationship with Professor Stiggler." He looked at Patterson. "Can I say something off the record?"

Now it was Thompson's turn to stammer. "No . . . No you certainly may not."

Everett thought about it for a moment, and then decided, what the heck. "Let me just say, that I am not now, and never have been involved with that repulsive woman on more than a professional basis. And let me further say that I would rather be castrated with an axe, and be dragged naked across a bed of nails than have anything more to do with her than necessary."

The room fell into a shocked silence, and Everett enjoyed the feeling of power that flooded through him. He was now completely in control. The look on Thompson's face was worth any amount of money. "Have I made that perfectly clear, young man?"

"Perfectly," said Thompson, trying to muster a smile. "Then let's . . ."

"Good," spat Everett.

Thompson opened his mouth and then closed it again. Then he said, "Let's move on to the evening of the fourteenth of March. At about eight PM were you present in Room four twenty-three of the University Center on the campus?"

"Yes."

"Please tell us what happened there."

"It was very simple, really. There was a convocation of the student review board, and they decided on an appropriate action concerning the case of David Shore's outburst. Since Mr. Shore displayed no contrition whatsoever, the students recommended expulsion. The administration complied."

"Didn't you find the punishment rather harsh?" asked Thompson.

Everett was enjoying himself, and the words strung themselves together in elaborate sentences. All of the arguments which had been used on him, the ones that were impossible to refute without sounding like a bigot, came pouring from his mouth. "Not necessarily, no. Given the crisis of hatred on our campus toward minorities of any sort, I feel that the students are in a better position than I am to decide what punishments should be meted out. Given the circumstances, Shore was extremely insulting to Professor Stiggler. It was beyond toleration. As I say, Mr. Shore appeared not the slightest bit apologetic about what he had done. The students made their decision, and I stand by it."

"Were there any minutes taken at the meeting?"

"Absolutely not," said Everett. "We wanted to give the students the ability to make decisions without fear of retaliation from the faculty."

"With no administration oversight?" asked Parker.

"I was the administration oversight, Mr. Thompson. It was my responsibility to make certain that things didn't get out of hand. They did not."

"And you feel that the decision of the board was a good one?" Thompson asked glumly.

"Under the circumstances, I feel they had no other option. I have no problem with what they did. None whatsoever."

Thompson looked at Friedman and Clarke, who both shook their heads. "Very well, then. I conclude this deposition at," he glanced at his watch, "three-ten PM." The court reporter turned off the tape recorder, and started to gather her things together.

Patterson nudged Everett, "That's it. We can go. You did just great."

Everett soared on the rush of power, and he grinned at Patterson. "I feel like having a hamburger with everything."

His lawyer chuckled. "I think that can be arranged. Let's get out of here."

As they walked through the door, Patterson turned back to Thompson and said, "First Amendment? Say your prayers, kid."

SEVEN

An hour later, Parker and the two associates were waiting for Diamonte in his office to give him the evening progress report. They weren't talking much. A queer feeling had descended over Parker, as if he were a survivor from Dresden or Hiroshima who had survived the firestorm by hiding in a deep hole, and emerged to find his world obliterated. He found it difficult to comprehend how his situation could have so radically altered in so short a period of time. Just a few hours earlier his life had been filled with such promise; the perfect case and a woman who seemed to go along with it. The professional and personal aspects of his life had seemed to be dovetailing into a beautiful and different pattern, elevated to the high plain which in the back of his mind he had always wanted to get to, but which had always been just beyond his grasp; the world where he himself was the master of all eventualities, not only those small triumphs in court or with women, but those in what could only be called the grander scheme of existence. It wasn't that Parker had expected (at least not seriously) any sort of worldly fame, but it had seemed to him that an avenue to the solidity that people normally associate with their parents had for a short time been open to him, and now had suddenly been closed off. Its loss brought sharply into focus how intensely he wanted it. He couldn't even imagine seeing Mary now, now that that road was closed. Although he did not consciously realize it, he more than anything feared that she would no longer respect him, that she would look at him with pity. He couldn't bring himself to accept this. He wanted to run away from her, from this damned case which had just self-destructed before his eyes, from himself, from everything; but there was nowhere to run, nowhere to go. His only remaining hope was that Diamonte would have something up his sleeve, some courtroom ace that would help him back onto the road again.

Diamonte swept into the room, his face beaming with pleasure, his demeanor that of a man of thirty-five who one day realizes just how much he loves his wife and children. "What an out*stan*ding day," he said, slamming the door behind him. He sat behind the desk and rubbed his hands with glee, oblivious to the funereal atmosphere of the room. "I just settled the Johnson suit. 7.5 million dollars for those people, and they deserved every penny of it." He raised his hand, held it for a moment, and then brought it crashing down onto the desk. "God, I love this job!" Then he perceived the mood of his junior colleagues, and the smile faded. "What happened?" he asked.

"Broadstreet didn't corroborate," said Parker. "It was as bad as it could have been."

The older lawyer deflated like a soufflé. "Details," he said.

Parker described the interview, becoming more depressed as he had to recount the specifics of the disaster. Diamonte's face steeled as he listened to the story. He picked up a pencil and tapped it on the table. There was a pause after Parker finished.

"Well," said Diamonte. "Well, well." He exhaled slowly. "Do you think he's telling the truth?" he asked.

"I don't know," said Parker. "I certainly don't want to believe him, but at this point I just don't know. Rick thought he was lying, at least he thought so at first. What do you think now?" he asked.

Friedman considered for a moment. "After listening to the whole thing," he said warily, "I'm not so sure. I would have sworn that he wasn't telling the truth when he described the outburst in the classroom. Where Shore called the woman a dyke. To be honest, I still don't think he's totally on the level about that. His story just doesn't make any sense. There wasn't enough provocation to make Shore go off the deep end like he was supposed to have. Besides," he went on, addressing himself to Diamonte, "The guy was a mess. He was sweating, he was nervous . . ."

"I've seen guys on the stand fall apart when I knew for a fact they were telling the truth," said Parker. "It doesn't mean anything."

"But he wasn't on the stand," said Friedman, a little heat creeping into his voice. "He was in the conference room, for Christ's sake."

"With a couple of lawyers who to the best of his knowledge wanted to make mincemeat out of him," was Parker's glum reply.

Diamonte looked at Clarke. "What did you think about him?"

"I was only in on the end. But from what I saw he seemed pretty determined."

"Determined like telling the truth determined?" asked Diamonte.

"Yeah. If he said what he said in front of a judge, the way he said it," she shook her head. "Nobody'd even question his sincerity. He'd sink us."

"But that was just at the end," Friedman insisted. "None of us have ever met this Stiggler woman, or even talked to her on the phone. I have no doubt that he can't stand her. The question is whether he was telling the truth about what happened in the classroom, and I still don't think that he was."

"But why not?" said Parker, throwing up his hands. "You say he's lying. I say he was just scared, and that after a few minutes went by he relaxed. Why the hell would he lie? He's gonna, he's going to lose money if Shore's kicked. That bastard of a father of his is going to pull the plug."

"I know that, Parker. But that first impression . . . I just can't get it out of my mind. That guy was lying! Until he got onto that bit about Stiggler, you had to drag everything out of him. He gave no details at all, nothing about his frame of mind, no incidental details of any kind. Nothing that would give him any credence."

Diamonte looked at Parker. "Is this true?"

Parker nodded. "It's true. But we're still left without a reason why."

"Because he's a lying sack of shit. That's why," said Friedman under his breath.

"No," said Parker. "Why would he lie?"

"That I can't answer," said Friedman. "But just because we can't ascertain motive doesn't mean that motive doesn't exist."

"Well," said Diamonte, "You're going to have to do something about him, because he's dangerous. What we need is more information."

"I've thought about that, too," said Parker. "But there's a problem. I can't very well subpoena an entire class of a hundred and fifty students. In a big room like that, half of them probably never even heard the original joke that caused this whole thing to snowball. The ones who did hear it were the ones who were sitting with Shore, and they're all friends of his. I wouldn't want to stack up their credibility against, well, I'm going to blow the girl clean out of the water, but there's still the teacher, whose motives may or may not be suspect, and there's the dean of the school for whom we have yet to determine any motive for perjury. The biggest problems I can think of with Shore's credibility are his youth and his personal interest in the case. A bunch of his drinking buddies aren't going to look very unbiased, if you know what I mean."

"Yes," said Diamonte. He put his fingertips together and thought for a minute. Parker hoped that this would be when the wily senior partner would pull the rabbit out of his hat and save the day, but in the end he looked at the two associates and said, "Any suggestions?"

Parker sagged. Friedman shook his head, and Clarke said that she wanted some more time to think about it. This was Parker's sentiment also. "Is the law library open tomorrow?" he asked.

"I don't think so," said Aimee. "It's Good Friday."

"Oh, damn," said Parker. "That's right. And I'm supposed to go to the mountains this weekend."

"Maybe it'll do you some good," said Diamonte. "Get away. Think about all of this. Why don't we meet again on Monday, and we'll see what you've come up with."

Parker, Rick and Aimee all rose to leave, but Diamonte said, "A word with you, Parker." The two associates left the room, and Parker sat back down in his chair. Diamonte rose and came around to sit on the edge of his desk. He folded his arms. "Listen, Parker. I just want you to know that I understand your dilemma. This must be turning into a nightmare for you. If the dean's statement is true, not only is your First Amendment argument finished, but any due process angle is damaged as well. An independent council of students, as well as the administration, reviewed the case. I know you've thought about all of this. And I know that you're probably feeling a little more pressure because I was the one who gave you the case, and it's for someone I have personal dealings with." Diamonte glanced out of the window. "I don't know quite how to say this without it coming out patronizingly, but I just want you to know that I know what you're up against. I've known Art Shore for a long time, and we're friends in a way, but I know what kind of man he is. I have a feeling he's holding something on you."

Parker looked up at him in alarm. Diamonte patted the air with his hand. "I don't know what it is, but I want you to know that whatever it is, it's not going to change my feelings toward you in any way. You're a top-flight litigator, and I'll always stand by you. And if it turns out that you can't win this case, then my feeling is that the case can't be won. We must face the possibility that David is lying. If he is, and he did fly off the handle at his teacher, and he got caught for it, and that this is the punishment that they've given him, then that's it."

Parker nodded glumly at his feet. There was no way that he could explain to Diamonte that what Shore was holding on him was far bigger than anything that Diamonte could help him with. If it became known to the bar that Parker had lied on his application, as he had had to do in order to get his job with the city attorney's office, his license to practice law in Colorado would be revoked, and it was doubtful that he could find any other place to practice. Shore held his career in his hands. Everything hinged on his winning this case. Now, Diamonte was hinting at the possibility that the case was unwinnable. It was the worst thing he could have heard.

Diamonte misread Parker's dejection, and continued on in his most fatherly tone. "What I'm saying is that you don't have to win this one for me. When I first gave you this case, I told you that I wanted you to see the larger view, to see what the law was capable of. Getting some obnoxious kid reinstated at any cost wasn't what I had in mind." Diamonte rose from the edge of his desk and began pacing about the room. "I don't want this to sound maudlin," he said, "but I wanted to give you an idea about justice. It's easy to forget in this business that that's what we're all about. It's more than me and it's more than you. It's an obligation that we have to people to do what is right. It's why I've been a Democrat for my entire life. Of course we also have an obligation to David

Shore to see that he is adequately and zealously represented. And if it turns out that he's telling the truth, then we must do everything in our power to do what is right for him. But if not, I want you to know that I'll understand. So don't worry about it, huh?"

"Yeah," said Parker flatly. He didn't feel like elaborating.

"Go on home. Have a hell of a weekend, and I'll see you on Monday. Get out of here."

When Parker got to his house, it was still light out, but the air was cold and damp, and smelled like snow. He put a microwave dinner in the oven, fed the cat, and called Pidge to work out the arrangements for the weekend.

"Heyyy, Parker," said Pidge. "What's wrong with you? You sound bummed."

"Nothing," said Parker. "It's just this thing from work. It's got me kind of wrapped up."

"Is this still that case for your boss's friend?"

"It's really going to hell."

"Drag. Don't worry about it. You'll think of something. And anyway, the long weekend is here! The market is officially closed tomorrow, which means that my Friday has already arrived. In fact, I stopped off and had a few already. What's the plan for tonight?"

"I think I'm just going to stay in."

"We must have a bad connection here. For a second there I thought you said that you were just going to stay in. Oh. Is Mary there?"

"Nah, I haven't talked to her."

"Not what I've heard. I understand that you've talked to her quite a bit. I haven't seen you for a week. You missed the squash game."

"Oh, Christ, I forgot all about it. We were really tied up Tuesday. I'm really sorry."

"Don't worry about it," said Pidge. "Isn't she great?"

"Yeah," said Parker. "She's fine."

"I knew you'd like her. Anyway, I'm feeling good. Let's go out."

"I'm really not up for it."

"Come onnnn. Let's go out. Let's go to the Saddle and get blind and watch the cowboys beat up on each other. You can talk some cowgirl into making my dreams come true."

"Nah. I'm staying home. But we gotta work out the details for tomorrow."

"Alright. Be boring. Be a loser. Walk out on your best friend in his hour of need. See if I care." He sighed audibly. "Anyway, there's nothing to work out. You're bringing Mary, right?"

"Yeah. Do you just want to meet us up there?"

"Sounds fair enough. Why don't we meet at that bar next to the covered bridge at four?"

"Fine. You bringing anybody?"

"Depends on what I can find tonight."

Parker tried to muster some enthusiasm. "Harsh. Maybe you better just plan on scamming when we get up there. Last minute dates for weekends are disasters waiting to happen. If she turns out to be a pill, you still have to look at her for two days."

"We'll see how it goes. You bringing your good skis or your rocks?"

"Rocks. It's late in the season."

"Yeah."

"Yeah."

"We're gonna have a great time. See you tomorrow."

"See you."

"Hey Parker? Don't worry about that case. You'll think of something."

"I'll see you."

He hung up the phone and let the cat out. He took a bottle of scotch from the cabinet and filled a tumbler with ice, and as he had nothing higher upon which to place his faith, spent the next two hours drinking until he couldn't remember to be afraid.

*   *   *

In the morning, cool and damp, a breeze wafted in through the window over Parker's bed, settling a few snowflakes on his naked shoulders. As he woke, he had the sensation of swimming upward through water, the light gradually increasing in intensity until he broke the surface and realized that he was conscious. He lay with his eyes closed for a few moments in the pleasant, shady place between slumber and waking, and then remembered, with a start, how much he had had to drink the night before. He opened his eyes, and the headache hit immediately. He shut his eyes and drifted back into a half sleep.

When he crawled from beneath the comforter a half an hour later, he stumbled over the clothes piled at the foot of his bed, and lurched into the bathroom. His temples throbbed as though he had an alien inside of his head who was tramping heavily upon the backs of his eyeballs. He moved to turn on the light, but then thought the better of it. The inside of his mouth felt swollen and dried out so he opened the medicine cabinet for some mouthwash. He took a swig and swirled the liquid around his mouth. He lifted his head to gargle, but the noise thundered through his head and he almost choked. He spit the mouthwash out, his tongue so dried out that he felt the fluid running over it rather than tasting it, and ran the tap until the water was icy. He cupped his hands and splashed his face several times. Then he turned off the tap and dried his face with a towel.

As he put the mouthwash back into the medicine cabinet, he noticed the seal of cocaine which he had placed there the first night Mary had come over. He looked at himself in the mirror in the half light; his eyelids swollen and puffy, his face pale, hardly human. "Oh, yeah," he said, and opened the little triangular seal. There was about an eighth of a gram left over from the binge he had gone on with the two women the week before. What were their names, anyway? He couldn't recall. He scraped the cocaine into a neat little pile on the little mirror he kept with the metal straw in the cabinet. He chopped the powder ever finer with a razor blade, and then divided it into two chunky lines. He put the straw in his nose, bent over the counter, and sniffed sharply. For an instant, a trail burned into the sinuses on one side of his face. He gasped, but the pain was quickly followed by numbness. He bent over the counter again and repeated the process with the other nostril. Then he inhaled deeply a few times, dragging the effect into his lungs, quickening his heartbeat. Within twenty seconds, the headache was a dull memory.

He swallowed a few aspirin and washed them down with cold water. With any luck they would start to work before the white powder wore off, so that when the throbbing in his head returned it would be at least tolerable. He washed his mouth out again, and then went back into his room and pulled on some clothes. Then he staggered down the stairs to the kitchen to make himself something to eat. The cat followed him from the living room and rubbed itself against his legs.

Parker picked him up and rubbed his cheek against its silky fur. "I hope you're feeling better than I am," he said. "Do you want something to eat, sweetie? Want some nice cat crunchies? Alright. It's coming . . . iiiit's coming. Just let Parker fix himself a little cure-all." Parker opened a bottle of club soda, poured it into a glass with ice, and then shook in a few drops of bitters. He drank it off quickly, and sniffed deeply a few more times. The clean, bitter smell and taste of the cocaine dripped into his throat and made his heart jump again. His head cleared a little more.

He poured some food into the cat's dish and gave him some fresh water. The cat purred and arched his back as he ate. Parker then made up some blender hollandaise, a quick recipe he had memorized for emergencies such as this one, poached two eggs, and placed them atop an English muffin. He took the plate back through to the living room and sat down on the sofa to eat. Afterwards, he took a shower and changed into fresh clothes. He felt a little more human, but his head was beginning to pound again, his body crying out to him for another blast. He needed fresh supplies. He picked up the phone and dialed his dealer's number. It was never wise to come to that guy's house unannounced.

After the line rang a few times, an incredibly, unnaturally relaxed voice answered. "Yeah?"

"Hey, Tab, it's me," said Parker.

"Hello, me," the voice breathed slowly. "You're callin' mighty early."

Parker looked at his watch. "It's after eleven," he said. "Sorry, did I wake you up?"

A quiet laugh. "No, man. I never sleep. You need something?"

"Yeah. Can I come over?"

"You bet, man. Mi casa es su casa. Right? Mi casa es su casa. That's Spanish, man. It means my house is your house. You come on by." The phone went dead.

Parker pulled on his leather jacket, and was on his way out to the garage when the doorbell rang. He cursed, and went to the front door to answer it. Mary was standing there. It was a surprise, but on balance a pleasant one.

"Hi, honey," she said, and wrapped her arms around his neck. "You didn't call last night. When I didn't hear from you I went out and I saw Clay and he told me you were staying home. You OK?"

"I'm fine. I just wasn't up for going out." Her cheeks were cold but she felt warm and soft in his arms, and her eyes radiated concern. He kissed her. "Did you actually go to the Saddle?"

"No, what's that?"

"It's this cowboy bar that Pidge drags me to sometimes. He said something about it last night.

"We didn't go there. I found him at this really loud club down by the tracks. I missed you. What did you do?"

"I wound up drinking half a bottle of scotch and passing out. I'm kind of hung over. And I want to go to bed with you right now."

She looked at him with a little surprise, and then gave her simple, honest smile. "OK," she said. "Sure."

"But I can't. I was just on my way out the door. I have to go someplace real quick. Do you want to wait for me?"

"Can I come with you?" she asked.

He didn't really want her to, but he didn't know how to tell her why. He had never heard her say anything that would indicate that she had any knowledge about drugs, or any experience with them. She was that sort of person. Ironically, it was one of the things he found most attractive about her.

"I guess it would be OK."

"What's wrong?"

"Nothing. It's fine. Let's go."

Tab's house was a few miles away from Parker's, in a post-war neighborhood that had been designed at a time when home-ownership in the suburbs was still a dream for most. His was a square, brick house, on a cheerless street lined with identical square, brick houses with small lawns in front of them. Under the lightly falling snow that was already beginning to taper off, the grass was just starting to turn green around the edges. Several of the yards had cyclone fences around them, and some had faded, plastic toys on them, grimly sitting by themselves on the otherwise deserted street. Parker pulled up in front of one of the houses.

"Wait here for me, OK?" said Parker. "I'll be out in a couple of minutes."

He looked up the street in both directions to make sure there was no one around, and then walked into the short driveway, and up the stairs on the front stoop. He rang the bell. After a long minute, the door opened. Parker's dealer stood about five feet ten, and thin. His face had the same translucency it always did, with a few dot-like freckles scattered over his small, sharp nose. He had almost no facial hair except for a few tiny whiskers which might doubtfully be coaxed into growing a mous-

tache of sorts. In total, the face was either youthful or ef-
feminate, difficult to say which. His movements were
slow and deliberate, as was his speech, and betrayed his
addiction, except for the short, quick jerk he used to flick
his long, almost matted hair from his eyes. The glassy
eyes took in Parker without expression.

"It's me, Parker."

"I know who you are," said Tab, a dazed smile ooz-
ing over his face. "Come on in, man." He beckoned
Parker into the living room, where two other men were
sitting on one of the run-down looking sofas. "You caught
me in the middle of some business. Just, you know, have
a seat. I'll take that," he said, lifting an enormous revolver
from the table next to the chair and slipping it into the
back of his waistband. He turned to the two on the couch.
"This guy here is like the lord of the litigators. Heh. Yeah,
the lord of the litigators. He even used to work for the
D.A.'s office, if you can believe that. Now he's working
for some firm somewhere. Heh. Lawyers, man. Lawyers
are tooooo much. He knows where the best shit is,
though. And he always comes back to me. Yes he does.
He'll make sure you all don't fuck with me. And these guys
here are selling Bolivia's finest export, which should interest you, Parker. Although it doesn't interest me, being
a vice that I don't particularly indulge in."

"What the fuck is this, man?" said one of the men
on the other couch, with a suspicious glance at Parker.

"It's no problem, man," said Tab, leaning back on
the couch. "Me and Parker go way back. Wayyyy back.
He's just a worker bee. But he's seen it all before. Now
let's take a look at this shit."

The suspicious one shot another look at Parker, and
then nodded to his associate, who pulled a large baggie

from the inside pocket of his overcoat and set it on the coffee table. Inside was a smaller white parcel, about eight inches long and a couple thick. "It's the best," the man in the overcoat said arrogantly.

Tab unwrapped the package, took a pocket knife and inserted the tip into it. He extracted about a half a teaspoonful and dumped it onto the glass. He looked at Parker. "You want a taste, man?"

Parker took a bill from his wallet, laid it over the pile, and then scraped across the top, powdering it. Then he cut out a line, bent over the table and snorted it. It burned a trail into his face. He shook his head. "Tastes pretty good."

"Well, we will see," said Tab. He stood up and went into the kitchen, emerging a few seconds later with a bottle of Clorox and spotlessly clean beaker. He poured the bleach into the tumbler. "Have you seen this before?"

"No. Well on TV, but they never really show what it's supposed to do."

"Heh," Tab laughed. "He's seen it on TV, man. Heh heh. That's real cool. Well watch this. See, you take a little bit and drop it on the top. And then you wait for a minute to see what . . . oooo yesss. Yessssss. That's very nice. See the stuff that falls through first, and stays looking like powder? That, to the trained chemist's eye, is some lactose that these boys, or someone else, has put in to increase the yield. There's always somebody stepping on something. But it's not bad, there's very little. But this other stuff, here, and here, that's pure cocaine. Look how it dissolves and falls through the bleach in shreds. Little streamers of perfection. Isn't it beautiful, man? Like a beautiful wedding veil. Mmmmmm. Yes. Beautiful."

"Hey, Tab," said Parker. "I gotta run."

"Oh, yeah. Hey. Of course. I've already got an eight-ball cut out for you. Let me grab it." He went through a doorway and came back holding a little seal in his hand.

Parker handed him two hundred and fifty dollars. "I better give this to you before I forget."

Tab chuckled languorously. "Yeah. You better do that." He took the money and put it into one of his pockets. Then he lay back again against his couch. There was an uncomfortable pause, and Parker was about to get up to leave, when there was a knock on the door. Tab instantly sat upright, reaching behind his back for the gun. He looked at the two suppliers. "Who the fuck is that?" he said. The dreamy quality had vanished from his voice, and his eyes were opened wide, darting around the room. He pointed the gun at the two other dealers, who lifted their hands.

"Hey, we didn't bring anybody else. It ain't us, man. It ain't fucking us. Just take it easy. Maybe it's just some dude selling encyclopedias or something."

The knock came again. Tab jumped across the room, still holding the gun on the two on the sofa. He put his ear to the door. The knock came again, louder. Tab leapt back, facing the door. He shifted the gun to his left hand and gently put his right hand on the knob. In one quick motion he jerked the door open and leveled the gun out on the stoop, where Mary was standing. "Who the fuck are you?"

Mary looked like a deer caught in the headlights of a truck. She swallowed and looked about the room, her eyes shifting from Parker to the coffee table and back to the enormous gun pointed at her face. "I'm . . . I was . . ."

"She's with me, Tab," said Parker. "She's with me. Just relax."

"Who the fuck is she?" Tab shouted, not taking his eyes off of her face.

"She's my girlfriend, man," Parker said. "She's with me. Just relax. She's OK. She doesn't know anything about this."

"You brought your fucking woman here?" He was still pointing the gun at her. "What the fuck's the matter with you?"

"Tab," said Parker. "Relax! Just relax, man. It's cool."

Tab held his position for a few seconds, and then shifted the gun upright. He uncocked it. "Yeah," he said. "It's cool. It's cool." He slid the gun back into his waistband, and then ran his hand through his hair. "Yeah. It's cool."

Mary's body seemed to sag a little. She leaned up against the doorframe. One of the dealers on the couch exhaled loudly and slumped back in his seat. He looked at Parker and shook his head, as if he couldn't believe his stupidity. The other dealer stared at the coffee table.

Parker stood up. "We were just leaving."

Tab nodded slowly. "I'll see you later, huh?"

Mary looked wide-eyed at Parker as he gently took her arm and walked her out to the car. He opened the door for her and helped her into the seat. As they drove away Parker didn't know what to say to her, but he knew that he would have to say something. He pulled the car over.

"I don't know what to say, Mary. I'm so sorry that that happened. If I'd known, I never would have let you come. I'm so sorry."

"Yeah." Her face was pale, and Parker could see that she was still shaking. She stared out the windshield and didn't look over at him. "Yeah," she said again.

Parker reached over gently and took her hand. "It's over now."

"Yeah." She didn't say anything else for a while, and Parker, wisely perhaps, didn't say anything either. After a moment or two, Mary said, "Did you get what you needed?"

He was about to say that it wasn't something that he needed, but he realized how stupid that would sound considering how close she had just come to being killed. "I got it."

"Well, then, let's go home, OK?"

"Oh, Honey, I'm so sorry."

"I know."

"You sure?"

"Yeah. Let's go."

Parker eased the car out into the street. A few snowflakes landed on the windshield and melted. He flicked the wipers once, and then reached over to hold her hand again. "You sure you're OK?"

"Yeah . . . no . . . I don't . . ." she stammered quietly. Then she said, "What did you buy?"

Parker didn't want to answer, because he felt ashamed. "Cocaine," he said.

"Can I see it?"

He could feel his cheeks redden. "Um, sure." He reached into his pocket and pulled out the seal. "Here."

Mary turned the pouch over in her hand a few times, and then carefully unfolded it. "I knew people who did it when I was in school, but nobody ever showed it to me. I guess they thought I was too virginal or something." She tilted the seal to one side. "It doesn't really look like much. Was this what was on the table? You know, back there?"

"Yes," said Parker. He had no idea how he was supposed to feel. "The two other guys were doing a deal with . . . With the other guy."

"How much was there?"

"I don't know. Probably about a half a kilo."

Mary was still looking at the powder in her hands. "How much would that be worth?"

"About fifty thousand dollars."

"Hmm." It was almost a laugh, but one devoid of amusement. "Lot of money." She folded the seal up slowly and handed it back to Parker, who put it into his pocket again. "Was the guy with the gun all coked up or something?"

"No. He's a um, he's a junkie. Heroin."

"Oh. Do you do that, too?"

Parker pulled the car over again and set the brake. He could not concentrate both on this conversation, which was about to get very serious, and on driving. "I don't want to lie to you, Mary."

"I don't want you to lie to me either. But I'd like to know. Do you do heroin, too?"

"Sometimes."

"A lot?"

"No. Only sometimes. The last time was about a month ago. Before that, about three months."

"Not more?"

"No."

"Why not?"

"Because I don't want to end up like that guy back there."

Mary was looking at him now, her expression one of pure innocence. "Isn't it, well, doesn't it make you addicted?"

"That's kind of hard to explain," Parker said quietly. "I can feel why people get addicted to it, when I do it. But I just never do it very much. I know what would happen to me if I did. It's pretty stupid, I guess."

"Then why?"

"I don't know. I guess I never had a reason not to."

Mary nodded, and then sat in silence for a few seconds. "You OK?" she asked.

Parker smiled, surprised at her for asking such a thoughtful question. "Me? I'm fine. He didn't pull a gun on me. I'm more worried about you."

"I'll be all right." She smiled back at him. "Honest."

He drew her to him in a hug. "Oh, Honey. I'm so sorry."

She hugged him tightly, and then pulled back to face him. She was blushing slightly.

"What is it?" Parker asked.

"It's kind of embarrassing."

"What?"

"Well, it's just that, well . . . hmmm." She bit her lip and looked away. "It kind of just . . . um . . . I guess, turned me on a little."

Parker managed to keep a straight face for about three seconds, and then the two of them burst out laughing. They were still giggling twenty minutes later when they drove into the garage.

EIGHT

Everett was still soaring as he made his way through the snowflakes from the parking lot to Old Main. They swirled around him mischievously, sometimes darting between the brim of the fedora he wore on cold days and the top of his muffler, to sting his face and make him blink. It was a Friday morning, Good Friday, as it turned out, not that the University took any notice of the Easter weekend. Spring Break had traditionally been held during this time, but the faculty had decided several years earlier that tying the vacation to so religious a holiday was too exclusionary to the students who did not happen to hold Christian beliefs. For the same reason, Christmas Vacation had been renamed Winter Break. Some professors had at the time also tried to eliminate the Thanksgiving holiday in the fall, or to at least rename it Harvest Break, in order to protect the sensitivity of foreign students, but the idea had been a bit too silly for the rank and file to accept, and the movement had died. Spring Break was quite a bit easier to reschedule, and none of the students minded waiting until April, since the week-long vacation was viewed by most of them primarily as an excuse to go someplace warm and drink themselves stupid.

Despite the gentle snowfall that had blown up overnight, Everett felt warm inside, partly due to his triumph at the depositional hearing, and partly because of his conditioning to cold after the long winter. The snow wasn't even sticking to the grass, and the cement sidewalks were only wet, the tiny flakes melting into a brown stain as they fell. Everyone seemed to sense that the snow would end quickly and be followed by a warm afternoon; it often happened that way with Spring storms. Some of the students were even wearing shorts as they shuttled about between the buildings. Everett was in a benevolent mood as he watched them walking quickly to class, some of them reading as they went, eager to have their minds challenged by new ideas.

By the time he got to the Quad, the construction workers were gearing up for their day, most wearing blue jeans and heavy, muddy boots. They were living in their own world, oblivious to the students, intent on the task at hand, and Everett, for once, felt not the slightest bit of animosity toward them. He, after all, now understood that their world was a part of his world, too. They had their work and he had his. He had a full day ahead of him, and he rather looked forward to doing his job well.

At the entrance to Old Main he picked up a copy of the campus paper and tucked it under his arm as he ascended the broad wooden staircase to the third floor. Several people said good morning to him, and seemed surprised at his animated replies. He turned into the last door on the third floor hallway, said hello to Joyce and complimented her on her appearance. He hung up his hat and coat on the peg, sat down behind his desk, and spread the newspaper out in front of him. There, on the front page, he read the following story:

Dean Endorses Student's Dismissal

Dean Everett Broadstreet testified Thursday that a student review board acted properly when it dismissed undergraduate David Shore two weeks ago.

Under oath at an official meeting with Shore's attorney, the dean explained the circumstances surrounding Shore's expulsion, and confirmed that he saw "no problem" with the Board's action.

Shore's family filed suit with the University within days of their son's expulsion. Their attorney has claimed that the University's action violates the First Amendment's free speech provision.

Attorneys for the University, in a prepared statement issued yesterday, claimed that "Shore was belligerent and insulting" to Professor Daphne Stiggler of the Women's Studies Department during a recent class. The statement goes on to call any First Amendment question in this case "Ludicrous."

In transcripts of Thursday's meeting made available to the Sentinel, Dean Broadstreet, who was present at the class and witnessed the altercation, detailed the events in Stiggler's classroom. He claimed that

"Dr. Stiggler showed admirable restraint," while Shore and his friends acted "in a most disruptive manner." When asked to leave the classroom, Shore stated "I don't have to take this from a fat old dyke like you." Shore then stormed from the room.

Shore's attorney, with the Denver firm of Byrd, Templeton and Diamonte, was unavailable for comment.

"I'll just bet that he was," Everett said to himself. He pushed the newspaper away with satisfaction and turned in his chair to watch the construction workers scurrying around. The snow had almost stopped, and already the light had grown in intensity, burning through the mist and casting shadows. One of the cement trucks rumbled into life. It was attached to some sort of snorkel-like device which pumped concrete up to the sixth floor of the tower. One of the workmen behind the truck, by his bearing Everett guessed that he was a foreman of some sort, had a walkie-talkie in his hand, with which he was obviously talking to one of the men at the other end of the snorkel. The man was looking upward, gesturing with his free hand. Occasionally, he had to hold the radio to his ear to hear over the roar of the engine. If Everett sat right up close to the window and leaned on the credenza, and craned his neck upward, he could see the other man high in the tower directing the flow of cement. He held onto a vertical steel i-beam, standing on the edge of the building, looking down at the truck, apparently unconcerned with his precarious position.

Everett was amazed that the man could seem so nonchalant. He reached into his desk drawer and took out his glasses so that he could get a better look at the worker high above him. Now Everett could see that the man had no safety device on, except for his hardhat, and that there was indeed no railing in front of him. The mason suddenly started laughing into the radio and pointing downward, where a great blob of cement had swelled over the top of the mixer and landed on the foreman's boots. Everett also smiled as the foreman called over to another man with a green garden hose. The dean could just hear the man's voice through the window. "Hey, Charlie! You wanna give me a little help here?" The other worker brought the hose over and washed down the man's feet. The foreman looked back up at the worker in the tower and said something into the radio. The two of them both burst into laughter. Then the foreman began pointing again and talking. The man upstairs waved and walked back into the building.

For a moment, Everett envied these men and their simple lives. But then, as he thought about it, he realized that their lives were no more simple than his own. Their work was dangerous and precise, and if they failed to be cautious, they could be physically injured, or perhaps make a building that would be structurally unsound. Still, they seemed happy. Perhaps it was because at the end of the day they could point to something and say, "I made that, and I did a good job." Everett had sometimes had that feeling when he was teaching. Now, he supposed, he was the foreman who always had cement dropping into his shoes. But the foreman outside had laughed. Everett realized that he rarely laughed at himself. Perhaps that was what Stein had always meant about not taking himself and his life so seriously. Perhaps if he allowed himself to bend happily sometimes, instead of being so straightlaced and formal, some of his employees might laugh with him. Perhaps the world might laugh with him.

He had certainly taken the first step, hadn't he? His eyes glanced back over the text of his newspaper story, and he almost chuckled. Such eagerness on the part of the reporters to say this or say that, and the truth be damned. If the quotes weren't exactly right, so what? This was the way the world was! People who worked hard and people who didn't, those who cared and those who were careless, priests and thieves, all tracking the courses of their lives, like sailors who had more or less control of the tiller. Everett had his hands firmly on the wheel for the first time in his life, and he wasn't going to let go easily. There was, of course, one piece of the puzzle missing, but he wouldn't remember it until later in the day.

Upon return to the campus after his lunch with the chancellor, Everett could hear the garbled sound of a bullhorn, a faint and indistinct roaring, coming from the direction of the Square. It sounded almost like a pep rally of some kind, like the voice of a cheerleader exhorting a crowd of fans, but such things never happened on the campus outside of football season, and then only on game days. Everett decided to investigate, and took a turn off of the walkway to Old Main. A light breeze was blowing, chasing away the chill air of the morning and replacing it with warmth, and as the zephyr swirled and dipped, the voice over the bullhorn was now clear and now muffled to the point where the dean could hardly hear it. As he passed the stone buildings with their ivy-covered facades, the voice gradually cleared until as he rounded the final corner at the Physics building and came into view of the Square he could hear the speaker distinctly.

The Square was bordered on all sides by buildings, and was a convenient midday meeting place for most of the students in the Arts and Sciences school, because one of the bordering buildings contained the Student Center and cafeteria; a new building commissioned during the last decade by the president. Whether because of it's disjointed architectural style or because so many students ate there, it was nicknamed the "Mess." On sunny afternoons, like this one was turning out to be, most students took their lunch and ate on the steps by the fountain in the center of the Square, socializing to one degree or another, playing hacky-sack or frisbee, or listening to the haranguers who came there on some days to curse the crowd because they were too conservative or liberal, too religious or secular, or too committed or uncommitted to whatever revolution the haranguer was selling. On most occasions, people in the crowd would shout back at the speakers, summoning all of their collegiate wit, and contributing to the carnival atmosphere. Professors often came and listened as well, enjoying the show, but by an unwritten rule they seldom if ever challenged the speakers. This was a game for graduate students and for those undergraduates who were especially well-read or especially foolish.

Usually, however, the haranguers were solitary individuals and their attacks on the peace were at least outwardly impromptu. As Everett cleared the corner of the Physics building, and saw what was taking place in the Square, he realized that something more organized was going on. A crowd of about fifty people were gathered around the fountain, looking up at a husky young woman with dreadlocks who stood, bullhorn in hand, on the steps. A few of the people had placards which they were holding up. Everett didn't have on his distance glasses, and so couldn't read the signs, but it was fairly evident that a formal demonstration was taking place. It seemed to be concerned with women's rights, a common theme. The dean stood for a moment and watched, and after a moment, since he had other things planned for the afternoon, and since the demonstration was small and orderly, and since the woman wasn't saying anything Everett hadn't heard a hundred times before, he turned and walked back to his office.

As he entered the foyer, Joyce looked up from her typing and said, "Oh, Dean, President Fowler called about a half an hour ago. It sounded urgent, but he said he would be away from the mansion and would call you back."

"That's fine, Joyce. Just buzz me when he does. Did you get all of the readmit files together?"

"They're on you desk, sir."

He opened his office door, and the sound of the construction burst upon him. He sighed, closed the door, and sat behind his enormous desk. In front of him, in a stack about four inches thick, were the files from students who had been previously dismissed from the University and now were asking for readmission. There was an assistant dean whose solitary job was to sort through these files, a young man with a bulldog face, whose disposition had been permanently soured by his continual contact with indolent students. These young people would stop at nothing— no lie was too extraordinary— to ingratiate themselves with the system so as to avoid a spell with the Department of Continuing Education. Cont Ed was designed as an outreach program to give people in the community access to college-level courses, but in practice acted as a sort of Corrections Department for the University. Most wayward freshmen who drank themselves into deficient grade point averages found their way into Cont Ed's night-school classes, another name for University purgatory, where sloth was burned out of them through the taking of classes in which they had little or no interest, but which they needed to pass with high marks in order to lift their cumulative GPA's to acceptable levels.

For some students, however, there was another possible course of action. The University had a program for a limited number of students in which the dismissee was allowed to attend regular classes during the day, and thereby avoid purgatory. Competition for the spots was fierce, and the stack in front of Everett, which he examined every month, represented those cases that the assistant dean found to have some degree of validity, perhaps five percent of the total number. Most people in these files were hard-luck cases, students who had been forced to drop out for family emergencies and the like, but who had not had the presence of mind to inform the school beforehand and had simply stopped attending classes, and had then been given a string of F's. But in Everett's opinion, any student who was that stupid had little business attending the University in the first place. A few of the cases were children of alumni or students who came from wealthy families from whom the school could profit by accepting them on a conditional basis. The assistant dean flagged these files by cryptically writing a small dollar sign or capital 'A' on the cover. It was an unfair system, and one which the administration would heatedly deny. Everett hated being a part of it, but, as his friend Stein would say, money made the University go round.

Everett adjusted his reading glasses and took the top file from the stack. The student's name was Joshua Wagner, and the cover had no other notation. The dean opened the file, winced as he read the grammatical errors in the boy's handwritten cover letter, and then ran his hand over the crown of his skull. It was going to be a long afternoon.

About a half an hour and three files later, his phone buzzed. Before he was able to reach for the button, his door flew open and President Fowler stormed in. Everett could see Joyce peering around the doorway at him in surprise. She shrugged her shoulders. Without preamble, Fowler launched in, "Do you have any idea what's going on at the Square?"

"Glad to see you, too, Robert," said Everett. Joyce closed the door.

"Don't get smart with me, Dean. Have you heard what's going on out there?"

"I can't hear much of anything over that," said Everett, waving his arm in the direction of the construction site. "But I did see a small demonstration in the Square after lunch. What of it?"

"A small demonstration? There's over four hundred students out there, and they're screaming to have that little turd David Shore removed from campus. They say there are television cameras coming. What are you going to do about it?"

Everett raised his eyebrows. He hadn't expected this. "I uh . . . What do you want me to do about it, Robert?"

"I want you to stop them. I want you to get out there and tell them to disperse. I want you to do your god-damned job! That's what I want you to do!"

Everett almost laughed. Stopping a demonstration like this was next to impossible; indeed, administration presence usually fanned the flames. "Have you talked to Stiggler about this? She was the one who wanted to get rid of him so badly."

"No. I left a message at her department for her to meet us in the Physics building. She may be over there now."

"Us?" asked Everett. He was in an impertinent mood, and annoyed that Fowler should come busting into his office shouting at him. Who did he think that he was? "Us?" he repeated. "What exactly do you expect me to do about this? The students don't like me. I'm old, white, and male. Or hadn't you noticed?"

Fowler seemed to notice him for the first time. There was a strange look in his eyes as he examined the dean's face. "What's gotten into you, Everett?" he asked.

"Nothing that shouldn't have gotten into me a long time ago."

"I see," said Fowler, his voice now educated and rational. "Well might I please presume upon you to accompany me to the Physics building? I could use your help."

"If you put it that way, Robert, I'd be glad to come." Everett carefully put his reading glasses into their case and stood up. "Shall we go?" The amazed look on Fowler's face was beautiful.

Once clear of the construction noise, the bullhorn was audible again, and as the two administrators walked silently toward its source it grew louder. Shouts could also be heard, although the words were unclear. Fowler led the way to the back door of the Physics building and up the dark staircase to the second floor. The building was almost deserted. They made their way to the side of the building that fronted on the Square and into a classroom. A large periodic table hung next to the blackboard, which was covered with mathematical equations. Everett looked at them with interest, as he always did when looking at theoretical math, as if it were a secret code that outsiders couldn't understand. He belonged to a club that could, and just seeing the differentials gave him a feeling of superiority. Not just anyone could understand them; not Fowler, well, maybe Fowler could since he was an architect, but certainly not Stiggler, who had turned from the windows as they walked into the room. Everett had never noticed how short she was. Even Fowler, who was barely five feet six, seemed to tower over her. She looked concerned and unhappy.

"Jack's down there talking to them now," she said, "trying to find out what started this."

"You mean you had nothing to do with it?" asked Fowler, visibly surprised.

"No!" she cried. "Of course not! We aren't any more interested in publicity than you are. We would have told you beforehand."

"Like you did with Biddlebody?" said Everett coldly. "Forgive me, but your record for honesty leaves a bit to be desired."

"No more so, perhaps, then yours does, Dean," said Beetle, who had at that moment walked into the room. He crossed to the windows.

Everett eyed him steadily. "I've had good professors," he said.

Beetle's steely eyes met his, and looked for a moment as if he couldn't quite believe what he was seeing, but was very pleased to see it. A smile spread across his face. "My, my," he said. "Someone certainly ate his Wheaties this morning."

Fowler looked from one to the other with growing impatience. "I don't know what exactly is going on between you two," he said, "and quite frankly I don't care. But you've been out there, Jack, and I need you to tell me what's happening."

It took Beetle a moment to pull his eyes away from Everett's. "Well, Bob," he said when he did, "They seem to be in a tizzy because Shore's back on campus."

"Can you make them go away?" Fowler asked.

The childlike tone of the question made Beetle smile. "No, Mr. President. I don't believe that I can. But if you want to hear something truly astounding, the one person who might be able to make them 'go away' is standing right next to you." He shifted his gaze back to Everett.

"*Me?*" asked Everett.

"Yes indeed," said Beetle, his face glowing with amusement. "I think if you went out there and said a few words, you might be able to make them see reason."

"Me?" asked Everett again. "They don't like me. I'm a white male."

"You really *are* feeling feisty today. I happen to be a white male, too. We all have our crosses to bear. But today you're a hero. You fought the law for them. It was in the paper and everything. Congratulations. As far as those kids are concerned you're the man of the year."

"Oh my God," said Fowler. He was staring out of the window at the crowd. "A television crew has arrived. Whatever we do we're going to have to do it fast. Everett, I want you to please go out and talk to them."

"What shall I say?"

"You'll think of something. Come on. We'll all go down there and see what we can do." He led the way out of the room and down the hall. He was speaking to Beetle, who was walking next to him. Everett and Stiggler brought up the rear.

"You know," she said, "I saw what you said about me at that meeting. Other people saw it too," she added softly. "I had no idea that you felt that way about me."

"Now you know," said Everett.

"And I didn't know you could be so hurtful." Her beautiful eyes were growing wet around the corners, making them even more lovely.

Everett stopped and stared at her with contempt. He couldn't believe that she, of all people, was saying this. "Maybe it just took me a while to get tired of being kicked in the teeth."

"Would you two hurry up!" called Fowler. He and Beetle were already at the top of the stairs. They waited for Everett to catch up, he left Daphne standing there, and then the three white males hustled down and out the front doors into the Square.

The scene that greeted Everett was far less impressive than it had been from the window overlooking the gathering. While there was a core of perhaps two hundred students who were listening to the speakers and participating in the rally, most of the rest of the young people were idlers who were content to watch. Their mood could hardly be described as outraged or even sympathetic. As Everett brushed through the skirts of the crowd he caught fragments of the conversations, and it was apparent that most of them were discussing other things: "Yeah, the T.A.s a total dweeb . . . I can give you those notes . . . We're gonna meet for beers over at . . . Why don't you come over to my place . . ." Comments hardly indicative of student agony.

Further in, more people were paying attention, but looked disgusted at the proceedings. They would occasionally shout things at the protesters: "Don't you have homework?" and "Go to Class!" and one young man gave a succinct cry of "Fuck Off!" His friends smiled approvingly. Still, even these people seemed disinclined to do any more to stop the protesters; this was light opera to them, divine comedy.

Between this group and the core of protesters there was a space of a few feet, as if the ones on the outside didn't want to be confused with the participants, and the ones on the inside felt that huddling together would increase the purity of their collective rage. Beetle, who was leading the way, had to push a path for Fowler and Broadstreet to get through. At the front of the semicircle, Beetle shouted something in Fowler's ear and held his hand against the little man's chest. Then he turned and climbed a few steps above the heads of the crowd.

A cheer went up as he came into view. Beetle turned and waved. The speaker, a shirtless man of around twenty or so wearing baggy cutoff khakis and what appeared to be a vest made in the style of the kind that comes with a three piece suit, but fronted with some sort of flowered pattern, took little notice as Beetle walked up to him. He was shouting into the orange bullhorn, " . . . and I'll tell you this, children, WE AIN'T GONNA TAKE IT ANY MORE! Let me hear you say POWER!"

A cry came back from the inner circle, "Power!" Outside the circle came another "Fuck You!"

"Let me hear you say POWER!"

"Power!"

"Jerkwad! Fuck head!"

"POWER TO THE PEOPLE! C'mon ya'll! POWER TO THE PEOPLE!"

All around Everett the protesters took up the chant, "POWer to the PEOple! POWer to the PEOple! POWer to the PEOple! POWer to the PEOple! POWer to the PEOple!"

Their voices so drowned out everything else that Everett could no longer hear the vulgarities from the outer circle. The speaker, satisfied that the momentum would be sustained let the bullhorn fall to his side. He and Beetle began shouting into each other's ears. Beetle gestured back at Fowler. The young man shook his head. "Come on!" Beetle seemed to be shouting, raising his hand in exasperation. The young man wouldn't budge. He held the bullhorn back, as if he feared that Beetle might make a grab for it.

"POWer to the PEOple! POWer to the PEOple!" shouted the crowd.

Beetle then gestured at Everett. He looked imploringly into the young man's face. The speaker looked at Everett and smiled. He held the bullhorn out to him, with a look on his face that said, "Do you want it?" Fowler shouted in his ear, "Let me talk first!" Everett looked at the young man and pointed at Fowler. The young man looked from one to the other of them, as if thinking it over, and then held the bullhorn to his mouth to address the crowd, which was still chanting "POWer to the PEOple" with lusty abandon.

"People!" he began, but then realizing that his voice blended in too much with the chanting, changed to, "Children! CHILDREN! Children, the administration wants to have a word. I don't know what they want to say . . ." He paused, grinning. "Go back to class!" came a voice from outside the circle. "That's probably right," he said, to a titter of appreciative laughter from the demonstrators. "But let's listen anyway . . . President Fowler?" He held out the bullhorn as Fowler ascended the steps. The crowd began to boo.

"Students!" The crowd booed and hissed, completely drowning him out. "Students, please!" The crowd grew louder, some now shouting things at him, unintelligible curses. Fowler looked pleadingly at the speaker who had handed him the bullhorn. The crowd, sensing victory, cheered. "Students! Students! STUDENTS!" The cheers gradually died down. "Students, please . . . Thank you. Let me just say that the administration is in complete . . ." he had to think of the proper word, "solidarity with you. We feel as strongly about this issue as you do. But you have to understand that our hands are tied . . ."

"BOOOOOO . . ."

"Students, please . . ."

" . . . OOOOOO!"

"PLEASE! Students! How can I express my sympathy if you don't even let . . ."

"BOOOOOO!" The students were in no mood to let him express anything. A few cries rose above the din.

"Fuck You!"

"Up Yours!"

"Go back to your fucking mansion!"

This one obviously surprised the little man. He looked stunned and fearful that the crowd might attack his house . . . It certainly wasn't beyond the realm of possibility . . . "Students, please! Thank you. Now, I've brought my close personal friend, Dean Everett Broadstreet, who has a few things to say. He's taken time out of his busy schedule to come and speak to you. No one has worked more tirelessly for your cause than he has, so please, give him your attention. Dean Broadstreet?"

The crowd cheered as Everett ascended. How different this sensation was! To be wanted! Loved! They love me! Fowler handed him the bullhorn and put his hand around Everett's neck, pulling him down. To the observers it appeared to be an embrace, but Fowler hissed furiously into Everett's ear, "Just say something noncommittal, and then get the little bastards to disperse." He stood back and smiled at the dean for the benefit of the crowd. Everett returned the smile, feeling a wave of scorn sweeping over him. He turned and faced the crowd.

Although he couldn't see much further than the back of the inner circle, hampered as he was by the fact that he had again forgotten to bring his glasses, he could see that toward the back of the crowd several policemen had arrived, their black uniforms sharp against the blurry, earth-toned background of students. In the front of the crowd the demonstrators quieted, beaming at him, waiting to hear him speak. He held the megaphone to his mouth and clicked the trigger.

"Uh . . . Hello."

Several people laughed in a friendly, encouraging way. "Hi Dean," someone said.

"Hi there," answered Everett. "I um, my. It's good to see you so enthusiastic. And it's nice to be on your side."

The demonstrators laughed and clapped. Without waiting for the noise to die down, he continued, "If I'd known that testifying made one so popular I would have had myself subpoenaed a long time ago." More cheers from the crowd. The news crew had pushed its way to the front row, and were pointing their equipment at him.

The cameraman turned on the light, which looked to Everett like a blue piece of the sun stuck about eight feet in front of his nose.

"Could you turn that off, please?" he said, holding his hand up to shield his eyes. The cameraman ignored him. "Please, I can't see." The cameraman acted as if he hadn't heard him. One of the demonstrators grabbed him, and said, "Turn off that damned light or we'll turn it off for you." The man, seeing that he was surrounded, hastily extinguished the lamp.

Everett glanced over at Fowler, who gave him the thumbs up sign. "We really don't need that, do we?" Everett asked the crowd. "Thank you. Now, honestly, I know that you all feel very strongly about what has been happening with the Shore case, but you have to understand that the University has no choice in the matter. You must understand that I personally know the damage that his presence is causing to people of good faith." Everett had the feeling that his sentences were beginning to get tangled up, but he ploughed on. The crowd adored him. "I know from my own experience what sort of a person he is, and I wish that we could do something to block his presence here. Unfortunately, though, things don't always go the way we would like. We have been ordered by the courts to reinstate him, but it is, and I have to stress this, it is a temporary thing. We feel strongly that the Universi . . ."

"You lying sack of shit!" came a voice from the outer circle. "You fucking bastard!"

Everett had to squint to see who was yelling, and when the boy's features resolved themselves, the dean realized that they belonged to David Shore, who was standing with a group of his friends. "You fucking bastard!" he cried again. "How could you do this to me? What the hell did I ever do to you, man?"

The words stung Everett. In all his plottings and calculations, in all his wavering over what to do, and in his bitter satisfaction at the way events were turning, he had forgotten the boy whose life might be irrevocably changed by his lie. Apprehension, banished for one blissful day, crept back into his heart. But almost as quickly came resolve not to be removed from his pleasant surroundings. The boy was not strictly innocent; Everett hadn't exactly lied— he had merely stretched the truth. And he hadn't been close enough to hear what actually happened in the classroom. Not really. Strength and righteousness pushed back the concern. "This isn't the time, David," he called over the heads of the crowd.

"When's it gonna be time, Dean?" shouted David. "When I'm long gone? After you've ruined my life? You can *get fucked* if you think I'm going to sit back and watch!"

The crowd, confused at first, began to realize what was happening. The young man who had been leading the rally when Everett arrived, suddenly pointed his finger. "That's him! That's David Shore!" As Everett watched, parts of the inner circle began to surge toward the object of their rage. The dean remembered his bullhorn. "No!" he shouted. "Please! This isn't the way!"

The crowd, however, was beyond control. Like a huge amoeba, it swelled and pushed outward as if trying to surround its prey and swallow it. Policemen moved in between the demonstrators and Shore's position. Other students, from the outside circle, began to move in as well. It looked like the beginning of a huge brawl. The policemen were holding their batons horizontally, trying to push back the demonstrators. Everett could hear voices shouting curses, not only at Shore, but at the officers as well. "Pigs! Pigs! Pigs!" The blond activist grabbed the bullhorn back from Everett and shouted into it: "No justice, no peace! No justice, no peace!" The demonstrators took up the chant, and soon all sound was drowned in the rhythmic roar:

"No justice, no peace! No justice, no peace! No justice, no peace!"

The camera crew, momentarily forgotten, started filming again, following the action as it lurched back from the fountain. Everett squinted his eyes and saw that the police officers were growing desperate. A few fights were starting around their perimeter. One of the policemen shouted hotly at Shore and his friends who were standing their ground, not wanting to show weakness. It was obvious that the policemen wanted them out of there for their own good. After a tense moment filled with sweating and scuffling and chanting, Shore's group seemed to agree. They began to edge backward and make their way to the rear of the circle. With the pressure to hold them back somewhat released, the demonstrators surged forward and diluted, the officers giving ground until the violence seemed controllable.

At the extreme limit of his vision, Everett could see David and his knot of friends exiting the Square around the Physics building. They passed within a few feet of Professor Stiggler, who sat alone on the steps with her arms about her knees. One of the boys shouted something at her but she shook her head and put her face in her hands. A few protesters followed, but the situation seemed largely defused. Much of the enthusiasm of the remaining demonstrators was spent. They dispersed slowly, clearing out of the Square in small groups, some laughing with delight, some cursing at their own impotence. The party was over.

Fowler sidled up to Everett, his small hand gripping the dean's triceps through the heavy material of his blazer. "Jesus Christ," said the little man. "I'm getting too old for this."

NINE

The town of Vail isn't quite visible from the top of the pass that leads into the valley, but after the race down the freeway, through the descending turns and over the bridges, it starts to sprawl along the banks of the Gore Creek, five or six miles of condominiums and massive vacation homes scattered into the forest like shot from a hunting party of giants. At the very center of the pattern, the bull's-eye, so to speak, the woods give way to the village itself, huddled below a mountain whose trees have been removed in great swathes, white in winter, zebra striped, following the million-dollar contours of the largest single ski-resort in Colorado, and one of the largest in the world. Vail was the brainchild of a veteran turned developer, who, after seeing the Alps, decided to build a Bavarian village in the heart of the Rockies. Given the unfortunate whim of geography that parked Vail solidly in the western United States, the result is an unusual amalgam of faux-European architecture and blue-corn-tortilla-chip restaurants. It is the sort of place where the mind doesn't reel at the sight of a tow-headed ski-bum in lederhosen dancing the Mexican Hat Dance for the tourists. The town hasn't exactly the glamour status of Aspen, whose Victorian houses are at least authentic, but it still draws great numbers of visitors eager to glide down runs several miles in length.

Parker and Mary drove into the valley at a little before five o'clock, or perhaps 'flew' would be the more appropriate verb, since Mary was at the wheel. This was her first chance in the driver's seat of the Porsche, and she tore down the interstate grinning with glee, her dark hair whipping about her face in the breeze. She would glance over at Parker from time to time, laughing at his obvious unease. "When was the last time you timed this thing?" she shouted over the rush of the wind as they shot into a curve a few miles from the East Vail exit. The engine popped as it decelerated.

"Oh . . ." Parker began, and then gripped the handle on the door as the wheels started to drift out of the turn, "Ohhhhhh. . . . !" The car snapped back into the fall line, and Parker exhaled. "It's been about six months, but if you'll pull over now I'll do it right here! I'm sure you don't want to drive it if . . . *Christ!*" The car began to skid into another turn, the tires scratching for a hold in the sand on the pavement.

"No! It's just right! Watch this! Watch my foot! Parker! Parker! Watch my foot!" As they came into the next curve, she slammed the car into a lower gear, her right foot rolling between the brake and the accelerator. The engine abruptly screamed and then fell as the car slowed, and then rapidly rose again as she stepped on the gas. The car jumped out of the turn. Parker watched the operation out of the corner of his eye, the force of the turn pulling him deeper into his seat. "Isn't that great!" she cried. "My brother taught me that! The trick in these rear-engine cars is to stay off the brake as much as you can."

"Thanks for the tip!" Parker shouted back, and he smiled, because her skill impressed him. She was impressing him a lot today. After the harrowing scene at his dealer's they had gone home and made giggly love in his kitchen because they couldn't wait long enough to get upstairs. She stirred within him again that strange combination of emotions where he felt half-man and half-child. It wasn't that she made him forget the troubles he was having at work, which had driven him to despair the day before. It was more that she made him feel that his troubles weren't so important—the crushing weight of simple adult existence melted in her arms, and he felt more alive than he could remember.

As they drove along he considered all of this, and his mind was drawn back repeatedly to their talk in the car after Tab had pulled the gun on her. This, too, had impressed him, more than she knew. Somehow she had walked the razor's edge between being judgmental (which would have completely turned him off) and being supportive (which would have turned her into another of his casual conquests, meaning that she would be casually discarded.) Her reaction couldn't have been better if she had been given a roadmap of his desires. He found himself wondering if she might be the *one*. He stretched his hand over and enclosed hers on the gear-shift. She smiled.

The road straightened out as it came onto the floor of the valley. The sunlight hit them in the face and reflected off the windows of the houses and the glittery ribbon of the river. "OK, slow down up here. We have to get off at the next exit."

She eased back on the throttle, slowing the car with the engine, working down through the gears as she got onto the off ramp. "Which way?" she asked in the sudden quiet and warmth.

"Left and go under the highway, and then left again at the stop sign, and then park in the big garage."

"This one?" she asked a moment later. She found a spot to pull the car into and they stepped out. Mary stretched and came slowly around and hugged him.

"Mmmmmm. That was fun, thanks. C'mon. Where do we meet Clay?"

They walked out of the structure arm in arm, still spent from making love before they left home and a little jittery from the drive. Parker stopped and pulled her tighter to him and kissed her again, wanting to tell her that he was falling in love with her, and yet not wanting to for fear that the feeling would go away if he did. She looked into his eyes, understanding. "I know," she whispered. "Come on. We're really late."

Parker led her through the covered bridge that crossed the Gore in town, and to a little doorway set into a wall of stucco-faced shops. It was very dark inside, and crowded. About half of the people were still wearing the tight-fitting, brightly colored clothing which the season's aimless breeze of fashion had blown onto the pages of ski magazines, deeming them crucial for enjoyment on the slopes. The others, dressed in heavy sweaters and Levis, blended into the noisy, smoky darkness. Parker and Mary stood in the doorway for a second, waiting for their eyes to adjust.

"There he is!" came a voice cutting over the others in the darkness. It had a familiar ring, and Parker thought he recognized it. He squinted toward the end of the bar. "Yo! Parker! We're down here!" A hand raised, and Parker could see that it was attached to Luke Guilford, a fraternity brother whom he hadn't seen in years. He was pressed up against the bar at the far side of the room, wedged against the wall with two women and Clay. Pidge waved, and tried to smile, but his expression was ambivalent and Parker instantly discerned that there was a lot behind it. Pidge and Luke were both friends of his from college, and were both fraternity brothers, but they had never been particularly friendly with each other. Their relationship would have been better described as unfocused enmity, and the source of this emnity lay in the things that made each of them who they were. Strangely, they were also the reasons why Parker liked each of them, although in very different ways; Clay for his kindness and for his honesty, Luke for his almost complete lack of both. It was clear to Parker that the two of them had probably run into each other within the last hour, here in this room, and although they would never have sought each other's company, they were too well acquainted to simply say hello and then ignore one another. Seeing the two of them together caused a subtle change in Parker, a letdown after the easy pleasure he had felt while being alone with Mary. Confronted with the task of interacting with the two of them simultaneously, he rather felt that he had to choose sides, and the feeling seemed to him sophomoric, as it had felt to him in college. Only now, at twenty-nine, and perhaps as much of an adult as he was ever likely to be, it seemed absurd to be forced into considering such ancient nonsense.

As usual, Luke's face betrayed nothing but friendly and casual ennui. He regarded Parker with such an even and unforced expression that his feelings regarding Clay were completely masked; when he chose to act on those feelings, whatever they might be, he would do so. Until that time they were as unimportant to him as whatever it was that made the sky blue or made the grass grow.

Pidge, however, had not had Luke's sort of up-bringing, neither its benefit nor its curse, depending on how one looked at it. And his great character flaw, his one tragic weakness, was that he had always wished he had. In college he had always felt the need for validation from the Luke Guilfords, from the mysterious universe of understatement, of power, of notoriety, of money, of all the things he imagined so important while growing up in Iowa. The fact that he so obviously wanted it had made it impossible to attain, and the thinly veiled desperation on Pidge's face, made so painfully apparent by its absence in Luke's, told Parker at once that he hadn't grown past that desire, had not made peace with himself about it, had not gained the strength one associates with adulthood. There was even a hint of appeal in his eyes, which Parker found frankly distasteful.

In the two seconds that it took for Parker to sum up all of this, he realized that he didn't want to deal with any of it. He had always been friends with Luke, and he wasn't going to snub him just to protect an aging boy who needed to grow up. If Pidge couldn't take care of himself, that was too damned bad. Parker waved, put his arm around Mary, and threaded his way through the crowd.

"Luke!" he cried. "It's been ages!" Without rising from his bar-stool, Luke extended his hand and Parker grasped it, holding it tightly for a second or two. Luke's long features creased into a grin. His hair was a little longer than Parker remembered, and his clothes were a little more refined than they had been in school, but he was otherwise unchanged. "I can't believe you're here," said Parker. "Where are you living now?"

Guilford's smile oozed into a smirk. "Manhattan," he answered, with a shake of his head that begged Parker not to rub it in. Luke had always sworn that he wouldn't go back to the city when he graduated.

"Get out!" said Parker, grinning.

Luke held his fists in front of him. "Every time I try to get out, they keep pulling me back in. Who are *you*?" he asked, meaning Mary.

Parker made the introductions. "Howja do?" said Luke, mocking his own accent and touching his forelock as if he had a cap to tip. "You look like a nice girl," he said. "How did you get mixed up with Parker?"

"Clay introduced us," said Mary.

"You know Pidge?" asked Luke, obviously surprised.

"Forever."

"I didn't know you knew any women, Pidge," said Luke casually. His natural sarcasm made the remark light, and Mary giggled, but Parker winced inwardly. Luke was the sort of person who, depending on mood, might keep pressing at such a theme until it ceased to be amusing. Parker moved to change the subject.

"And who are these ladies?" he asked, looking at the other women.

"This one's Jessie," said Luke, indicating the brunette standing beside his bar stool. She appeared to be in her early twenties, but something in her face, a shadow of intensity, made her seem both older and younger at the same time. Her hair was perfectly cut, her chin and cheekbones sharp. She was astonishingly beautiful. "Jess, this is Parker. He's a bud of mine from school."

She didn't say anything, and looked up at Parker from beneath her eyelids, as if she were searching for something. After a second or two one corner of her mouth twitched upward and she extended her hand, the nails of which were immaculately manicured. Parker felt an odd, tingling thrill at touching her, and as quickly as the sensation came, he felt guilty for it. Mary was, after all, standing right in front of him. He hoped she hadn't noticed what had just happened, and withdrew his hand hastily. One of Jessie's perfect eyebrows arched just enough that he noticed.

"This is Denise," said Clay, putting his arm around the thirtyish blond standing beside him. She was attractive enough, in an ordinary sort of way, but she would never be in the same league with Jessica.

Denise smiled and leaned against Clay, and Parker could see that Pidge felt proud he had been able to get her all by himself. He could also see that he was gathering the things he could lay claim to, Mary and Denise, around him like a shield. The three of them started talking together, and Parker settled against the bar close to

Luke. Jessica stood between them, facing Luke, so Parker couldn't see her face.

"So I hear you're a liar, er lawyer now," said Luke.

Parker grinned sheepishly.

"I really can't say that I'm surprised. With all the dope dealers you used to know, I'll bet you're billing hundreds of hours to Bogota, hmmm? Golden boy of the firm?"

"Wait for it," said Parker. "I started out with the D.A.'s office in Denver."

"You?" Luke had been one of his principle drug suppliers in school. "You?" he asked again. "Christ, you're not still there, are you?"

Parker shook his head. "Nah, I'm with a private firm now. Made partner a few months ago," he added with pride.

"Heh-heeeeyyy! Super!" He shook hands with Parker. "Where are my manners? Let me get you a drink. Jess, would you get us a couple?"

Jessica looked to the bartender, who was about ten feet away, and cleared her throat. It was a quiet, almost inaudible sound, but it cut across the noise of the bar like a note from a harp. The man instantly looked up from the well over which he was working. Jessica held up four fingers.

"Long Islands?" the bartender asked, ignoring the seething crowd in front of him.

Jessica nodded. The bartender smiled.

"Isn't she something?" asked Luke.

"Remarkable. Where did you find her?"

"Friend of a friend. Wait, you know her. Do you remember that one girl who had the poster of her father tacked to the ceiling over her bed?"

Parker remembered her well, but said, "I didn't really know her, but yeah."

"Jess is a friend of hers, from Foxcroft. We met at a party down in Soho. She just moved out here. So how do you like being a lawyer?" Luke asked.

"Some days better than others. Most days better than this one."

"What's up?"

"Nothing. Let's talk about something else. What are you doing now?"

Luke tilted the glass from his last drink into his mouth and sucked in an ice cube. "Trading," he answered thickly, wrapping his tongue around the ice and pushing it into his cheek. "Penny stock stuff. Herman's very pleased." Herman was Luke's father, a vast, shadowy, forbidding character who had always figured prominently in Luke's stories of home, owing in great part to Luke's mortal fear of him.

"Herman," said Parker, and chuckled. "God, I haven't heard that name in a while. How is old Herman?"

"Im*mense*. He's gained about eighty pounds, and he's still about five feet taller than I am. I think he'll keep getting bigger as I get older, like Santa."

"Was he the one set you up bilking people out of their life savings?"

Luke snorted and almost choked on the ice cube. "So you've heard about me," he said. "No, that was my idea. I don't see Herman much any more. He spends most of his time looming around the house up in Westchester." He paused and lit a cigarette, exhaling the smoke in a fluffy cloud. "Every once in a while he blows through the city on his way out to the Hamptons. I can always tell because it gets dark outside in the middle of the day. Ah. Booze."

The bartender set four enormous tumblers in front of them and squeezed a wedge of lemon into each. "Put 'em on your tab?" he asked.

"Yup," said Luke. He picked one of the glasses up and held it out to Mary, who was still talking with Clay and Denise. "Hey . . . Mary?"

"Mmmmm, thanks," she said. "What is it?"

"Long Island iced tea."

"What's in it?" asked Mary, taking the glass and looking through it.

"You've never had one before?" asked Luke. "You're in for a treat. All natural ingredients. Even has Vitamin C. Good and good for you." He raised his glass and touched it to hers. "Lachaim."

She took a sip. And coughed. "God. What's in this thing?"

"To tell you the truth, I can't say that I know the recipe. Parker?"

"No clue. Gin, I think. You know, Pidge?"

Pidge was smooshed between the end of the bar and the wall. He looked surprised to be asked. "Gin, vodka, rum . . . sweet and sour, I think, and uh, coke. Just a splash."

"That's it, Pigeon," said Luke. "Get behind the bar. This is your big chance. I always knew you had to have *some* sort of hidden talent."

Clay looked a little embarrassed, but covered it with an uncomfortable chuckle. Denise put her arm around him again. "How come everybody calls you 'Pigeon?'" she asked.

Luke turned back to Parker, who was pulling sharply at his drink. "Where are you staying?"

"Some house here in town. Speaking of which," he began, but then shook his head as the liquor hit the mark. "Sweet Jesus that's strong. Hey Pidge, where's the house at?"

Clay pushed his way past Mary and Denise. He put his elbows on the bar next to Luke, who ignored him. "It's real close to here. About two blocks. I'll draw you a map." He scribbled on a cocktail napkin and explained the directions to Parker.

"You going out tonight?" Luke asked.

"I don't know. I'm pretty whacked."

"Big night last night?"

"Hardly. I drank about a half a bottle of Scotch though."

"What, alone?"

"Just me, Justerini and Brooks."

"I can't say I like the sound of that," said Luke. "If you're feeling low, I've got plenty of nick. I can cut you an eighth."

"No need," said Parker, not telling him that he had his own supplies.

"Super. So . . . What's our plan for tonight? Drink a little?"

"Oh, what the hell."

Luke grinned. "It's so good to see you, man. Just like old times. Let's get a couple more of these poisonous drinks."

They had the couple, and a couple more, and after about two hours Parker was getting fairly blasted. At first, he was a little concerned that things might get ugly between Clay and Luke, but Luke barely said a word to Clay, clearly content to stay huddled in drunken companionship with his old friend. For Parker, it was an enormous release. Clay was his best friend, true, but Clay was always somewhat judgmental, and judgment was something in which Parker was profoundly uninterested at the moment. He noticed that Clay kept looking over at him, but as Parker grew steadily buzzed he found himself not caring. Mary came over once or twice, but Parker tried to keep her at a distance. She wasn't really drinking, which made him a little uncomfortable, but she seemed to understand that he wanted to talk with Luke, and she was talking quite a bit with Jessica, anyway. As Parker watched them, he briefly fantasized about the two of them.

Luke had just ordered another round when he asked, "So why were you drinking alone last night? What's the problem?"

Parker explained the situation, and Luke nodded in commiseration. "What's the guy's name?"

"Shore. Arthur Shore."

Luke clucked. "Don't tell me. About six-two? Silver hair? Really fair skin?"

"Yeah. How did you know?"

"I *know* that bastard. He's one of Herman's lawyers."

"No way!"

"No. I've met him. He's been to dinner at the house. He works for . . . wait a sec. I'll think of it . . . Beauchamp Tyler. He works for Beauchamp Tyler. Boy, he's a cold bastard, too. I'm glad I'm not in your shoes." He shook his head sadly, but then he started to smile. "So the kid called his Women's Studies teacher a dyke, huh?"

Parker started to laugh, in spite of himself. "He sure did. Can you believe it?"

Luke's laugh soared. "Oh, man. Ohhh, *man*. How classic is *that*? Kid's got balls, I'll say that for him."

Mary came over again a few minutes later. She whispered in Parker's ear, "Honey, can we go home? I'm really tired."

Parker was disappointed, but he was also getting very drunk, and he knew that she was right. It was time to go. He stood up. "Luke, it's been real."

"You're not leaving?"

"I am. You gonna be 'round tomorrow? You wanna ski?"

"I'm too old for that sort of thing." He considered for a moment. "Well, maybe. If I see you I'll see you. If not, meet us at the bar at the bottom of International afterwards. Around four."

Parker turned to tell Clay he and Mary were leaving, but he was gone. "Where's Pidge?"

"He and Denise went to dinner," said Mary.

"We'll see him later. Night, Luke. Nice to meet you, Jessica." Jessica smiled.

*   *   *

Parker awoke early the next morning, pleased to find that he was not at all hung over. He slipped out of bed, trying not to wake Mary, and went into the kitchen where he found Clay watching television. Clay glanced up at him without smiling.

"What's the matter with you?" asked Parker.

"Why did you take Mary to your dealer's house?"

"Oh. She told you about that, huh?"

"She told me she almost got her head blown off."

"Yeah. That was pretty ugly. She handled it well, though." Parker rummaged through one of the grocery bags and took out a box of cereal. He poured it into a bowl and poured some milk onto it, making it crackle. Pidge was still staring at him. "Look, will you lay off, Pidge?"

"I can't believe you were that stupid. Why did you bring her there of all places? She doesn't know anything about that stuff. I mean, what were you thinking?"

"It wasn't my idea. She just showed up at the house when I was on my way out the door. I figured she'd just wait in the car, but Tab was doing a deal and it got kind of long. She knocked on the door and Tab went bananas, that's all. She's OK." He grinned. "To tell you the truth, she surprised the hell out of me. I reckoned she'd flip out. I sure would have. She was really cool, though. It was the last thing I expected."

Pidge shook his head.

Parker tried to be conciliatory. "Look, I don't want to see her hurt any more than you do. I think I'm . . . I might be falling in love with her," he said, and instantly regretted it since saying it made him feel both goofy and exposed.

"Well, just be careful with her, you know? Try to keep her in one piece."

"Deal." He crunched his cornflakes for a moment or two. "So what time did you get home, young man?"

Pidge grinned. "About a half an hour ago, thank you very little. I just met Denise yesterday at the bar. She works about two blocks from my office. What do you think of her?" Pidge always needed validation.

"I think she's cute. I think she's just fine. I didn't talk to her much though."

"You didn't talk to her at all, Parker. You and Luke were too busy walking down memory lane. She'll be around this afternoon, though. I told her to meet us at the bottom of the hill at five."

"Luke wants to meet there, too."

"Oh." Clay's disappointment was evident.

"I wish you guys got along better," said Parker.

"I like him, I guess. I just don't think he likes me much."

Parker shrugged his shoulders. "You shouldn't care. He doesn't care about anything."

After Mary got up, the three of them headed for the slopes. It was already noon, and the air felt to be around sixty degrees. The sky overhead was almost black with blueness. The snow, melting into puddles of brilliance, had the consistency of an enormous white Slurpee. As Parker tossed his skis onto the ground they made a splash.

"Man, is the whole mountain like this?" he asked as he kicked into his bindings.

"Denise says it's not so bad higher up," said Pidge. "Let's go right to Mid-Vail, and then straight to the top, all right?"

"Yeah, what do you want to ski, like Riva's or the backside?"

"I think we oughta stay on this side. I reckon the bowls are probably really wet with all the sun on them. What do you think, Mary?"

"It's up to you, Parker," she said. He pushed his skis back from underneath him, stretching the backs of his legs and looking down at the snow.

"Let's go," said Parker.

When they got off the second lift, the world stretched out far below them in all directions. They set off to the East, hopped off a shallow cornice, and dropped into the first run. He was surprised to see that Mary went off of it as well, instead of taking the easier way around. The snow was much better here than it had been at the bottom of the mountain, heavy but manageable, and Parker relaxed, concentrating on his skis, weighting them and unweighting them in turn, taking pleasure as the edges carved quiet semicircles in the snow. He went for about five minutes without stopping, and then pulled up at a catwalk to catch his breath. He looked around and saw that he was alone. He didn't know if the others were in front of him or behind him, or even if they were on the same run. The slope fell sharply before him, and in the distance below he could see the lift that went up to the right. He waited for a few minutes, and when no one came, he pushed out over the edge, feeling the ground drop away beneath him, his speed accelerating until he checked it with a few quick turns. The icy wind swirling under his sunglasses caused his vision to cloud on the sides, until finally he could see nothing but the spot where he was looking, shooting through the blue shadows into the floor of the small valley toward the lift he had seen from above. He pulled up in a graceful arc and rubbed his eyes until his vision cleared. There were very few people around, a few other skiers meandering down the slope in the glaring light, sliding by him to get onto the lift. Parker stood and waited until it became clear that he had become separated from Mary and Clay. Then he got onto the lift, knowing that if he took it back up, it would put him above Riva's Ridge, the run he had mentioned at the bottom of the hill. If he were to find his friends, that was where they would be.

He skied alone for more than an hour, taking several runs down the same steep face. The snow here had been carved by countless skiers until huge moguls had formed, really big ones, soft and heavy today in the sunshine. They required from Parker intense concentration to keep from falling. His being became an odd unity of relaxation and vigilance as he lost himself and his troubles in the attempt at perfection, until work and conflict were far from his mind. At one point he stopped and lay in the snow and stared up into the dark featureless blue of the sky, relishing the solitude, and for a few, fleeting seconds he understood to the very depths of whatever soul he had that all of his troubles would turn out all right in the end. It was the same feeling that Mary gave him when they were alone together. Part of him wished that she were there with him, but at the same time he wasn't concerned; in a way she was with him all of the time. The feeling was comforting. He thought about the night before, and realized that he should have been better to Pidge, who was uncertain and needed his help. It was almost a pity, he thought, that they were going to meet Luke later. Parker felt more like being with his closer friends now.

A voice called across the silence, and he turned to face up the slope behind him. "Yo! Parker!" It was Luke, about fifty yards above him. Parker sighed to himself, but he raised his hand, and Luke pushed off toward him, his body casually lifting and falling through the bumps until he came to a stop next to Parker.

"Hey Luke," said Parker, getting to his feet. "You made it."

"How are you skiing?"

"Good. Real good. Have you seen Pidge?"

Luke shrugged and adjusted his shades. "Yeah, I saw him a while ago. I got away before he saw me. Hey, don't look at me that way. I know he's a friend of yours but spending time with that guy is like watching paint dry." He took a small canister that looked like a nasal sprayer from his pocket, put it to one of his nostrils and snorted sharply. He handed the canister to Parker. "Here. This'll put some lead in your pencil."

Parker hesitated for a second, not really wanting it, but not wanting to seem prudish, either. The clarity he had felt while he was alone was quickly fading, and as peace fled from the corners of his mind, mundane existence crept back into them. He took the canister and blasted it into his nose. The cocaine was extremely clean, and his heart raced. "Yow," he said. "Thanks. We really oughta find Pidge."

"I suppose, if you really want to."

"Why do you hate him so much?"

"Why? Why do you think? Because he's a loser. He always was a loser, and age hasn't improved him."

"He's not that bad."

"Yes he is." Luke pointed his skis through the fall line and sped off down the hill. Parker raced down after him.

They waited at the bottom of the run for fifteen minutes or so, and when Mary and Pidge didn't come, the two of them attacked Riva's again. They spent the rest of the afternoon there, skiing the bumps until the sun went behind the ridge and the snow began to crust over with ice.

"You 'bout ready to call it?" asked Luke. The tails of his skis had just slid out from under him, causing him to fall in a fairly spectacular fashion, and he was slow getting back to his feet. "I don't know how much more of this fun I can take."

"I'll race you to the bottom."

"Last one down buys the first round."

"Done."

Parker had a decent lead at the start, and tucked down the first catwalk to the next run, where he pulled up sharply and popped over the lip to the right. As the ground fell away he turned and saw Luke behind him about thirty feet. Luke took the turn more gradually, but kept more of his skis on the snow and preserved more of his speed. Halfway down the run they were almost even, both going very fast, but toward the bottom, where several runs intersected, the Ski Patrol had erected barriers to slow people down. There was quite a little traffic jam, with so many skiers trying to get through the barrier at the same time. Parker chose his line carefully, around a cluster of kids who were moving unpredictably toward the opening in the barrier. If he timed it right, he would be able to cut off Luke, skirt the other skiers, get through the opening, and force Luke to have to wait.

It worked perfectly. Parker shot through the opening and into the clearing beyond, and looked back in time to see Luke raise his fist in frustration. Parker shouted back at him with glee, without checking his speed. But as he turned to face downward again, disaster struck. Looming not twenty feet in front of him, a paltry distance considering Parker's velocity, a man was lazily drifting into Parker's fall line. There was absolutely nothing he could do to avoid a collision. The last things he remembered before slamming into him were, a: I wonder if he's going to sue me (the legal corridors of Parker's brain never fully at rest), and, b: I wonder if it's going to hurt.

Wham!

The two of them tumbled over each other a few times, and then came to a stop by the side of the run. The other man, cursing, struggled to remove his hat, which had somehow come down over his face. As he did so, and a pair of eyes glared at Parker, Parker relaxed.

"Hi, Pidge," he said.

Pidge groaned and leaned back into the snow. "You jerk."

A twinge of annoyance swept through Parker at seeing Pidge prostrate in the snow, at his having gotten in his way and snatching victory from him, at his not being friends with Luke and not handling himself well. He had to force the smile. "Sorry, pal. Did you break anything?"

"I don't think so. By some miracle."

Luke came by at this moment and cut a sharp turn above them, blanketing the two of them with a shower of snow. He laughed. "Looks like you're buying," he said as he looked down at them. "Thanks, Pigeon. I can always count on you to be in the wrong place at the right time."

* * *

By midnight that evening things were getting very, very bad. They were clustered, a largish group by now, maybe ten people or so, Parker, his friends, his girl friend, and assorted random revelers they had picked up along the way, squeezed around a table in some bar called The Hole, which was the fourth or fifth tavern of the night, and at about this time Parker was beginning to feel disgusted by most everything. The pleasure he had felt yesterday at meeting Luke had completely disappeared, and been replaced by fatigue. He was tired of trying to balance his feelings between Luke and Clay, tired of having to act as if he were enjoying himself, tired of worrying about his career, and due to the lateness of the hour, just plain tired.

He wanted to take Mary and leave, but Mary was chatting with Jessica and asked if they could stay a little longer. She seemed to be enjoying herself, which Parker resented. It didn't seem right to him that she should be having a good time when he wasn't. She was also drinking quite a bit, which both surprised and disturbed Parker. He didn't want her to act like the rest of his friends—he wanted her to be special, to be tuned in solely to his needs.

He wasn't even bothering to try to follow the conversation any more, which wasn't difficult to tune out since the bar was belting out seventies disco hits at an ear-splitting volume. Parker stared bleakly out across the frantic crowd on the dance floor and wished he were somewhere else.

Parker felt a hand on his shoulder, and a voice shouted into his ear. "Hey, waiter, get me a drink, will you?"

Standing behind him in the darkness was his young client, David Shore. The boy's face looked wrong, broken. One of his cheekbones was bruised and swollen.

"Christ," Parker shouted back. "What happened to you?"

"I have to talk to you. I tried to call but you weren't at home. Your office couldn't tell me where you were."

"Sorry, I didn't expect to hear from you. How did you get that shiner?"

"Could we go somewhere and talk? You know. Away from . . ." He nodded his head in the direction of Parker's friends.

"Sure," Parker answered, and then said to the table, "Listen, I'll be back in a little while."

Pidge lifted his chin. "What's up?"

"This is a client of mine," Parker answered. "I have to talk to him."

"Is he the . . ."

Parker nodded.

"We'll be here."

Outside in the dark, David said, "Let's get a cup of coffee." They went next door to a little restaurant and ordered. "Well," said David, "I've had an interesting couple of days. You're looking at public enemy number one. Some of the nonviolence crowd had a little rally yesterday to honor yours truly. What a nightmare."

"Is that where you got that?"

"Yeah. It happened afterwards. Broadstreet was up at the Square bullshitting the students about me, and I lost my temper. I started shouting at him. I feel pretty stupid about it now, but you know how it is. The notes from your meeting with him were in the campus paper, and I was pretty pissed off after I read them. You gotta know that he was lying. You know that, don't you?"

Parker looked at him for a moment, and then broke one of his cardinal rules about never asking a client directly if he is telling the truth. "Do I?"

Shore closed his eyes and shook his head. "Shit. Of course he's lying. The room was filled with students. Everybody saw it. I can't understand why he's doing this to me."

"Well I'll tell you something, David. We'd damn well better figure it out. Because when I deposed him the other day, he was pretty convincing."

"You don't believe me, then."

"Look, it's not that I don't believe you, but you've got to level with me. Is there anything you're leaving out?"

"No! That bitch lit into me. I mean, maybe I could have held my temper, but, no I'm not leaving anything out."

"Why do you think he's lying?"

"How the fuck should I know!" He said heatedly, and for a moment looked much like his father. Then his features relaxed. "I don't know, man. But he is. I mean, I read his statement in the paper. I couldn't believe it. And then, seeing him up in front of that crowd, I lost it. That's when all the fun started. The cops were there. It was like a riot scene. My friends and I split, but a bunch of the demonstrators followed us off the campus and started shoving us. It was real bad. That was one of the things I wanted to talk to you about. Those guys were crazy. There was even a chick with 'em. I think they might try to go after you."

Parker had to suppress a chuckle at the boy's earnest expression. "David, I live in Denver. I don't think they're going to come all that way just to rough me up. Do you want to press charges on them?"

David shrugged his shoulders. "What's the point? It was a brawl. Besides, I don't get scared easy, but these people are weird. I'm just gonna forget about it, and try and keep a low profile. Not that that's gonna be easy, now that I was on the tube and everything."

"What!"

"The news last night. Didn't you see?"

"Oh, God. No, I missed it. What'd they say?"

"It was just a little blurb about the demonstration and how the police had been called in and everything. They had pictures."

"Did they mention your name?"

"Yeah, but just in passing."

"Fuck," Parker hissed. "Did they interview you? You didn't talk to them, did you?"

"No. I don't think they could have found me anyway. I came up here right after it was over. Saw the story though, and I talked to dad about it. He's really pissed. That's the other thing I wanted to talk to you about. You know how he feels about the media and stuff. He just about blew a gasket when I told him, and said that he was going to have a talk with you. I wanted to let you know beforehand, you know?"

Great, thought Parker. Another session with King Sonofabitch. And then, a sort of sinking feeling of panic flowed into him; he was still at a point where he didn't know how he was going to win the case, and no great ideas had occurred to him. This was disastrous news.

His face must have betrayed his anxiety, because David continued, "He's not that bad. I've never seen him . . . no, take that back, I have seen him destroy people, but he's not out to get you. You just have to let him scream for a while. He'll get over it."

Parker almost sighed. "Yeah, I'll talk to him Monday."

There was silence for a moment, and Parker sipped at his coffee. He was finding it hard to concentrate. Finally, David stood up. "Look, I'll talk to you later, huh?" He tossed some money on the table and started to leave.

"David, don't worry about it. We'll figure it out."

"Better," said David.

Ten minutes after his departure, what was left of Parker's shaken confidence had completely collapsed. He tried to turn the problem over in his head, but he only came up with the question, echoing gloomily through the usually crowded corridors of his cerebral cortex: What am I going to do? What am I going to do? He kept testing the well, but it came up dry. First Amendment? Don't think so—not without a witness, forget it. What student would want to go against the dean? Or against the teacher of a class they were in? And who'd be credible? Some other students? Who? Subpoena the whole class? What the hell for? The kid's probably lying to me anyway. Due process argument, shot. What am I going to do? Lack of counsel, maybe, weak though, especially without a credible fear of bias among board members. And Diamonte's voice—'getting some scumball reinstated at whatever cost . . . ' Shot. Collapse. What am I going to do? Shore's going to ruin me. He's going to do it. What am I going to do? What am I going to do?

The answer started quietly and grew louder: You're doomed.

When he looked back up at the clock on the wall, he realized he had been sitting there for forty-five minutes. He dragged himself out of the booth and back to the bar. The noise hit him like a wall. The sea of people and the crazy lights and all of the noise. He felt disoriented. He walked the long way around where Shore's friends had been, keeping an eye out for them because he didn't want to see them, but they were gone now and he made his way toward his table.

"Hey Parker!" shouted Luke. "I thought you'd gotten lost. Who was that kid?"

"Client."

"Is he the 'dyke' kid? What a stud!"

Parker simply shook his head and sat down. He stared at the table.

"Lighten up! It can't be that bad."

Only my whole life, thought Parker.

"Is there something wrong with Parker?" Mary smiled at him crookedly. "What's wrong, honey?" she said. She slipped trying to stand up and knocked over several of the drinks on the table, one of which fell into Parker's lap. She didn't seem to notice. He thrust her away.

"Just sit down, will you?" he said with contempt. He suddenly understood just how acutely he despised weakness. "Just . . . I don't know, have another drink or something." He got up and headed for the bathroom. Inside, it was quieter, and bright. He took a handful of paper towels from the rack and began to wipe off his pants. From one the stalls he heard a loud sniff, a groan, and then laughter. A man and two women came out. When they saw him they grinned. One of them inhaled deeply and said, "It's for my sinuses." They all laughed again and went out. Parker looked at himself in the mirror, and decided he could see nothing in his reflection that he liked. He wanted to dissolve again, just like he had the other day in Diamonte's office. He felt for his wallet and extracted the eightball lying in its folds. As he headed for the stall, the door opened again, and Jessica walked in.

"Thought I'd find you here," she said. He realized that it was the first time she had spoken to him directly. Her voice was soft and beguiling. "You OK?"

Parker palmed the seal. "Yeah. Fine. Just a little wet, that's all."

"Mary's a little buzzed."

"Don't remind me."

"Just so I know you're OK." She looked at him expectantly for a second, making no move to leave, and Parker knew she knew what he was doing.

"Yeah," said Parker. "I'm OK. Listen, do you uh, do you want any of this?" He opened his palm for her.

"You read my mind." She followed him into the last stall and closed the door. The space was so confined that they were almost touching as he handed her the seal. "Help yourself."

"Ooooo. Nice and rocky. I like that." She laid a little on the tank of the toilet and handed him back the seal. She reached into her little purse and pulled out a credit card and a bill which she used to powder the cocaine. Then, rolling the bill into a tube she bent over the toilet and inhaled, once on each side. Then she stood up and breathed deeply. "Thanks." She handed him the bill. "You know, you look like you've got more on your mind than a tipsy girlfriend. Your friend says you've got big problems."

After snorting the rest of the powder, he stood up and faced her. "You might say." He didn't feel like elaborating.

She looked thoughtfully at him for a moment before lowering her voice and saying, "I've got something that'll help with problems better than this stuff. Coke makes you too tense."

"What did you have in mind?" he asked, but even as he said the words he knew what was coming. He could see it in her eyes.

"Got a little something back at my place. You know what I mean?"

"I think so."

"Do you want to?" she whispered.

"How do you fix him?"

"I chase him. You want to chase him with me?"

Parker exhaled and leaned against the wall of the stall. His teeth were beginning to grind. The cocaine was pounding through his system, and what she was suggesting gave him an almost sexual excitement. "Oh,

God," he murmured. "Like you can't know. But how's it going to look. I mean, I can't just go off with you and leave her."

"Mary's OK. She'll understand."

Parker laughed dully, a short, flat sound. "Are you kidding?" he said. "Mary? I'm a pretty bad influence on her, but she's not ready for *that*."

"I've been talking to her. You might be surprised at how much she understands. Or might. But anyway, your friend, what's his name, Clay, he'll look after her." Her voice took on a glacial edge. "Hey, I don't do this with everybody."

Parker made his decision. The temptation was too great. "OK, let's do it."

Her face relaxed into a smile, sliding over her features in expectation. "Cool. Let's go."

The sudden darkness of the club after the brightness of the men's room was like a tangible substance, an inky quantity with faces floating in and out of its surface. Jessica disappeared into it and Parker followed her back towards the table. She took his arm and stopped him. "Do you want me to say your goodbyes for you?"

Parker weighed this for a moment. He knew it would look bad, but the urge to run was strong in him. "How?"

"I'll just tell them you're upset or something. Don't worry. I can do this."

"OK. I'll see you outside."

He pulled his coat around him under a streetlight by the door and waited. Pidge came out a moment or so later.

"Oh, there you are. What's up? The chick said you were going to bail."

"Yeah, I just can't handle this scene right now."

"What about Mary?"

"I don't think she'd notice if I left. Not in her condition."

He smiled. "I know. She's a little looped. You better take her home."

"I can't, Pidge."

"Why not?"

Jessica emerged from the bar, and Parker glanced at her. Pidge's face twisted with disgust and amazement. "You . . . you *fucker*. You're going to leave with another girl?"

"It's not like that, man. We're not going to do that."

"Well why . . ." A new comprehension dawned on his face. "You're going to go *fix?*"

Parker couldn't bring himself to say anything. He stared at the ground.

"Let me get this straight. You're going to leave that girl in there, that really nice girl, who's had too much to drink, probably because she wants to keep up with you, by the way, you're going to leave her so you can go off with this whore and fucking shoot up?" Parker could see the anger building in him.

"Hey, why don't you watch your mouth."

"I'm real sorry if I offended you," he said sarcastically to Jess.

"Keep your voice down, you idiot. You don't know what you're talking about. You think I should bring her along to see this?"

"I don't think you should be doing this at all! I think you oughta go in there and take care of somebody who needs you."

Parker's frustration was beginning to get the better of him. "Look, what do you want from me? This is the way I am. If you didn't want her to meet me, you shouldn't have introduced me to her. You were the one who pushed us to get together."

"Yeah, because I thought she might be good for you. I thought she might inject a little decency into your pathetic life."

"What a crock of shit. You wanted me to go out with her because you can't have her and you still want to be close. 'Take care of her Parker,'" he mocked. "'Leave her in one piece, Parker.' Why don't you just admit that you don't think you're good enough for her. It'd be the truth, wouldn't it? You don't have the confidence she needs, and you don't have the nerve. You know deep down that she'd never be happy raising a family of loser choirboys like you."

The punch came so quickly that Parker didn't have time to duck. It caught him squarely on the jaw, he saw a light, and then realized he was on the ground. When he opened his eyes, the best friend he had in the world was already inside, and Jess was kneeling over him.

"Your buddy has a good right," she said. "You want to go talk to him?"

Parker got to his feet and dusted himself off. "What the hell for?"

*   *   *

"So what'd you tell her?" Parker asked.

"Tell who?" Jessica answered absently. She was bending over the coffee table while she inserted a little spoon into the creamy colored pile.

"Mary."

"You worry about her too much. She'll be fine. I don't . . ." She lifted the little spoonful onto a piece of aluminum foil. "There. I don't think you have anything to worry about with her. I told her I'd see her next week."

"Was she upset at all?"

"No. Not really. Maybe a little. She just wants you to like her. So like her. Here."

She handed him the foil and a delicate glass tube. Parker took it, a little reluctantly now. He held it above the candle, bending over it, straw poised, as apprehension tore at his anger. Should I be doing this? And again and again . . . an eternity of questions lapses in the second, just one second that it takes for the powder to melt and turn to tar, running down the foil like a brown, bubbling tear. He could see Clay's face as he cursed him, Mary's as she sat at the table, and as they had made love. Mary as he knew she would look now, unhappy, disappointed with herself and him . . . No. No, no, no! The hell with the Pigeon's moralizing, to hell with him, to hell with her. She'll live. The tar begins to smoke, an infinite number of highs escaping, unused, so much useless vapor . . .

"You're losing it. Go!" Jessica commands.

He inhales in reflex, and is instantly committed. He feels the smoke collect in a tingling pool in his lungs hesitating for a moment, and then gathering strength, moving through his blood vessels, a creature within him tingling like a million golden needles of pleasure, collecting, growing, and finally moving upward, upward to his neck, his chin, he can feel his lips tingling before it comes oooooohhh . . . Hisssss, like a warm, wet towel of perfect weight falling upon his brain, blocking out all but pleasure, and then he himself is moving upward in the spiral to the next world, beyond indecision, an arrival into the perfect world he seemed to have left only a moment before, the warm embrace he remembers so well. He sails ever upward until he dissolves on the air, a trickle of piano notes, lilting and rising to the point where pain doesn't even exist in the airy attics of dreams, just a little like being high, but then again, no, nothing like that, not like that, at all.

TEN

T he letters began on Monday.

They started with a single leaf, a simple paragraph caught upon the op-ed page of the campus paper, as stuck with all the innocent determination of time as a fly in amber. But that single leaf would take on an existence of its own, like a flea which bites a giant and leaves him cursed with some incurable malady, its infection breeding inside of him until consumption and death become inevitable. In the careless act of turning a page Everett's fate was sealed, his demise ensured, for had he not opened the campus paper on Monday, seated behind his desk, trying to ignore the rattling windows and generally unaware of the titanic forces building about him, would it have ever happened? Had he not seen it, not connected it with the meta-narrative of his life, would that first letter have existed? It was a diverting philosophical idea that he had heard bandied about the University in recent years, the idea of solipsism, that reality is a human construction. It was a logical extension of the hermeneutics that Jack Beetle had become famous for teaching. Hermeneutics after all denied the existence of truth as an absolute because of its necessary component of interpretation. No one person can experience any event, view any piece of art, or read any piece of literature without the lens of one's own particular background getting in the way. Therefore, Beetle would argue, no two people will see the same things in Chaucer's *Canterbury Tales* or in Dante's *Inferno;* rather, people will only see what they themselves are prepared to see, and since the preparation lies in an individual's background, it is therefore purely subjective. Beetle (and others like him) had made quite a splash in the world of letters by linking hermeneutics to English Literature, and in one whack giving professors a logical justification for any lunatic interpretation of any piece of writing, a justification for declaring that Marvel Comics had as much literary value as Shakespeare, and a justification for declaring the entire canon racist, sexist, and bigoted beyond the possibility of repair.

These ideas, known as "deconstruction," "post-modernism" or "post-structuralism," twisted deeply into the corridors of late twentieth-century academe. History, much to Stein's chagrin, was also a popular target of the deconstructors, who argued that the facts of any single event were unknowable to anyone who had not seen the event themselves. Furthermore, the logic went, those individuals who had witnessed an event would face the impossible task of disregarding their own biases in relating the details of the event, and then overcoming the biases of the person to whom they were relating the experience. Over the course of time, the various stories which we refer to as "History" had been gradually assembled and shaped into "Meta-narratives" designed to reinforce the power-structure of society. Once the elegant simplicity of this argument took hold, history texts could be dismissed as hopelessly biased, and a legitimacy was given to those professors who purposely distorted eyewitness accounts in an effort to guide the student to a higher plane of awareness. After all, since all accounts are biased, no bias can be any worse than any other, and it would be almost immoral to give a student information without helping the student to see how the information is vital to the world view. Since fact is clearly in the province of individual perspective, there can be no such thing as fact, and in the absence of fact, the concept of reality becomes less concrete. Reality, say the postmodernists, is not real, and it never was. Our realities have been constructed for us, and we are doomed to work within them.

Again, an interesting philosophical idea, one which Everett had spent less than eight minutes of his entire life considering.

He certainly wasn't considering it Monday morning as he snatched a few minutes from his busy schedule to leaf through the paper and see which way the wind was blowing after the Friday afternoon debacle. He had no warning of what was coming, the riot incident had been played down, if anything, and the campus paper devoted more space in that issue to effective techniques for snowboarding in deep powder than to the gentle breeze of campus activism. The stories were the same as they always were, the advertisements in their proper places, everything normal, and Everett dawdled through the pages, hesitating for a moment to examine a picture of a co-ed in a bikini and ski boots, before turning the page to the editorials, and even then he only half-focused until he came to the little letter. How tiny it seemed, three inches long in the fine print . . . But how radical its effect on poor Everett!

> *Editor:*
>
> *I read with interest the story about how Dean Broadstreet testified that Professor Stiggler had acted reasonably in the classroom over the disruption caused by A & S student David Shore. I'd like to thank the Dean for giving me a good chuckle, because his statement was the most ridiculous nonsense that I have seen in years. I was in that classroom, and just to set the record straight, for anyone who's interested, and it was Stiggler who came unglued. She did not eject Shore, he quite reasonably stood up of his own volition and left the room as anybody else would have after listening to the insults she levelled at him and his family. Writing this letter will probably cost me my grade in that class, but I'm too pissed off to care anymore. For three years I have swam through waves of bullshit dreamed up by malcontent professors and applauded by an obliging administration. If someone doesn't put their foot down soon, the entire University's going to drown in it.*
>
> *Sincerely,*
> *John Post, Junior, History*

Sweet mother of God, thought Everett. For a moment, he couldn't believe the letter was real. He looked back at it again. And then again. And then a fourth time. There could be no doubt; it was real, all right. Having ascertained that he was not in fact dreaming, and that someone had had the audacity of penning such a scandalous document, several thoughts flashed through Everett's mind. First, could it be a plant from one of Shore's friends? He could find out if the student had actually been in the class by checking in the computer across from Joyce's desk. He stood up, intending to go check, but then sat down again. How would it look? Everett never looked into the computer himself. He didn't even know the password to get himself into the system. Joyce always checked such things for him. It would look strange for him to go poking around in there now . . . I wonder if Joyce knows? She hadn't looked at him differently this morning; she rarely read the paper, being one of those sorts who remains happily ignorant of the push and pull of campus politics, but still, what if she had read it today? Everett stood up again and tiptoed across his office floor. He could barely hear over the building noise, but he was suspiciously certain of his footfalls in the office. If she heard him she might turn around and face the door. Quietly, quietly . . . He put his ear to the wood. He couldn't hear anything, but then, there it was . . . tap taptaptap tap tap . . . She was typing, which would mean her back was to his door. If he opened the door carefully, he might be able to see if the paper was on her desk. He put his hand on the knob carefully . . . and . . .

Bang! The door swung open, catching him in the forehead. He fell back, clutching at his head. Little Joyce filled the doorway. "I'm terribly sorry, Dean," she said, but she looked at him strangely . . . She knew! Or maybe not . . . Maybe she was just surprised because he was skulking by the door . . . How do you explain this one, Everett?

"My fault, Joyce, I was . . . uh . . . just looking at uh at this . . ." No good! She's looking at you as if you've lost your mind. Play the pain card. "Ow. You really got me, there." That's right, her expression has changed to one of concern, the old maternal instinct kicking in.

"Are you all right?" her brown eyes, ageless and aged, radiating worry. Perfect, Joyce!

"Yes, of course." Now! Look on her desk while the door is open and see if the paper is lying on her . . . Damn! There it is! But maybe it's just sitting there . . . She's looking that look again . . . Take the offensive! "What did you need, Joyce?"

"Professor Matthews has had something come up and he wants to know if he might come in earlier." Matthews! Matthews was an art professor who wanted the school to fund a sabbatical for him in Indonesia, of all places. Matthews! Indonesia! What the hell do I care about Matthews and Indonesia!

"For when?" asked Everett. And who's that student typing? I've never seen her before.

"Ten minutes from now," said Joyce, every square inch of her pulsating with efficiency. We must use every minute given to us! she seemed to say. "There was nothing on your schedule since Dr. Horning cancelled. Do you think you might be able to squeeze him in?"

It was more than a question. She knew better than he did if he was able to do so, since she was in complete and total control of his schedule. But I want to look in the computer! he wanted to scream. But I can't because you're here! And so is that student! Everyone's here! Everyone is in my office! How can I make you all leave!

Wait! I know!

"Yes, certainly. I'll see him as soon as he can get here."

"Thank you, Dean. I'll call him right away." She turned and started to bustle toward her desk.

"Joyce, after you call him, could you run down and get the allocation sheet from finance please?" There. That'll take her at least ten minutes.

"Allocation sheet?"

"Yes, the budget approved for travel this semester. The one that President Fowler sent last month." He tried a sheepish smile. "So I'll know if we can afford to send Mr. Matthews away."

"Yes, sir."

He closed the door and then gingerly placed his ear against it for a moment. He heard her make the call, hang up the phone, and then slide her chair back. Now!

He opened the door again. "Oh, Joyce, before you go, could you show me how to get into the system?" He laid his hand on the computer, which sat on a small desk of its own by his door.

"Right now, Dean? If there's something you need I can gladly get it for you." She was giving him the same incredulous expression. *Does she know?*

"No, I only have to check one record quickly. For something I was doing before. It'll only take me a minute, and I really need that sheet from finance."

"If it will only take a minute, I'm sure I can do it for you before I go."

No, dammit! Stop it! Just give me the damned word! "Really, Joyce. I'd be glad to do it myself. And I need that sheet. I've used the computer before. I just need to know the uh . . . You know." He nodded elaborately at the back of the girl who was typing.

This caused Joyce no end of confusion, until a light seemed to come to her. "Oh, I see." She led him back into his office and closed the door. Taking his arm with surprising firmness she leaned close to him. "You know how to log onto the system, don't you?"

"Yes. It's on the menu, isn't it?"

Joyce's voice dropped to a husky whisper. "Right. At the prompt, type in PLATO. That's the password this week. OK?"

She departed, and as soon as she had cleared the door into the hallway he sat himself in front of the terminal, shaking. The young student seemed to take no notice of him. He turned on the machine, chose "Student Records" from the display, and watched as a new window opened. "At prompt, type access key."

He tapped in P-L-A-T-O. A new window welcomed him into the student record system. "Type in Student Name, Last name first, First name last."

He couldn't remember the student's name. Hurry! He dashed into his office, checked the name again, and rushed back to the computer terminal. The student, alerted to his suspicious behavior by the noise of his sudden departure and re-arrival, looked at him from the typewriter.

"This is confidential. Could you please turn around?"

She shrugged and went back to her work.

"Post, John," Everett entered. The computer seemed to take forever as it considered this name.

"There are three John Posts in the University," the machine informed him.

"Specify student number, or, if unknown, department."

Another quick trip into the office and back again. "History," he typed. Another interminable delay. Then, the machine clicked a few times and made a humming noise. The screen flashed. "Post, John. Student number 0109278625-3746. Please select desired information from menu."

Everett took the mouse and moved it to "Academic Records." The machine hummed again, and then stopped. Everett wanted to pick it up and shake it to make it hurry. Joyce would be back at any moment. Finally, it brought up the youth's record. Another smaller window lit up. "Select desired year." Everett punched it in. The machine had to think about this for a moment before it came back, "Unable to comply. Select 'Schedule' from main directory. Press escape to exit." Everett almost cried out. He hit the escape button with force. When the screen cleared, he hastily hit "Schedule" from the menu. A new screen welcomed him to academic scheduling. "Please enter student ID number." I don't know his ID number! He hit enter, and a new window asked, "Please enter student ID number, or if unknown, student name, last name first, first name last."

The door to the hallway opened, and Everett's heart almost stopped, but looking up he realized that it was only the student, leaving. Good riddance! He typed in Post's name again, specified the department when asked, and was a little surprised when the screen cleared almost immediately and displayed the boy's current list of classes and times. Sure enough, there it was, "WMNS

EXP AMRCA—WS 1011." The little drip was in fact registered into the class. He pushed the escape button. A new window asked, "Make changes?" It was a sore temptation, but he selected "No," and exited the system. He stood up and raced into his office, almost slamming the door behind him.

Barely a minute later, someone knocked gently on the door, so softly that he almost didn't hear it above the construction noise. "Yes?" he called out.

The door swung open again and admitted Professor Matthews. He was in his early forties, and his complexion was of the leathery sort that some men develop around that age. He had a remarkable head of hair, though, a thick, silvery sweep that lifted from his brow in a graceful, Byronic arch and swooshed backward to a termination below the collar of the heavy, blue work shirt he wore. He seemed ill at ease, fittingly, Everett thought, since he was about to ask the University for a full professor's salary of fifty-three thousand dollars, plus traveling expenses, to head for a tropical paradise and examine primitive pictures for the better part of a year. He shifted from one foot to the other, and squinted through the construction noise as if it could make him hear better.

"Excuse me, Dean," he called out. "I was supposed to come and see you right away. My name is George Matthews."

"From the Art Department," replied Everett. "I've been expecting you. Come in, please."

After shutting the door, he approached the desk and slouched into one of the chairs. Everett looked at him stolidly for a few seconds, and then George, evidently realizing he was no longer in a studio, called himself to attention and sat up straight.

"Now then, Professor, what can I do for you?"

"Have you read the letter I sent you?"

"Yes, I remember doing so, but I don't have it here with me. My secretary has filed it away, and she's not here at present. Would you refresh my memory?"

George looked uneasily around the room, and then refocused his attention on Everett's face. "Well, Dean, as you may be aware, our department has been gaining a good deal of prestige among similar institutions as a fine school for fine arts. We've made great strides in terms of developing our sensitivity to indigenous people's cultures, but that being said, we really have no one in the department with more than a passing expertise in indigenous people's arts in South East Asia."

Everett was in no mood to hear this line of discussion, especially from this Byronic fop who managed to work in the code words 'indigenous peoples' twice in one sentence. The dean had the annoying feeling that the big gun code word, 'diversity,' couldn't be too far behind, but he let the professor continue.

"So, that being said, we in the department, well, I, was wondering how the administration would feel about sending someone to study this culture. Specifically, in Indonesia, which, being so large and spread out that it encompasses such extraordinary diversity." *Aha*, thought Everett. "I have some pictures I'd like to show you." Matthews reached into his satchel and extracted a thick folder. He pulled out a stack of pictures which looked as though they had been raided from someone's collection of *National Geographic*. After leafing through them, he placed several on the blotter in front of Everett, who glanced at them impassively. "Look at this, Dean. This is Borobudur. An incredible building designed by a kingdom that's now almost forgotten." George's voice became animated as he described it. "Isn't it amazing? A scholar could spend years just studying the carvings on the walls, and not even scratch the surface. And here, the Wayang puppets, an integral part of Indonesian socialization."

Everett studied the photograph, which looked to him like a gilt representation of some colossal insect. "The Wayang is the shadow puppet show. They use it to represent the forces of good and evil through traditional stories."

"A puppet show."

George looked up and smiled, the sarcasm in Everett's voice lost on him. "Yes, isn't it interesting? The stories represent Krishna, which is fascinating in itself, since Indonesia is a Muslim country. Whole villages come out to watch. I saw it many years ago."

"I take it you have spent time in this part of the world."

"Yes, when I was a student. The trip truly opened my mind."

Everett guessed that this would have taken place during the seventies. Which meant that he had probably spent his time smoking marijuana and laying about like a bum. He had heard stories. He wondered whether Matthews had been a draft dodger. "And now you want to go back again?"

"Very much, sir."

Before Everett could reply, Joyce came in and handed him the allocation sheet he had asked for. She left without a word and closed the door behind her. Everett looked the paper over. "Professor Matthews, how many people in your department are on sabbatical this year?"

A good deal of George's enthusiasm faded away. "Two, sir. But Professor Donaldson will be returning in the fall," he added hopefully.

"And Professors Carlisle and Johnson will be leaving, correct?"

"Yes, sir."

"Which means that from a department with twelve full professors, fully twenty-five percent will be absent during the fall term. I'm sure you see where I'm going with this."

"Yes, sir."

"You see, the legislature has been extremely critical of giving sabbaticals lately, as I'm sure you are aware. I just don't think that we can afford to have one third of the senior faculty from a department gone at one time. If you are interested in taking a leave of absence, I might be able to consider it . . ." he let the phrase hang in the air for a moment.

Matthews shook his head. "I could never afford it, sir."

On fifty thousand dollars a year with three months off in the summer? thought Everett. "Then, I'm afraid I have to say I'm sorry."

George sadly collected his pictures. "I'm sorry too, Dean, but I thought that you, who have taken such steps to ensure sensitivity on campus would have been willing to help this through."

What in the world did he mean by that? The letter! The Byronic Fop has read the letter, and now he thinks I'm an easy mark! He thinks he can waltz in here and indigenous-peoples me and get whatever he wants! The nerve! Everett could feel his face reddening. "Whatever I have done has been for the good of the University, Professor Matthews. I'm sure that you'll keep that in mind."

George thrust the pictures back into the satchel and gave a little chuckle, so quietly that Everett barely heard it. What did *that* mean? "Is there something else on your mind, Professor Matthews?"

The man hesitated, and then said, "It's just that it always seems to come down to money, doesn't it?"

Huh? What's he babbling about?

"I mean," George continued, as he inserted the clip on his case to lock it, "I know that this would be good for the department. And I think you know that, too. But it seems as though there's never enough money for the good programs."

Oh thank heaven. He's just upset about the money. Everett shrugged elaborately, as if to say, 'My hands are tied.' He watched the man depart. But now, left alone for a few precious moments, he began to brood. The letter! I wonder who's seen it. It was so small, really. A few inches buried in the newspaper. Who takes the time to read those things, anyway? Don't kid yourself. Everybody reads them. But still, it was so small. And who is this kid? Does he have some sort of chip on his shoulder? Everett took out the paper again and reread the letter. 'Malcontent professors.' Welcome to the real world, Everett thought. Or at least to the real university. No doubt about it, this kid is probably just a freak. He's unimportant . . . But what if there are others? No way. Maybe, though. No way. Who knows? And who has read the letter?

"Who has read the letter?" became a sort of motto for him as he stumbled through the rest of the day. He didn't want to see anyone, and spent the afternoon in his office. He sat behind his desk as if it were a bunker to protect him from the prying looks he could imagine on people's faces. There were only a few people on his appointment book, and Joyce dutifully sent them in, but Everett wasn't going out under any circumstances. Every passing moment helped to lull the sinking feeling out of him, and as four o'clock drew near, the earliest hour he could go home without having to explain himself to Joyce, he felt almost confident again. On his walk to his car, he had another moment of anxiety as he had to confront unfiltered humanity; a few pockets of students wandering on campus. He tried to tell by their faces if they had read the letter, but they all ignored him. Blissful anonymity.

It was not to last.

Tuesday morning, three more letters, all along the lines of the first.

Wednesday the count increased to a total of nine. This was not an isolated incident, now, and the whole school seemed to be talking about it. Everett, to his horror, was rapidly becoming a character, an object of speculation. There was no doubting the looks on the faces at this point. They all knew. Even Joyce, who had taken to giving him sideways glances he could feel more than he could see. She seemed willing to keep up the charade that all was well, however. She never mentioned the gossip, and she certainly never asked him if he wanted to talk about it. Instead, she kept his appointments coming in to see him, asking this or that, spending long moments staring at him through the din which was now becoming a secondary feature of his office; he himself being the main attraction.

By Wednesday afternoon, the noise in Everett's office reached a crescendo of excruciating intensity. Apart from the normal din of the cement mixers which gargled and rattled and roared in an orgy of sound, and the various trucks which beep-beep-beeped intermittently while backing, and apart from the normal shaking of the windows in their frames behind him, and apart from the disinterested shouts of the army of workmen, quite apart from all this, a new sound seemed to have been specially conceived to torment poor Everett while he suffered. About a half an hour after he returned from lunch, a peculiar banging noise began which cut through all of the other sounds coming from the tower. BANG . . . BANG BANG BANG . . . BANG. BANG. BANG. It sounded like gunfire. Everett spun around in his chair and tried to spy the instrument that could be responsible for such ferocious volume, but he could see nothing except the construction workers going about their business, apparently unconcerned about this latest assault upon their eardrums.

It was perhaps unfair that the new sound had begun just at this particular moment, as Everett had been hunched over his immaculate desk reading the latest letter in the campaign for his demise, and his morale was exceptionally low. He had spent his midday at a lunch meeting with several professors representing the foreign language departments, the intention of which had been to discuss some additions to the core curriculum, but the professors had been if anything, distracted by his presence. They all seemed to be looking at him out of the corners of their eyes, as if hesitant to say anything in his presence, and wanting far more to talk about him than about curriculum. He found himself picking at his food and mopping his brow in a gloomy cloud of suspicion, playing every bit the criminal tortured by conscience.

Upon his return to Old Main, he had picked up a copy of the faculty newspaper, the *Guardian,* and after tearing it open to the forum page found a long letter written by the Assistant Dean of the law school, Elliot Posner. Most of the letter addressed the constitutionality of the speech code board, and echoed some of the questions that Rasnikov had echoed at the Teller meeting. The language was technical and legalistic, however, and demanded from Everett a level of concentration that the racket from across the quad denied him. As he came to the last paragraph, he realized that the writer was talking about him, saying that the nature of such a subjective body encouraged people in authority to "see what they wish to see," and ignore objective reality. Just as it dawned on Everett that this assistant dean, this Elliot Posner, was calling him a liar, the banging noise began.

After a moment, the new sound died away, and Everett started to re-examine the letter, but it started right up again in earnest. BANG. BANG. BANG BA BANG BANG BA BA BANG. It sounded as if it were right outside his window. He stood up, collected the papers and thrust them into his briefcase. It was worth braving the sea of looks to get out of the office and away to somewhere quiet. "Joyce, if anyone needs me, I'll be at the University Club."

She clearly thought he was retreating, but by that time, growing accustomed as he was to being stared at, the dean didn't even notice.

Inside the club he found Stein at one of the tables, and Everett slumped into a chair opposite him. Stein was mumbling to himself, but stopped as he noticed Everett's arrival. Everett was afraid that with his current untouchable status his friend would make small talk and find a pretext to leave, but as their eyes met, his friend's face cracked into a small smile.

"The beleaguered warrior leaves the sanctuary of the fort," said Stein with a grin, but then his expression sobered. "How are you?" he asked, meaning it.

"Well, nobody's burned me in effigy yet," Everett answered, trying to muster a smile. "I suppose I should be thankful for that, at least." He wanted to change the subject quickly. "You seem preoccupied."

"Yes, I was just looking at this thing that was stuffed into my mailbox." He handed a xeroxed flier across the table. "What do you think? You want to go with me?"

The piece of paper announced a seminar being given by a visiting professor, Ms. Yorumba Khaleel, who would be speaking on the African-American Womynist Perspective in European history. A date was given, and a room number.

"You don't really want to go, do you?" asked Everett as he slid the paper back to his friend.

Stein looked at Everett with surprise, and then chuckled. "No, I don't think so." He watched Everett for a few seconds, and then continued: "You're serious, aren't you? You really think I'd go to something like that?"

Everett shrugged. "No, but you never know. Half your department will be there. Khaleel's got a good reputation."

"For what?" It was more of a statement than a question, and Stein said it with bitterness. Everett didn't say anything; if his friend was in a mood to splash away at the neo-liberal foundation of late twentieth-century academia, that was his business. It wouldn't do any good, anyway, and Everett was beyond caring anymore. He was glad of the silence that stretched into several minutes.

Finally, Stein sat up in his chair and looked across at Everett, his face serious and intense, his voice quiet.

"Everett, when are you going to wake up and see what this is really all about?"

"What what is all about?"

"This whole sordid diversion that academia is taking has nothing to do with liberalism or conservatism. It's much bigger. Much bigger indeed. What we have here is the eternal struggle, my friend. Good against evil."

Everett tried hard not to roll his eyes, and quickly looked around the room to make sure no one was listening. Stein's good and evil theories were well-known enough among his enemies to make life embarrassing for his friends. "I don't know if many of the other professors would agree with you, considering that they mostly consider you so far out in right field," Everett replied quietly.

Stein smiled ruefully. "Well, maybe I am. But that doesn't mean I'm wrong. How many of those professors that you're referring to got their doctorate degrees after 1970? Do any of them really know anything about history? They have degrees in 'disciplines' that hadn't even existed when they began as undergraduates. You remember those days. Have to get rid of academic elitism. Have to make higher education more accessible to the masses. Hell, Everett, I actually believed some of that stuff. But somewhere along the line, pedestrian concerns like '*veritas*' and 'historical integrity' got thrown by the wayside.

And now we have this whole movement of deconstructionists who argue that history itself is impossible to know. They justify absurdly subjective grading practices by saying the subject matter is subjective. How many department meetings have you been to where some fool gets up and starts in on the anti-testing litany? Over in history, I have to listen to these thirty-year-old PhDs chastise me for assigning so much reading material in my 300 level classes. Everett, I've got students coming into my survey course who God as my witness can't even read! Two years ago, I had a T.A. tell me that I shouldn't rely so much on essay questions, because they put students who couldn't write well at a disadvantage. How in the world can there be students at this level who can't write well? Doesn't that bother you? Do you remember when we were in high school? We all knew how to write well or we didn't graduate. We even had good penmanship."

"Some people would say that we spent too much time teaching things like penmanship, and not enough on teaching tolerance for people whose cultural background didn't allow them to be good at such things."

"Oh, what nonsense," Stein snorted. "'Cultural background?' You don't honestly believe that, do you?"

"I don't know, anymore. I just don't know."

"Everett, you cannot tolerate falsehood or ignorance. Some questions do have a single right answer. You're a mathematician for heaven's sake. Two and two always equal four. A squared plus B squared always equals C squared. Hitler was a bad guy. There are some things that just simply are, and it doesn't matter whether your skin is white or black or brown or green or blue. There is no cultural background that predisposes one for failure in anything. And that the idea that there is one has gained a footing in the academic community of all places just proves that there is some sort of mass hysteria involved. I'm telling you, there is something fundamentally wrong here.

"Everett, if I look at the last hundred years or so of western history, it seems that there has been a movement among intelligentsia to get away from dogmatic prescriptions of right and wrong, to move towards a core morality that transcends, I don't know, religion I suppose, in the traditional sense, and I have agreed with that movement. Too much misery has been caused by cold celibates who didn't give a damn about right or wrong, and who cloaked their own aggrandizement in the scarlet robes of the church. But something else is happening now. The new reformation was always driven by the desire to get to the core truths of human existence, with a tacit understanding that there was a fundamental decency that was necessarily rooted in a belief in whatever people chose to believe as God. But now, it seems to me that the academy has taken a hideous turn toward nihilism. We are no longer driven by good. It is . . . it's *evil*. Look at your own reaction, look at your face right now because I used that word. No one seems to believe any more that evil is real, that it can exist. People forget the sorts of things humanity has been capable of when left to its own devices. You know, it's only twenty years since Pol Pot declared that God was dead and made a good run at murdering a third of his entire population. And the intellectual crowd wrings its hands and says how awful he was, and at the same time makes half-hearted feints down the same road, restricting dissension and telling children that religion is the opiate of the masses and that morality is absolutely relative. I sometimes think that they're trying to edge out history requirements so that people won't see the big picture and realize what's going on."

Everett sighed. "Evil as you see it, with your cultural background as a white male in a western society with a religious tradition that believes that there is such a thing as good and such a thing as evil. And, I might add, a libertarian political perspective that holds the individual as the most important unit in society."

"Perhaps. But I would remind you that my religious tradition is not the same as yours, and historically my people have been considered as outsiders in your society, both as a collective group and as individuals. And as far as my political feelings are concerned, again, I don't think that this has anything to do with liberalism or conservatism. The desire on the part of some to dominate thought itself is neither new nor partisan. Stalin or McCarthy. The John Birchers or the politically correct. They all seek to destroy the one thing that makes humans free. I consider them to be evil. And, yes, I consider evil to be an absolute. But if you deny the existence of absolutes, don't you also have to deny the legitimacy of the university ideal as a search for truth?"

Everett could see where he was going, and answered carefully. "No, because I reject the premise that truth is an absolute."

"That must have been very convenient for you when you were giving your deposition."

"I didn't lie!" Everett shouted, and then realized that the conversations around him had died away, and that many people in the room were looking at him. "I didn't lie," he repeated quietly. "You were in that meeting over in Teller. You heard what that girl said. It was the same thing as what I testified."

"I remember all right. I remember a scared little girl who couldn't take her eyes off of Stiggler for more than a second at a time. It was as if she couldn't think of anything more calamitous than saying something Stiggler would disapprove of. Not exactly what I would call a credible witness."

"So you think I perjured myself."

"Let's just say that the vehemence of those who disagree with how you saw things is enough to give anyone second thoughts."

"Well, I don't think I have to stay here while you call me a liar."

"Oh, sit down, Everett. I'm one of the only friends you've got anymore. All I'm saying is that I think you have a credibility problem right now, and I think you're being set up for a fall."

Everett slumped back into his chair. "So do I. What do you think I should do?"

Stein shook his head. "I don't know. But I do think that the next time you're called to the stand, during the hearing, you'd better think very carefully about what you say. And if there's any room for error in your previous statement, you'd better come clean."

"And have everyone say that I lied in my deposition?"

"They're already saying that. Look, the only thing I can see you getting out of this is maybe getting your honor back. Think about it. If they put Gretchen Van Doorn on the stand, Shore's lawyer is going to pulverize her. I've even heard a rumor that she slept with young

Mr. Shore, and that Shore dumped her. If there's any truth to it at all, her testimony will be totally suspect. Judging by the letters I've seen in the paper, there is an overwhelming supply of witnesses, impartial ones, who will dispute her account. So in the end, it will come down to Stiggler's word against an ocean of dissent. Even if you side with Stiggler, she'll still probably lose, and you will have gained nothing. As I see it, you might as well come clean, say that you were pressured to alter your testimony, and hope that this whole thing blows over. And even if it doesn't you'll have done the right thing. Because that's about all you've got left."

Everett's heart sank through his belly and into his toes. "Dear God," he said. "What an infernal mess. How do these things happen, Stein? You go through life working hard, building up the power and the ability to do whatever you want, and then in a day, just one day, everything falls apart."

"It's not the doing things that's the problem, Everett. The great fallacy of power is the belief that power enables one to do whatever he wants. Anyone can do what they want to. Power means having the ability to ride out the consequences. What's that line from *Lear*? 'As flies to wanton boys are we to the Gods.'" Stein looked at his watch. "Listen, I have to go. I've got a class." He stood up and walked around the table behind Everett's chair. He put his hands on Everett's shoulders and squeezed them gently. "Think about what I've said." Then he was gone.

ELEVEN

When Parker started to come to, light was slamming against his eyelids, and in a half-conscious effort he turned to escape it, until he realized that he had fallen asleep on the couch, someone's couch, and that the couch was under a window, and that the sun was streaming in on him. He rolled upright, slowly, carefully, and after a short but intense consideration of the merits of the idea, struggled to his feet. A wave of nausea swept over him. There didn't seem to be anyone else in the apartment, and he searched the rooms for a few frantic seconds to find a toilet. When he did, he collapsed onto the tiles and retched into the bowl, heaving and shaking until his eyes felt as if they were pushing out of their sockets. Finally he passed out on the cold floor.

He was in the same position when he woke up again, and though the nausea had passed, waking brought profound disorientation. He wondered for a few moments where he was. He was alone in an apartment in the mountains. He squinted outside, in Vail. What am I doing in Vail? In the living room he found the stained aluminum foil and the candle on the table. That explained a few things. Recollection began to filter back to him, slowly, slowly, answering the questions as soon as he thought to ask them. The girl, what's her name, Jessica, is gone. I am alone. My friends are not here. My friends did not come. I have to get out of here.

He walked out of the apartment and into the street in a daze. There were hundreds of people walking about, random people he didn't know. Except that they were all carrying skis on their shoulders, and wearing the appropriate attire, their numbers and apparent single-mindedness of purpose might have placed them on a busy street in any large city. He stopped one of them, a middle-aged woman who was walking by herself. "Excuse me, could you tell me the time, please?"

In the expression on her face he could see how terrible he looked. "It's three-thirty," she said without stopping to check.

That couldn't be right. It was light out. People were going skiing, or rather, coming away from skiing. Parker pulled his coat around him. The sun made it feel hot, but he liked the feeling. It didn't make any sense, though. Why was the sun out? He walked against the tide of the people, moving toward the base of the mountain. Then, in a rush, he remembered many things. He lurched over to a wall and leaned against it while he worked everything through. He remembered that he had been in a fight last night. He remembered that he had left Mary . . . Mary. So much for Mary, he thought. If I didn't blow that, Pidge blew it for me. Then, in what would have seemed obvious to anyone in full possession of their faculties, but required from Parker a burst of inspiration, it occurred to him that it was afternoon. The sun was in the west, and everyone had finished skiing. They were going home. Parker wanted to go home, too. He felt exposed and unsafe in the sunshine with nowhere in this alien cityscape to hole up in and hide until his cognitive functions returned enough to give him a measure of security in his dealings with others. As it was they could all look inside of him, and it appeared to him that many of them were trying to do so. They turned to stare at him as they walked by, pinning him to the wall like an insect on a card. With as much strength as he could muster he pushed himself back into the street, where he altered his course to the direction of the house Pidge had rented.

His trek took him past the last bar he had been in the night before. In the daylight, the building seemed almost deserted; the doors closed, the darkened windows giving the effect of being boarded up and abandoned. He kept walking, his legs now beginning to ache from the simple but inexorable exertion of motion. With each step he remembered more, and each recollection compelled him to move faster, to find an escape. The events of the previous evening were beginning to have an uncomfortable clarity to them. Another street, and another, and finally the corner. He could see the house from here, and his car, parked in front. The street was empty. He stopped and rested for a moment, panting a little. As much as he wanted to be inside now, to occupy a corner of the earth where he belonged and could recuperate, he

273

knew that the next few minutes were going to be bad, and loaded with questions and awful feelings. Then he squared his shoulders and walked the last twenty yards.

The door was locked. For a few seconds, he didn't know what to do, but then he remembered that he had had a key. And here it was, still in his pocket. It was strange to him how so many things were different, but how so many of them were still the same. He had checked out of the world for a time, but he was checking back in again. In his absence, the planet had turned a few degrees, and some things were now different to him, but most things were still the same. The key was in his pocket. He took it out and put it in the lock. He took a deep breath. This was going to be bad.

There was no one home and there was no note. His things were still in his room, just as he had left them, but everything else was gone, as if a surgeon had come in and cut out all of the things that didn't belong to him, and could possibly do him damage. He stuffed his clothes into his bag and took his skis out to the car. After loading everything, he started up the engine and put the car into gear. He didn't stop until he got home.

* * *

His disorientation was gone by the next morning, but considering the fear that had replaced it, it might have been more comfortable for Parker to have stayed lethargic and stupid with only a mild and unfocused sensation of dread. The prospects of the day hung sharpened panic above his head like the blade of a guillotine. He took a shower and then, while shaving, checked the well of his imagination to see if it had come up with any new angles he might use on the Shore case, but it came up dry again. The only idea which presented itself was the thought that he could argue that David had been unable to bring counsel with him to the disciplinary board, and had therefore had his rights violated. Such an attack might work, but it would almost certainly require adjudication, which meant time, and time was a luxury which he did not have. This case needed to be dismissed quickly—he didn't even want to contemplate the possibility of a trial. And the nagging voice came back to him—why bother? Why prolong the inevitable? The fat, balding picture of the Dean's face came back into his recollection. Why would he lie? Why would he lie? The thought of using an attack based on lack of adequate counsel in the present case seemed so thin, so unbelievably weak, that he almost felt ashamed for considering it. It was peripheral garbage, nibbling around the edges of the problem when he needed an attack on the jugular. Still, it had to be considered; that and subpoenaing a large cross-section of students to see if any backed up David's account of the day in class. Parker's mind checked and rechecked, shuffling the deck over and over again, but no matter how he examined it, the University had all of the aces. As he considered the prospect of explaining to David's father that this was the best he could come up with, his knees literally went weak, and he had to hold on to the vanity to steady himself until the feeling passed.

When he got to the office Linda looked up at him from her desk. "What happened to your jaw?" she asked, without preamble.

His problems with her seemed at the moment so inconsequential that he didn't even want to talk to her. She was like a little mosquito buzzing in his ear. But if he didn't say anything, if he ignored her, he knew that she would talk about him to the other people in his office, and that was something he wanted even less. He gave a non-committal shrug. "Skiing. I fell." He started to walk into his office.

"Are you OK?" she asked.

"Yeah, fine."

"Oh, Parker?" she called out, summoning him back to the door. "Shore called. He asked if you could call him at home."

Oh great. The old tyrant wasn't wasting any time. And if he was at home, missing a day of work, it must mean that he was in an exceptionally bad mood. "At home? Did he leave a number?"

"No, I assumed you'd have it on your Rolodex."

"Why would I have his home number? The only number I've got for him is at Beauchamp Tyler. Would you check with Mrs. Pringle and see if Jim has it?"

"Parker. Wake up. David Shore. Not Arthur Shore, David Shore. He wants you to call him right away."

Parker went into the office and dialed the number. The boy answered on the first ring. "Hello?"

"Yeah, David, It's . . ."

"Parker! Where have you been? I've been trying to get ahold of you."

"I just walked in the . . ."

"Forget about it. We've got him!"

"What?"

"You heard me, I said we got him!"

"Got who?"

"You wanted corroboration? Well I've got corroboration in spades. I'm gonna fax you something right now, OK?"

"David, wait a second. What are you . . ." But David had hung up.

Feeling somewhat bewildered, Parker went down the hall to the storage room where the office fax machines were kept. There were two of them, and one of them was ringing as he came in. There was a pause as the machine answered, and then began to spit out a curl of paper. It appeared to be a page cut from a newspaper, with one story outlined in a broad strokes. Across the bottom of the page was the hand-written note: "YES!"

Parker tore off the paper and read through it. A symphony started to play inside of him, before he got a grip on himself. He raced back to his office and dialed David's number.

"We got him!" said the student. "Do you finally believe me?"

"OK, hold on for a second. I want you to tell me exactly who this guy Post is." Please say you don't know him, Parker thought. Please, please say you don't know him.

"How should I know? I never heard of him. I don't even think he's greek," he added, in a tone which suggested that this might cast doubt upon Mr. Post's sanity. "I guess he's just some dude in the class."

"Do you know how we can get ahold of him?"

"I'm way ahead of you. There are three John Posts listed in the phone book. Here are the numbers. Do you have a pen?"

"Yeah, go ahead." Shore listed the numbers.

"Do you have any way of knowing which one is the one we want?"

"I've been thinking about that. The first one is an on-campus exchange. The guy in the paper says he's a junior, so I doubt that he's living in the dorms. The third one is listed on Gold Dust Road, but that's way up in

Five Mile Canyon, which is outside of town. It's possible that this is the right guy, because sometimes students score these big houses up there. But I go to parties a lot up there, and I think I'd know him if he was the right one. But the second guy, he lives two blocks off campus. I think he's the one."

While he was talking, Rick and Aimee walked into Parker's office and sat down. Parker pushed the fax across the desk, and Rick picked it up and read it. A triumphant grin spread across his features as he did so. He handed the paper to Aimee.

David was still speaking. "So what do you think, now, Parker?"

"I don't know, but I got a good feeling."

"Yeah, me too. Hey, I gotta go."

"Listen, are you gonna be around later this afternoon?"

David laughed. "Are you kidding? I've got Women's Studies this afternoon, and this is one day I'm not going to blow it off."

Parker couldn't help chuckling, but he said, "Listen, don't get too nasty to her. This thing isn't over yet. I'll call you at around five. Oh, hey, I almost forgot. Has anybody else tried to talk to you about this? I mean press or anything?"

"As a matter of fact, I have a message sitting here from some dude at channel five. He must have called while I was at my eight o'clock. What do you want me to do about it?"

"I want you to ignore it. I don't want you to say anything to him, or to anybody else who might want to talk to you about it. Don't even call him back. I don't think they can make too much of a story out of you if you refuse to talk to them. And I'd imagine the school wants to keep this as quiet as possible. Hopefully they'll forget about you."

He hung up the phone and faced the two associates, rubbing his hands together. "OK, kids. I think we got ourselves a ballgame."

Aimee finished reading the fax and laid it on the desk. "I'd love to talk to this guy."

"Good. Because that is going to be your primary target for the day." Parker leaned back in his chair, and the wheels which had been frozen for days began to turn. He tossed the legal pad with the phone numbers across the desk. "David thinks that his number will be one of these three. Try the second one first. He's probably in class, and it may be hard to catch him, but keep trying. Feel him out. See how willing he is going to be to giving us a statement. And if he's amenable, see if he can't give us a line on some other people in the class who might also be willing."

"What do you want me to do?" asked Rick.

"First of all, I want to make sure that there's no possibility that this is some kind of mistake or that the guy is a scam artist. So I want you to get a list of the other students in the class from the University, and make sure his name is on it. Now that there's been some publicity, it's always possible that he could be a crackpot. I don't want to make any obvious mistakes, you know? Don't take anything for granted."

"Did you see the story on the news?"

Parker winced. "No, I missed it. But I ran into David up in Vail and he told me all about it. He also said that his father just about went into orbit when he heard that his son had become a celebrity. Which leads me to the next point on the agenda. I'm not exactly thrilled at the prospect of another session with that bastard, if you know what I mean. So if all of this starts to pan out, the witnesses and everything . . ." He paused.

"What's wrong?" asked Aimee.

"Nothing. I just have this fear of getting too far ahead of ourselves at this point. But I'll tell you, if it is at all possible, I want this thing to be finished by the end of the week. Which means that I want to pitch a settlement to Patterson by Thursday. That'll give him enough time to talk to his people and get back to us. So today I want to concentrate on putting together a convincing brief. I'm pretty sure we've got him, but I want it to look good and scary."

Rick nodded. "Are you going to ask them for anything out of the ordinary?"

"Like what?" asked Parker.

"I think we should demand that the administration and that professor be forced to take First Amendment sensitivity training."

Parker laughed out loud. "Do they have such a thing?"

"I heard that there was a group in California that was doing pro bono work for students on PC campuses out there, and they actually got it into a settlement."

Parker thought about it for a second, but then he shook his head. "I have to admit that it has a certain appeal, but I don't want to risk the publicity."

"It was just a thought."

"Yeah. One thing I do want though is to get David out of that class. I want the school to amend his graduation requirements so he doesn't have to take it. There's no way he can get a fair shake in there, now. But we can talk about all this later. Right now, just get ahold of Post and the class list. I'm going to go talk to Diamond Jim and give him a rundown on what's happened. I'll talk to you in an hour or so." He got up before they did and started up the hallway to the senior partner's office, but Linda stopped him. She was laying down the receiver of her telephone.

"Parker, are you parked in the right space today?"

The question was so mundane that he hardly heard it. "Huh?"

"Your car. Did you park in the right place?"

"Sure. Why?"

"I just got this weird call from building maintenance asking what kind of car you drove, so I told them and . . ."

"Yeah, whatever, I'm in the right spot. Take care of it if they call back."

"That's what I . . ."

Parker turned her off and resumed his walk to Diamonte's office, where he encountered the formidable presence of Diamond Jim's secretary, Mrs. Pringle, who guarded his door during office hours. Mrs. Pringle was something of a legend in the firm, having been there longer than anyone but the named partners, and everyone, including Parker, and quite probably including Diamonte himself, was a little afraid of her. Not that she was in any way overtly threatening; she was quite amiable, but she had that particular streak of steel that used to be referred to as 'finishing' back when young women of good families were installed as a matter of course in schools like Madeira and Hollins. Nor did she fit into the stereotype of the cold and inevitably unmarried older woman. She was married, to all appearances happily so,

and at office functions she squired her husband attentively, at all times projecting the image of the perfect
wife. For Mrs. Pringle did everything perfectly, and
therein lay the source of her subtle intimidation. Everything about her was perfect, and more devastating to the
morale of those mortals around her, not only was she
perfect, she was in all ways naturally so. Her hair, long
ago turned gray, was pulled into a tidy but somewhat
voluptuous bun at the nape of her neck. Her face might
never have seen makeup in its perfect span of years. Her
hands were manicured, but her fingernails were unpol-
ished. Most of all, she seemed to have an air of comprehension of all that she came into contact with; her eyes
were clear and shrewd, in a way that reminded Parker of
Mary's, in whose he had always seen a glimmer of that
understanding which makes women far more intelligent
than men, and which causes thoughtful men to aspire to
be better than their natures.

Parker asked if he could see Mr. Diamonte (Mrs.
Pringle was the kind of person with whom one felt awkward using Christian names), and the senior secretary informed him that the senior partner was on the phone and
asked Parker if he would care to take a seat and wait,
which Parker did. Mrs. Pringle tidied a few things on her
desk, and then, as if to pass the time, asked Parker how
he felt about his recent ascension to the rank of partner.

From anyone else, it would have seemed like old
news, since his promotion had happened some four
months earlier, but since she had probably known that
he was going to be promoted before anyone else in the
firm did, and since she had been with the firm for so
long that time for her flowed in more expansive waves,
the question dropped comfortably from her lips and

onto the floor, where Parker picked it up and turned it over a few times.

"I'm still in shock," Parker said with the self-deprecating diplomacy that Mrs. Pringle's demeanor elicited. "I can't imagine that I deserved it."

"I'm sure you'll be a credit to the firm, Mr. Thompson. We all get what we deserve."

"I certainly hope not," Parker replied, pushing a diplomatic grin onto his face.

She returned the smile, letting several quiet seconds with her eyes locked on his elapse before saying, "Mr. Diamonte is free now. You may go right in." How she had known without looking at the phone that Diamonte had finished was a mystery.

Parker thanked her and stepped into the office, where Diamonte rose from his seat and walked around to sit on the edge of his desk. "Any news?" he asked, as Parker sat in the chair in front of him.

"Yeah, maybe some really good news." He handed the fax to his boss and waited as he read it.

Diamonte's eyebrows raised. "Have you checked it out?"

"Aimee's calling the guy right now. She's going to see if he'll be willing to give us a statement, and if he can recommend anyone else in the class who can help us out. Rick is getting a class list to make sure that this Post kid was actually there. We'll see how it goes."

Diamonte nodded. "Assuming it's all on the level, how do you want to proceed?"

"To tell you the truth, I feel a lot more secure in subpoenaing other students in the class if it comes down to it. But it may not be necessary, if Post is able to give us some names. If he does, I'll stay late tonight if I have to to get ahold of them. If all goes well, and it looks like we've got a good list of witnesses, I'm going to offer a settlement on Thursday."

"Excellent."

Parker shifted in his chair. "Not that I want to assume too much, but the one thing that's bothering me is why the Dean would have lied when I interviewed him."

The older attorney shrugged. "If you wrap this up quickly, I doubt we'll ever know. It doesn't matter, anyway. Since Art is so nervous about publicity, I believe that the wiser course would be to forget about it."

"Yeah," said Parker. He took a deep breath. "By the way, speaking of Mr. Shore, I don't know quite how to ask for this, and I don't want you to think I'm chickening out, but evidently there was a brief item on the news about David Friday night . . ."

"Uh-huh," said Diamonte. "I saw it. There was a demonstration up there on Friday afternoon."

"Yeah, well, I was wondering if um, you might be able to . . . um . . ."

Diamonte grinned. "Ye-e-esss?"

"Well, could you talk to him for me? I don't know if I could handle another . . ."

"Relax, son. I just got off the phone with him. Don't sweat it."

The air left Parker's body in a hurry. "Thanks a million."

"Don't mention it." Diamonte shrugged again. "My job. And he's not so much of a bastard with me. I've known him too long. You just have to remember that people like Art will do *anything* in order to get what they want. The normal rules of civilized conduct don't apply.

The trick is to make sure that they don't get anything on you, or better, to get something on them. Like I did."

Parker's eyes widened a little. He looked at the old lawyer, who had always seemed so upright and fatherly, in a totally different light. "What? What did he do?"

Diamonte crossed his arms and pursed his lips thoughtfully. "I'll tell you what. You tell me what he's got on you, and I'll tell you what I've got on him."

Parker laughed. "OK, I see your point." He rose to leave. "Listen, thanks again. I'll get out of your hair."

As he started to go, Diamonte took a critical look at Parker's face. "What happened to your chin? Here." He pointed to his jaw.

"I've been telling everybody else that I fell while I was skiing. The truth is that my best friend clocked me. I really deserved it."

"Oh, the passion of youth."

Parker spent the rest of the morning drafting the outline of a settlement proposal to give to Patterson. It wasn't until after lunch that Aimee returned to give her progress.

"Post is a go," she said without preamble. "It took me a while to catch up with him, but he agreed to give us a statement."

"How did he feel?" Parker asked.

"Reluctant," Aimee replied. "But sincere."

"What do you mean by reluctant?"

"Difficult to explain. I just got the feeling that he wanted to do this, but he didn't want to do this, if you know what I mean."

"You don't think he could be blowing smoke, do you?"

"Oh no, not at all. I'm positive he was there. I kept my questions vague, and he replied with extremely direct answers. He could have read Shore's statement. I mean, I don't think he did, but what he said matched exactly. He's our man."

"So why do you think he's reluctant?"

"I don't know. I just get this feeling. Like, when I asked him if there were other people in the class who we could talk to, he got a little evasive. At one point he said to me, 'You don't know the kind of pressure we're under.' He told me that he was willing to go on the record, because he was so angry, but that he didn't think a lot of people would be. I get the feeling there's some kind of coercion to go along. Of course, it could just be his apprehension about contradicting a teacher who's still going to give him a grade in the class."

Parker picked up his phone and dialed Friedman's office. "Hey Rick, come on down here, would you?" He turned again to Aimee. "I want to hear what he came up with. So did Post cough up any names?"

"Yeah, eventually. But he said not to expect too much." She tore a sheet from the legal pad she was carrying and handed it to him. "Here they are. Three of them."

"Well, it's a start," Parker murmured.

Rick came in in an excited rush. "Oh, Jesus. You gotta hear this. After I left here this morning, I called Patterson to make sure that I wouldn't have any problems getting a roster from David's class, right? So that all worked out until I called the University. Some stupid broad, sorry Aimee, in the administration office starts giving me the total run-around. She says to me that she can't give me that information because of privacy rules or whatever. She says it's administrative policy. So I tell her to call Patterson's office and she'd see that it was all OK. But she says that Patterson had already called and told her to turn the information over to me. So I'm like, you know, what's the problem? So she tells me that she has to check with her supervisor before she can give me the information. So she winds up jerking me around for an hour before she finally calls back and tells me, like she's doing me some colossal favor, that I can pick up the roster this afternoon. So I'm like, 'what?' like I don't have anything better to do than to spend four hours driving way the hell up there and back again. So I tell her I want her to fax it to me. And she tells me that it's against department policy. I just about hit the roof. She's getting really stubborn now, and we're starting to go round and round, so finally I look back at my notes, you know, to find her name, and I say to her 'Look Mrs. Price, this is part of an ongoing investigation, and if I don't have that list in my hand in five minutes, I'm going to walk across the street to the courthouse and have a warrant issued for your arrest for obstruction of justice.' And she actually *believed* me! I didn't even know her first name! I swear, you have to be certifiable before any arm of the government will give you a job. Anyway, here's the list. It came over the fax less than a minute after I hung up with her. She must've had it in her hands the whole time."

"Well?" asked Parker.

"Well what?"

"Is Post on the list?"

"Oh. Yes, he is. Right here. I spent the rest of the morning at the library getting addresses for these people. I'm about three quarters of the way through."

"OK. Finish it up and let me know when you're done. Aimee, see if you can get ahold of the other people Post recommended we try. I'm going to go ahead and call him right now."

After they had left, Parker picked up the receiver and dialed the number. When the phone stopped ringing, there was an uncomfortable silence for several seconds. Finally, after what seemed like an awfully long time, Parker said, "Hello?"

A quiet, suspicious voice answered. "Hello."

"Hello," Parker said again. "Is John Post at home?"

There was another pause. Then, "Who?"

"John Post. Is this the John Post residence?"

"Who's calling?"

"I think I must have the wrong number," Parker said, and hung up the phone. He redialed, and the phone rang several times. Someone picked it up with an audible click, and the same voice, now a little angry, said, "Look, man, what do you want from me?"

"I'm sorry, my name is Thompson, I'm an attorney, and I'm trying to find a student named John Post. Does he live there?"

"Oh, yeah, you're that guy's lawyer, right?" The voice became more accommodating. "Yeah, this is me. I'm John."

"Hi, John. Like I said, my name's Parker Thompson, and yes, I'm David Shore's attorney. I was wondering if I might have a little of your time."

The voice deflated a little. "Yeah, whatever."

"If you're busy I can call later . . ."

"No, no. It's not that. Just, you know, what can I do for you?"

"You can tell me what happened that day in your Women's Studies class."

"Hell, you know what happened there as well as I do. And I already told that woman who called." Post became suddenly anxious. "She did work for you, didn't she? That Aimee person?"

"Yes, she's an associate here. And she told me basically what you told her, but I'd still like to get it straight from you, if you don't mind."

"All right. The professor flipped out, which isn't that unusual. Your client and a bunch of his friends started laughing about something during a lecture on the theory of rape. The professor, Stiggler, tore into him and told him that he was a rapist, and I think she said that his father was a rapist, too. He was trying to blow it off, but she went on and on. I think it was that thing she said about his father that set him off. He said something about fat dykes having power in universities, and then he took off. You know. He split. Stiggler turned about as white as a sheet, and she said some more stuff about him after he left, about how fraternities were your basic rape camps, and how until people are wised up to this, the status of women will never improve. Yadda yadda. The class broke up early. That's about all, I guess."

The killer instinct in Parker was unleashed. His free hand was clenched around a pencil, shaking it in triumph. "Would you be willing to come down here and give us a formal statement?"

Post sighed. "Yeah, I suppose. When?"

"As soon as possible. Tomorrow, if you can make it."

"My Tuesday Thursday schedule is pretty light. I can come in the afternoon, say four o'clock?"

"Four o'clock is fine," said Parker. "Do you have a car?"

"Yeah."

Parker gave him the address of the firm. "We'll pay for your gas."

"Thanks," said the student, without enthusiasm.

"Now," said Parker, "Is there anybody else in the class who you can think of who might be willing to come forward and talk about this?"

"I wouldn't hold my breath."

"Why not? It sounds pretty clear that this kid is getting railroaded, doesn't it?"

"Oh, yeah. He' getting the shaft all right. Everybody knows that."

"Then why do you think people will be reluctant to talk?"

"Jeez, you guys just don't get it, do you? That kid Shore doesn't have anything to lose here. He doesn't have to worry about his grades or his future or anything. For all I know, he can probably buy them. I mean, don't get the feeling I'm doing this because I like him. I don't. I think people like him are parasites. Those pigs come here and drive around in their BMW's and get anything they want, they ignore everything that's going on, drink their way through college and get degrees and go off to whatever world they live in. People like me have to work for it, and if I get kicked out of school for talking to you like this, and you better believe that's a very real possibility as far as I'm concerned, I don't have any place to go, and I'm scared shitless. But I just get so . . . fucking . . . pissed sometimes at the crap they expect us to go along with . . . This stupid temper of mine has gotten me into a mess, and because I've got some stupid sense of integrity, I'm gonna go through with it, I'm gonna give you your statement and I guess I'll testify or whatever. But don't expect too many other people to do it. You think we don't understand what's going on here? That kid Shore stood up because he probably thinks nothing can happen to him, because he's got money, and look what they did to him. They tried to throw his ass out of school. You think we don't understand that? You think we didn't get the message? And the only reason, the *only* reason why he didn't just disappear is because he's got enough money to go out and hire somebody to fix it for him. If it had been somebody like me, I would have been out of here like a shot, and nobody ever would have noticed."

Post's voice became soft, and bitter. "I've been here for two and a half years now, and man have I seen some things. And I keep waiting for things to change. But the older I get, the more I realize that it just ain't gonna happen. No matter how many stories you read about in the papers or in the magazines about all the stupid shit that's happening on campuses, nothing ever changes. Nobody cares. And I'm beginning to wonder if I do."

Parker was silent for a moment. "I don't know what to say to you," he said.

"Hey, I don't mean to yell at you. You're doing your job. It's just that this is all starting to come down on me. I got some pretty weird calls this morning."

"What do you mean?" Parker asked.

"Well, one dude called up and told me I was a fascist, and I guess I can get over that, but then, like three different times, some chick called up and just said 'You're next.' It was pretty creepy."

"Did you think about calling the police?"

"Are you kidding? Call the University cops? Haven't you been listening to me?"

"You don't live on campus. Call the regular police department. Tell them what happened."

"Yeah, whatever."

"Look, John, I can't give you advice, because it would be a conflict of interest for me to do so, but I really would recommend that you call them. I know you're scared, but I don't think it could hurt you."

Post didn't say anything.

"And I'll tell you something else . . ." Parker paused, trying to find the right words that would lead him around an ethical breach. "I can't talk about this case with you, or how it relates to you. But when this is over, if something happens to you, give me a call and I'll represent you. Pro bono. Or, if I can't, I'll put you onto someone who will."

"Yeah, sure." It was clear that Post didn't believe him. After a second or two he gave a short sigh of resignation.

Parker got off the phone and arranged to have a court reporter present during the interview he had set up. He was reasonably certain that Post was exaggerating his fears about his own academic safety, but he was equally sure that he would give an excellent deposition, and on the almost inconceivable chance that the case went to trial, he would make an excellent witness.

Later in the day, Parker stuck his head into Aimee's office and asked if she had had any luck with other candidates. She told him that she had only been able to get in touch with two of them. One who she had talked to had flatly refused to speak with her about the incident, but the other one had said that she would think about it. This last one had, however told her in confidence that there was no doubt that Shore had been provoked.

"Did you tell any of them that their names had been given to us by Post?" Parker asked.

"No. I told them that we were calling students at random."

"Great." Parker checked his watch. It was after five. "Why don't you go on home."

"Hey, you want to go get a drink or something?"

Parker weighed the invitation. He couldn't be sure how much she was offering, and he didn't want to assume that she was making any sort of serious advance. Regardless, though, it was a personal gesture, and represented a step toward friendship, and meant that some of the animosity he had felt from her since he had made partner had dissipated. It was a relief. "No," he said. "I want to call David. But I'll take a rain check."

She smiled. "Sure. See you tomorrow."

By the time Parker got off the phone and had written a few notes on what he wanted to include in the settlement proposal it was fairly late, and he was the last to leave the office. He walked down the darkened corridors alone in a mixture of elation and anxiety; elation over the case and the salvation of his career, and anxiety over his personal life, which had come adrift. He wondered if he would see Mary again, and felt a loss when he concluded that he probably wouldn't, and if he ever did their meeting would take place in the inevitable cloud of resentment and sorrow, surrounded by people who wouldn't understand, and that the pain he would feel would have to be born internally.

Still, he thought, it happens, and he tried to put it out of his mind. The elevator took him into the parking garage, dark and almost deserted. There was a car parked on the other side of his own, and as he walked toward them he started to fish his keys from his pocket. The jingling sound echoed off of the concrete. When he was about twenty feet from the Porsche, he heard a faint sound from the far side of the garage, and then what he thought was someone calling his name. For a moment he thought he had imagined it, but it came again distinctly.

"Parker?" It sounded like a woman.

He took a few steps toward the voice. "Yes? Is anyone there?"

A car engine started, and at the same time a young man stood up on the other side of his Porsche. By his attire, he looked to be about twenty years old, but he had a stocking pulled over his face. Parker's heart froze—he thought he was about to be robbed. The boy didn't have a gun, though. In his hand he had a bottle of orange-colored fluid with a rag stuffed in the top. The car at the far side of the garage pulled out and began coming toward them, accelerating. Parker moved to get out of the way.

"Fuck you," said the boy.

"Huh?" said Parker. He still didn't understand what was happening.

The boy took a lighter and lit the rag. He dropped the bottle through the passenger side window of the Porsche and bolted for the car.

"Hey! What are you doing!" He looked back at his car and saw a sheet of fire erupt inside. "No! Noooo!" Without thinking he ran toward it and yanked the door open. The heat caused him to stagger back, stunning him. He wasn't thinking clearly. All he could think about was how much he loved his car, how many hours he had put into it. For some reason he thought that if he could pull the bottle out it would make the fire stop. He knelt down and saw a piece of it lying on the seat. He grabbed for it and screamed in pain. The gasoline was on his hand and he could see it burning. There was some on the shoulder of his jacket, too, and he could smell the hair burning on his head.

"Help!" he started screaming. "Help! Help! Oh God somebody help me!" He jumped around in agony, beating at his clothes, and each time he hit his hand the pain was worse than he could believe. He couldn't stop screaming. "Help me! Oh God, help me!"

A man came running into the garage and saw what was happening. "Holy shit!" He tore off his jacket and wrapped it around Parker, and then pushed him onto the ground and rolled him over. "It's OK, it's OK," he said. "It's OK. You're gonna be OK. It's out now. It's out." He took the coat off of Parker and looked at him. "Oh sweet Jesus," he said. "Don't move. I'll call an ambulance."

At the hospital, the doctors bandaged his arm and the side of his head, covering one of his eyes, and gave him a shot of something to take the pain away. It felt a little like heroin, but he was wide awake. They told him that the burns were mostly first and second degree, and would heal without much scarring, and that his ear would be fine. His right hand was worse, though. They wanted him to come back the next day to check on it. Then they put him in a cab and sent him home.

Mary's car was parked in front of his house, and he stared dully at it for a few minutes before going inside. The cabby asked him if he was all right. "Fine," said Parker. He stumbled toward the door, and then realized that Mary was there. The thought of seeing her felt indescribably wonderful. She will take care of me. He opened the door.

"Mary?" His voice sounds so thick in the darkness he can hardly hear himself. He tries again, louder. Deep breath. "Mary?"

"Upstairs, honey."

"I can't come up there." She can't hear you. Find the stairs. Oh my hand. Oh it hurts so bad. Sooo bad. Don't cry. You can't let anyone see you cry. Find the stairs. The railing. Use the railing. Slowly, slowly. Oh my hand. One at a time. Someone's laughing. She's laughing. Something's wrong. I hear two of her. Nervous. I can't hear. There's no light. The light will make it louder. It's so dark. Last step. Voices. But there's still two of them. I'm hearing things that aren't there. I hurt so bad. I see two of her. One's under the covers but she's there. She's naked and so pale and she looks so skinny. Why are there two of her? She doesn't look right.

"We wanted to surprise you, honey."

"I can't see."

She's on her knees on the bed and she leans forward. Her breasts lean forward. She's naked and she doesn't look right. Is there someone else there?

"Oh my God! What's happened to you?" The light's on now I can see I can hear and What's she doing here. She's lying under the covers and she's naked now she's . . .

Oh no. Oh no turn away and make it stop. I hurt so bad but I have to get away and make it stop. I'm down the stairs now and the living room is so big and there's no place to hide and make it stop. I want to go to sleep. I am asleep. I am dreaming and it hurts so bad but I'm not asleep and now she's here. I can hear her footsteps on the floor slap slap slap the light's on and Mary's here. Shake my head and wake up. Shake my head Ahhhh, I am awake. I'm awake.

Mary was bending over him where he sat in the corner, his bathrobe wrapped around her. "Parker, what's happened? What's happened to you?"

"What's she doing here?" The words came out thick, as if his mouth was filled with pebbles. He focused his eye onto her face.

"Come on, Parker. Come in and lie down. You're burned. I think you're in shock or something."

He stayed where he was. "I'm OK. Is she here?"

"Who?"

"Jessica. Is she here?"

"No, she's still upstairs. Can you see?"

"I'm OK. Why did you bring her here?"

"We'll talk about it later." She started to tug at his other arm, the one that wasn't bandaged. "I want you to . . ."

He yanked his arm away, and winced from the pain. He started to feel very angry. "I said I'm OK. We'll talk about it right fucking now. Why did you bring that cunt into my house!"

She stepped back as if he had slapped her. "Maybe because I thought you wanted me to."

"You don't know what I want. You haven't got any idea of what I want."

"I can't believe I'm hearing this. It's not like you've never done it before. Clay tells me you've practically made a hobby of it. Jess said you'd like it. And that I'd like it. And I think maybe I would."

"You wanted to? You? What do I care what you want?"

Her voice softened a little. "I thought you cared a great deal."

"Maybe I did." He felt very, very tired. His head sank between his knees.

She misinterpreted his quietness, and huddled down next to him. He ignored her as she began to whisper to him. "Don't you see that for my whole life people have been expecting something from me, have been expecting me to act a certain way, but I can't do that. No one could. It makes you feel like you're dead. I don't want to be like that anymore. I'm so tired of being the girl on the outside. When we met the first time, you wouldn't even talk to me. I wanted you to talk to me so much, and you wouldn't because I was dead. I want to be alive like you. You're the most alive person I've ever known. I love you, Parker. I want to be with you."

Parker slowly raised his head and looked into her eyes, just a few inches from his own. "I want you to go upstairs and put your clothes on. I want you to get your friend and I want you to go away. And I never, ever, want to see you again."

She looked at him with mute appeal, but he turned his face away. He heard her go upstairs, and then a few minutes later come back down. She and Jessica stood there for a few seconds, but he couldn't look at her. She took a few steps forward and dropped the sweater he had loaned her onto the floor next to him. "This is yours," she said. Then she and Jessica turned and walked away. He heard the door close.

His cat walked down the stairs and crossed the room to him. He rubbed his tail against Parker's legs, and then, eliciting no response from his owner, sat down beside him and started to wash his paw. Parker picked up the sweater and held it to his face. He could smell her perfume in it, and it made him cry, very, very quietly.

* * *

After his appointment at the hospital, Parker walked over to Welton Place to see Clay. The news wasn't all bad. He would probably have some scarring on his neck, but his face would heal without disfigurement. That was the word that the doctor had used. His hand, however, would need some work, and he already had an indication of just how painful that work would be when the doctor removed the bandage. Fighting to keep from crying out he had watched the cloth come away from his arm, and then looked in disbelief at the blistered ruin of his fingers. They would never look normal again. But at least they wouldn't have to be removed.

Diamonte had been more upset than he, and had tried to force him to fill out a police report. Parker had convinced him that it wouldn't be a good idea; he had no idea of what the kid looked like, and he couldn't even remember the kind of car he had seen in the garage. And there was always the looming specter of publicity. Parker had been burned, and a lot of the fight had gone out of him. He didn't want to risk losing his career as well as his lover and his appearance. Diamonte had finally dropped it.

So here was Parker heading for the fern bar in the hopes of meeting with his best friend and burying the hatchet. He hadn't talked to Pidge since the night in Vail, and he wasn't sure that he would be there, but he knew his friend, and felt confident that he would be waiting for him.

He was, and as Parker navigated the terrace, trying to ignore the looks of revulsion at his face from the beautiful people sitting at the tables, he could see from the side that Pidge's jaw was set and he looked angry. "Hey pal," he said, and collapsed into a chair.

Pidge looked up, and the anger changed to shock. "Jesus Christ, " he mumbled. "What happened?"

"Had a spot of difficulty with the Porsche."

"It blew up?"

"It had a little help. Some kids firebombed it."

"Oh my God. Are you going to be OK?"

"I don't know. Don't think I'll be your best-looking friend anymore though."

"Oh Lord. Let me get you a drink."

"Just a coke, huh? I'm already on pain killers, and I've got work to do this afternoon."

"Yeah, anything you say," said Pidge. He went into the bar and emerged with a soda. "Who was it?"

"I can't really remember. I think it was some students who were dissatisfied with the judicial process."

"Did you talk to the cops?"

Parker sipped the drink through the straw. "Nah. Didn't see much point in it."

"But you've got to. You can't let someone get away with something like that."

This line of discussion was making Parker tired. "I don't want to talk about it."

"But you . . ."

"Hey. I don't want to talk about it. I have my reasons."

Pidge looked as if he wanted to say something, but changed his mind. He shrugged, and they lapsed into a long silence. They ordered lunch, and Pidge finally asked.

"Have you talked to her?"

Parker had been waiting for the question, but it still made him sad to think about it. "Yeah," he answered. "I talked to her."

"You guys OK?"

"No."

"Sorry."

"Me too."

Parker could see that there was a struggle building in his friend; Clay was dying to say it, but he hadn't counted on Parker's being so incapacitated and weak. After a while, he couldn't resist. "It is your own fault, you know."

"I know," said Parker. There was another silence as the waiter brought their food. "I'm sorry, Pidge. About everything."

Pidge shrugged his shoulders kindly. "Forget about it." A few minutes later he asked, "So how about this thing with the University?" Pidge asked. "You gonna win?"

Parker leaned back in his chair, and felt the sunlight on his face. It burned a little, but it was all right. He saw the shafts stabbing into the darkness between the buildings, and realized how beautiful the light was. "The case feels pretty strong," he said.

TWELVE

W hen Everett was a child he loved airplanes.

He knew them all, too. The P-38 with its elegant twin fuselage; the P-40 Tigershark; the hardy Corsair of the Marine; the 51 Mustang that could fly at 30,000 feet and could outrun and outclimb anything else in the sky. And he knew the enemy planes, too. The Stuka, the Messerschmidt, and the Faulk-Wolfe; the Judy and the Zeke. Everett knew them all, and to the amazement of his childhood friends, and the amusement of their parents, he could recite the declassified statistics for each one, how fast, how far, how high. He had made models of them, painstakingly cutting the tiny strips of wood, and gluing them together into frames, perfect frames, for making a substandard airplane would have been the only sacrilege he knew. Then covering each plane with tissue paper, and coating the tissue with dope, always being careful not to spill any so his mother wouldn't scold him. And then suspending each plane from the ceiling of his room where he could gaze at them and wonder, and dream. For, as a little boy, growing up in World War Two, he knew that the only thing in the world worth being was a pilot. And the only kind of pilot worth being was a fighter pilot.

But that had been when he was very young, when his dreams were youthful and honest and simple, when the future was something that simply happened, not something that had to be planned for. And then, in the blink of an eye, Everett was twenty, and in college, and faced with the challenge of charting a course for life. It was a terrifying prospect. He flirted with the idea of going into the business world, along with most of his undergraduate friends, but there was something inside him that rebelled at the notion. He had tried to rationalize it as being a dislike of such straight-jacketed regimentation, the fashionable cry of young people of any era who view the world of their elders with distaste. But in moments of uncomfortable clarity Everett knew that this was not the case for him. He saw these men who wore suits and made decisions, who played the corporate game, as enviable characters. They had taken the plunge and, for better or worse, jumped from the high dive into life. Everett couldn't bring himself to do more than look at the pool. What if he were to fail? What if he were to be fired? Or worse, what if he were to work for years and years at a boring and repetitive job only to realize in late middle age that he was a no-one? A nonentity? What if his life amounted to nothing? He who had wanted to be a fighter pilot as a little boy, he who had had such great dreams?

Then, another blink of an eye, and ten more years had got behind him, and Everett was still in school, but on the other side of the desk. He was beginning to realize that among the successful in academe there were two basic types of people: the true intellects, who daydreamed brilliance; and the half intellects, those who had enough grounding in common sense that they could ensure the university's smooth operation. He knew enough about the true intellects (a friend of his from Northwestern, Stein, was one) to know that he would never be one of them. He hadn't nearly enough imagination, and more importantly, he knew that he would never have the muse that called them into their own peculiar worlds. So, driven by the ambition to rise above the second-raters, he had consciously started working toward a position in administration. Everett rarely begrudged the intellectuals the awesome voltage of their brainpower, because he knew that without people like him, they couldn't exist. And he knew that he had at least been able to ante into the game by completing his doctorate.

But deep down he always knew that the success he found in academia was founded on the depressing fact that he was a coward.

Six decades of existence, Everett thought, and it all comes down to this.

He was finding it difficult to concentrate on the matter at hand, difficult to focus on the fact that his life, as he had known it, was creaking and straining in collapse, like some ungainly prehistoric bird falling slowly into the ground, its tendons severed, its muscles useless. The harder he tried to look into the future, the deeper he was dragged into his past, a region where thought was easier to accomplish, gliding over his years in academia, especially the early years when he had known uncertainty and consciously feared failure, and had wondered if the career path he was choosing was the correct one. How honest those years were, how blessed and simple. He had not known such simple fear for years, and he didn't feel it now, when perhaps he should have.

Now I am old, he thought. Where shall I go? What shall I do? Maybe I can teach math in a high school someplace. Wouldn't that be nice? Statistics for the young minds, or maybe trig or geometry. Or algebra. He hadn't thought about teaching algebra for years. He smiled at the thought of it.

"Are you listening to me?" asked President Fowler. Fowler was worked up, a little lump of anger and impotence sitting in his chair behind his desk in his airy home office. The veins stood out in his temples. What a little fool he is, Everett thought.

"No, Bob, I'm not listening to you," he said.

"You're not . . . You're . . . Let me just say that I am astonished that you can be so cavalier at a time like this. After you have so severely damaged the reputation of such an august . . ."

But then again, no. What high school would be interested in someone like him? Too old. No relevant experience. No experience at all in teaching for the last twenty years. Maybe an administrative post somewhere, maybe in the private sector. I'll have to leave Colorado, though. My name's been ruined here. Once a liar . . . He shook his head sadly. Then he realized that he would have to sell his house. I'll have to call a real estate agent.

And then people will be coming through my home to look at it. And they'll all know me.

" . . . institution. I can well imagine the feelings of guilt you must have. The damage you've caused. But let me just say that shaking your head will not be enough this time. Not enough by half. You don't even realize . . ."

What a mess. Nowhere to go. He fastened his eyes upon Fowler's face.

"the extent of what you have done." Fowler's face twisted in frustration as he had to say the words. "We've lost . . . *Funding!* I've already had three calls today from organizations that politely told me that they could no longer support the tower, or any other projects on campus. What the hell am I gonna do with that goddamned monstrosity on the quad if I can't get the money to finish it? Dick Whittaker from the State House called. He oversees the Committee on Higher Education. Said that he has grave doubts about the institution. Wants to do an audit. How could you do it, Broadstreet?"

"Do what?"

"Lie and lie and lie again. To me, to our attorney, repeatedly. How could you have slandered that poor young man's reputation?"

Everett actually laughed, and then he became sober. "In all honesty, I'm glad that things worked out for him. In all of this, I'm glad that he'll be OK."

"I'm sure he'll be glad to hear that when he sues you."

"Is he going to?"

"Dan says he probably will. You, me, Stiggler, the college. What hurts me the most is that if I had only known, if I had only known, I would have done everything in my power to help him. And now I'll never be able to make him understand that. I am as much of a victim in this as he is. We are all victims of you, and whatever twisted agenda you've cooked . . ."

Everett was growing tired of this. He wished that Fowler would do it and get it over with.

" . . . up for the school. You are an odious, evil person. I have never taken such pleasure in firing someone."

Everett looked up. "I'm out?"

"Yes."

"Finally." He stood up to leave.

"And let me just say . . ."

"No," said Everett. As he walked to the front door of the house, he could hear Fowler shouting at him.

" . . . Vacate the office by the end of the day or I'll have you thrown out! Did you hear me? Did you? Did you!"

Everett stopped at his house to collect a few boxes, and then drove over to the campus, where he parked his car. The boxes were awkward and difficult to carry. He tried to tuck them under his arm, but they kept sliding down and dragging on the ground. He stopped several times to adjust his grip on them, but in the end he had to hold them in front of himself with a hand on either side, as if they were a big sign. Faculty members still on campus glanced at him as they walked by, their conversations coming to a halt. They all knew what the boxes meant.

Fortunately, Joyce had left for the day, so he was spared the humiliation of having to explain to her what had happened. He dragged the boxes into the office and pushed them into shape, fixing the bottoms with scotch tape. He sank into his chair and stared out of the window at the tower, now deserted and quiet.

His door opened suddenly, and a custodian entered. He seemed surprised to see Everett in the office. "Oh, excuse me," he said. "Are you Dean Broadstreet?"

"Not precisely," Everett mumbled.

"Pardon?"

"Yes, I'm Broadstreet. What do you want?"

"Excuse me," the custodian repeated. He dug into his coveralls and produced a sheet of yellow paper. "I got this work order here to change the locks on this door."

"I see." Fowler wasn't wasting any time.

"If you don't mind the inconvenience, sir, I'd like to do it now if it's OK with you. I have a pretty tight schedule."

"Sure," said Everett.

"Thanks. I won't be a minute." He set his tool box on the floor and took out a screwdriver. Everett watched for a while as the man disassembled the doorknob and the deadbolt. The custodian went about his work quickly, glancing at Everett from time to time, and perhaps feeling self-conscious at the silence finally said, "I guess someone got ahold of the wrong key, huh?"

"What?" asked Everett.

"I was just saying how I reckon that somebody got ahold of the wrong key, you know?"

Everett stared at him.

"I guess some students got the key and were trying to get in here, right? That's why you wanted the lock changed, right?"

"Oh," said Everett. He nodded dumbly.

The man tried the new lock a few times, and said, "There. You won't have any problems now. Have a nice weekend." He picked up his tools and left, leaving the door propped open. Everett thought about getting up to close it, but realized that when he started to take the boxes out to his car, it would be easier to have it opened. He went into Joyce's office and opened the door to the hallway as well, and kicked a wedge beneath it. Then he went back into his office and started to take the things off of his desk. He didn't want the heavy brass compass to be scuffed, so he wrapped it carefully in the day's copy of the campus newspaper before setting it into the box.

A door opened in the hallway, and as Everett looked up at the sound he saw Jack Beetle going by. Beetle looked into the office, and Everett thought he could detect a slight surprise or perhaps fear in his eyes as he hustled away. Everett hurried out into the hallway after him.

"Jack . . . Jack, wait a moment. I want a word with you."

Beetle paused for a second, and then turned around. "Well?" he said expectantly.

Everett wasn't exactly sure what he wanted to say, now that the moment had arrived. He stood in the darkened hallway, confused, and then finally stammered, "I just . . . I needed to know."

Beetle stared at him coldly, waiting, as Everett tried to marshal his thoughts. "What did you need to know?"

"Why did you do this to me? Why me?"

The younger man's eyes steeled in the darkness. "I don't know what you're talking about." He started to walk away.

"No! Wait! Please, Jack. Please!" Beetle ignored him, and Everett's control snapped. "You *owe* me, you little shit!"

At this Beetle stopped, turned, and walked back to Everett, an empty smile once more spreading into the lines of his face. "My, my, my. The great Dean stoops to the vulgar. I guess you're human after all. I've had my doubts. Well? What is it that you want to know? Why we ganged up on you? Why we destroyed you?"

"Well, yes . . . I suppose so." He felt embarrassed to express his vulnerability so openly.

Beetle leaned his head back in the manner of one who has heard a clever joke which he alone completely understands. He glanced down the darkened hallway as if to be sure that no one was around, and then he turned back to Everett. His eyes glimmered with malice and hatred. "You must be the most arrogant, pompous fool that I have met in my entire life. Don't you realize that I don't care about you? You're a nobody. A nothing. A relic, I admit, from an age that we want to forget, so I suppose I can take some small satisfaction that I had a hand in your removal. But don't kid yourself. I never cared enough about you to actively try to get rid of you. People like you are like a bad smell. They always blow away, in time."

"Is that so." Everett hadn't expected so personal a response, and he didn't know what else to say.

Beetle continued, the words pouring out of his mouth. "Yes. That is so. I mean, look at you. You never liked me, from the moment we met. I remember that moment. It was at a faculty orientation session twelve years ago. The old chancellor introduced us. You looked at me like I was a slug, tiny, worthless, inconsequential. Remember? You hated me. You hated why I was brought to this campus. You hated the people I brought with me. You hated everything we ever tried to accomplish. And you still do. But you never did anything about it. You were always more concerned with your image. In fact,

313

you always tried to be on the winning side. On my side. You're pathetic. A washed-up old fool trying to stay afloat while we tied bricks to your feet and laughed when you struggled. Grovelling like a worm in front of the president. No, we never had anything to worry about as far as you were concerned. You always did whatever we told you to, even when we didn't say it. Why would we do anything to you? Now, that friend of yours over in the history department, what's his name? Stein? He's the sort we have to keep our eyes on. He's brilliant, but his intelligence is muddied by compassion. He refuses to accept that the course we are charting is the correct one."

Beetle paused for a moment, as if deciding whether to continue. "You know, I don't know why I'm going to say this, seeing as I consider you to be such a dolt, but I'll try to lay it out for you." Beetle bit his lower lip, searching for the right words. "I know you want to know this, you want to know why I do the things I do. I don't think most people would see it this way, but I suppose the best way to put it is to say that it has to do with evolution. There is a proper way for humans to evolve from this point in history, and it involves washing away the insanity of the last five thousand years. We have finally reached a time when people are moving away from the hierarchical structure that has held them in shackles for all of recorded history. It is finally dawning on the masses that this, this earth, is all there is, and that all people have the potential to be superior. That's an important word—*superior*. The chain of command that has led people around like animals, always seeking the higher authority, the insane idea of God, is finally on its way out. It's a tough one for people to swallow, but it's true: There is no God. It doesn't exist. It never has. And the ludicrous notion of sin, which has kept people from achieving their destiny, and kept them comfortable in slavery, is disappearing from people's thoughts. It has already been practically removed from the language. Finally, finally, we are at a crossroads where the human race can escape the eddy in which it has been trapped by ignorance and fear. With the proper guidance, a new day will dawn when humankind will become the masters of right and wrong. We, my colleagues and I, are providing that guidance. Do you understand what I'm saying, Everett?"

"I think so."

"Forgive my pessimism, but I don't believe that you do. Not even here, surrounded by it, can you have any idea of what we've accomplished. In just fifty years, look how far we've come. From the first, vague stirrings of disbelief in particularly uncomfortable aspects of the moral code, to great segments of the population who view the idea of any moral code with suspicion. I know of students who will question whether Hitler was wrong to gas the Jews. Not from any weak sense of right and wrong, not from any unhealthy pity, but from the viewpoint that it is impossible to know what was on the minds of those who marched the wretched Jews into the showers! I'll bet when you were a young man, you wouldn't have believed that the masses could ever begin to think in this way. But they are. They're fed it every day on television, hour after hour, and they believe it. They *know* that the concept of morality is flawed. Even the great religions are moving away from the idea of sin. They're terrified of it because they can no longer explain it. Too many people are asking too many questions, and they find the gold in their coffers getting dangerously low. And those others, those bible-thumping fools who still buy the nonsense and use

315

it to prey on the weakness of fear are vilified in the press as dangerous or unstable, as well they should be. It's happening all around you. These are great days. Humanity is about to make a great leap."

"When I was a child, people like Hitler and Mussolini were saying the same things."

Beetle looked at Everett with scorn, and a great part of the fervor with which he was speaking seemed to die out of him. "Wrong again," he said. "They were not saying the same things. The idea of military conquest was stupid and irrelevant. But though you'll never hear me say it in front of anyone of substance, the fascists had some good ideas. Many of the early deconstructionists were fascists. Did you know that? It's true. Even old Paul de Man never apologized for writing propaganda for the Nazis in Belgium. There were many great intellectual fascists. Ezra Pound was one. So was Heidegger, the greatest philosopher since Nietzsche, and most likely the most important philosopher of this century. And you may remember that when you were a child there was a movement to keep us out of the Second World War, because at that time the concept of fascism was not considered to be in bad taste. Of course, we play that down as much as possible, since the term 'fascism' got away from them and was saddled with too negative a connotation. We can't afford to be connected with the word anymore. But I'll tell you, we've done the next best thing. We label those who oppose us as fascists, the classical Liberals who detest government and the like, even though to label them that way is ridiculous. Another great fascist once wrote that if you tell people anything long enough, they start to believe it. And he was right. Most people don't even know what the word fascist means, precisely. It's just something bad. We have forced that negative label on our opponents, and we win again."

"But I thought you were a Marxist."

Beetle shrugged. "I wouldn't call myself one. To be technically accurate, post-modernism actually developed as a denial of Marxism. I wouldn't call myself a fascist, either, though there are people who could easily label me as one. It doesn't matter. Both labels would be as accurate or inaccurate as the other. I mean, what's the point in a name? Names can be twisted and their meanings changed as quickly as people can make them up. Most people are too foolish to see that yet. I use a Marxist perspective as a teaching tool, because doing so creates in students doubt about things they had always accepted as self-evident. I have a political interest in sowing confusion, because confusion breeds apathy. But I am personally no more of a Marxist than I am a libertarian. I don't think there is a single word that expresses my philosophy. But then again, of course, words themselves are worthless. And as definitions change over time, the things that they define become less clear. Most people don't realize that. Most people are too foolish to see what's two feet in front of their noses."

Everett found himself astonished at this line of discussion. "You don't believe that they can be educated?"

Beetle chuckled in the darkness, a short hiss that cut through the space around him. "That's not exactly what I'm saying, but no. To be blunt, I do not. Not in the way you mean it. At present, people can be taught to do things, to perform functions, but most can't be taught to think in any sort of abstract manner. The meta-narrative is too firmly entrenched. They can perform a function in society, but they are not equipped to lead it, and it is madness to give them any substantive voice in its direction. As a group, as a *species*, they are important. As individuals, at this point in history, they are dangerous."

"But our history, the history of this country . . ." Everett began.

"Was an interesting experiment," Beetle interrupted. "But its time has come. The men who began this country, and the European philosophers who directed its foundation, were thinkers. I'll give them that. Jefferson, Madison, Hamilton . . . Even Adam Smith. They were brilliant. Visionary. But their hypotheses have failed. The Enlightenment concept of rational self-interest needs to yield to the concept of *ir*rational self-interest. I mean, let's face it. We are on the verge of extinction. As a species. We're destroying the very air we breathe, the water we drink. Our country has survived for as long as it has because up until recently the stakes were low. But now . . . Hell. Look around you. Do you really think that our survival should be allowed to continue in the hands of the free market? In the hands of the masses? Ultimately in the hands of people who get angry if a transmitter in a television station breaks down and some mind-numbing program is interrupted for twenty-three seconds? That's insane. And they don't even want the responsibility. What percentage of the adult population votes? And of the ones who actually do, how many of them really listen to the ideas that these so-called leaders express? twenty percent? thirty? Personally, I think that's fortunate, because it has kept a check on the danger of democracy. Most people will vote for whatever they're told to. Providing of course that in being told they are led to believe that they are making a free choice. Most buy their politicians with the same level of thought that they buy boxes of breakfast cereal. But I shudder to think about what would happen if more people became involved in the system. Do you actually believe that the future of this country, the most powerful country in the world, a country with the military capability to destroy the surface of the planet . . . Do you honestly think that the future of this country can be left in the hands of people who get impatient waiting for a microwave oven to finish cooking their food for them? Do you honestly believe it should?"

"So you think there will be some sort of revolution? Some push to change the government?"

"What kind of a fool do you take me for? Of course there won't be a revolution. Why bother? I'm trying to explain to you that these people don't even want the responsibility of cooking their own dinners. They're hardly going to organize themselves to take up arms against the government. How they ever managed to do it two hundred years ago is something I'll never understand. But of course, not that many of them did. The percentage of colonists who fought for the rebels was actually quite small. Anyway, as I was saying, the masses won't rise up. We have taken that responsibility from them, or at least from a large percentage of them. And the percentage is growing. We have organized the poor and the underclasses and now we take care of them because quite frankly they are currently incapable of taking care of themselves. Now we're beginning to take care of their children, teaching them just what they need to know. I must confess that I get a bit of a laugh when I see these sad-faced idiots lament the destruction of the educational system. It's not being destroyed, it's being refined.

"We are witnessing something incredible, epochal. We are seeing the beginnings of the next great intellectual movement, the true reformation, the one where we learn to live without God. It won't be completed in my lifetime, or in the lifetime of my children or of my children's children. But in a few hundred years humanity will fundamentally outgrow the psychological need for its parents. And when that happens, we will be able to truly explore the boundaries of technology. We won't be held back by the nagging suspicion that we really shouldn't do all of the things we are capable of. We will master life itself. And we will master death."

"But what you're saying doesn't make any sense," said Everett. "If the people are stupid, as you seem to think that they are, they will never become the masters of anything. Do you trust the people or do you hate them?"

"No, I don't hate them. I hate the lethargy that grips them. Voltaire once said something to the effect of, 'I detest the commoners. They spend their time dashing between the church and the public house, simply because there is singing in each.' I think that says it very well. The public has become drunk and slow. If we have to use that drunkenness to the advantage of a greater goal, so be it. The results are good. If they don't understand now, at least they are asking the right questions. Look for example at the so-called rise in spiritualism, people worshipping trees and making medicine circles in the deserts and performing witchcraft and all the rest of this idiocy. I think they are doing it because they've come adrift from their moorings, and just don't know how to finally cut away from the anchor. What can I say? We can't quickly undo a fear that has become so ingrained in society that people begin to think it natural.

I've talked to some of these people, and I don't think they know what they believe in. And that goes for more than spiritualism, by the way. Take Daphne Stiggler, for instance. That poor, misguided soul doesn't know what she stands for. I think it changes daily. But I know that fate can always count on sophists like her to foment disruption and confusion, which always seem to play into our hands. She's a marvel. She can say less with more words than most politicians. Even I have trouble keeping up with her sometimes. I have to admit, though, that I personally find association with her extremely distasteful. She's even tried to get me into bed a few times. Can you imagine anything more revolting than that? Still, it's all for a greater cause, and we all must sacrifice for the greater good.

"Which reminds me, I have to go meet with her now. Fowler wants some new ideas for funding for the tower. So, you miserable old fool, if there's nothing else .. ?"

Everett's mind seemed filled with thoughts, coming and going so fast that he had trouble gripping any of them. There seemed nothing he could say to refute Beetle's logic. At length, he shook his head dumbly. "No, I think I understand. But I hope history proves you wrong."

Beetle laughed. "History? We *invent* history. We never, ever lose. I would say that today is a win. If we were living during the Hellenic wars, I suppose now I would have to complete your humiliation by sodomizing you, the vanquished foe. But you're just not that important. Besides, I find the idea of sodomy disgusting. Don't you? Goodbye, Everett." Beetle turned and slipped into the darkness, his footfalls slowly fading away, until Everett heard a door opening, and then closing sharply.

Everett turned back to his office and sat behind his desk, surrounded by the trappings of respect that he had so long craved, and from which he was now separated. He knew what he had to do, but it took hours for him to build up the courage to do it, and he waited in the room where he had known tragedy until well after the darkness became complete. He needed to make a stand, to make one statement with his life that would regain his dignity. To do the right thing.

After a time he rose from his chair, and with his hands starting to shake, he unfastened his belt and removed it, feeling the buckle slide and catch on each belt-loop. He climbed on top of the desk where he could reach the beam in the ceiling. His arms began to shake and his knees trembled. He took the belt and looped it around the massive beam. The belt, however, was too short. With one end of it tied, there were only a few inches left over. He looked around the room from his vantage point high above it, and spied a length of nylon packaging twine in one of the boxes he had brought. He climbed down and retrieved it. Then he climbed back up and wrapped one end around the beam, tieing it securely. But then, when he tried to tie a noose into the other end, he found that he didn't know how. He tried to remember. Something about making one wrap over another and then wrapping the end over the whole thing leaving a loop on one side. It took him several attempts before he got it right, and when he did, he began to shake violently. He forced himself to place the loop around his neck. The twine felt sharp and rough against his throat. A thought suddenly occurred to him: what if he should jump off of the desk and then have the cord cut right through his neck? He had heard of that happening before, and he didn't want it to happen to him. Somehow, the thought of strangling to death was more pleasant, more comfortable than being decapitated. But then he realized he was being foolish. He wouldn't know either way. He leaned against the cord a little and felt it tighten. His heart started to race. He looked down at the desk and noticed that he had put his belt there when he had removed it from the beam. He didn't want to be found without his belt on, so he loosened the noose and slipped it back over his head, feeling again the roughness of the twine against his skin. After he had put on his belt, he started to place his head in the noose again, and again he started shaking violently. He knew that he would have to do this quickly or he wouldn't be able to do it at all. But as he was about to jump, he remembered that he hadn't left a note. He once again took off the noose and climbed back down. He took some paper out of his desk and laid it in front of him, seated himself, and tried to think about what to say. What salutation should I use? he wondered. He wrote "To whom it may concern," but then he decided that it didn't sound right. He crossed it out, and then decided that he didn't want to leave a suicide note that was imperfect or indecisive. He crumpled up the paper and threw it into the wastepaper basket, but then realized that people would find it there when they found his body. He picked it up and tried to decide what to do with it. After a moment or so, he tore it into little tiny pieces and put them into a neat pile on his desk. He would decide what to do with them later.

But another blank sheet was lying on his desk, and once again he had to think about what to write. He decided that he would think about the whole thing first, know just what to say, before committing anything to ink. The moments stretched out, and nothing came to mind. He had a feeling that the note would have to be perfect, the final summation of his life, and that he would have to include something about the pressure he had felt to lie about David Shore. He also wanted to mention something about what Beetle had said to him, something really incisive. But eloquence eluded him. He must have sat there for more than a half an hour before it dawned on him that he couldn't think of a single thing to say. With something akin to relief, he told himself that he didn't want to commit suicide without leaving a note. And that the pieces of the earlier note he had torn up would have to be removed. And that if he tried to kill himself with that twine, he would decapitate himself and make a mess. A mess that Joyce would probably find on Monday morning. He couldn't do that to her.

He scooped up the pieces of the note and put them in his pocket. He would throw them away later. Then he climbed back up onto the desk to remove the noose from the beam. But as his fingers worked at it, he found that he couldn't get it untied. The knot had become too tight when he had pulled at it. If he couldn't get it off, he would have to leave it hanging there, where people would find it and know that he had been unable to . . . that he had been too much of a coward to . . .

Everett pulled desperately at the knot, but the more he tried, the worse the situation became. The twine began to bite into the palms of his hands, leaving a deep red welt. Nothing would dislodge it from the beam. It would have to be cut away. He jumped off of the desk in a panic, and searched frantically for a knife of some kind. There wasn't even a letter opener at his desk. Nothing in his pockets. He rushed out to Joyce's office, brushing against the open door as he did so. There was nothing sharp in Joyce's desk, and in horrified disbelief he saw that he had knocked the door closed behind him. He had knocked it off the wedge when he bumped into it. With a sinking feeling, he knew that it would be locked, but he tried the knob anyway. It wouldn't turn. He didn't have the new key. He would have to come back on Monday morning and beg to be let back into his office so he could collect his things, and when they opened the door for him they would see the noose, empty and pregnant with meaning, dangling above his desk. He could hardly imagine the humiliation.

But ironically, as he left the outer office, his face burning with shame, he had conquered his fear of death. Fear is about worrying that things might get worse. And Everett knew that life was as close to hell as he would ever get.